STICKS & STONES

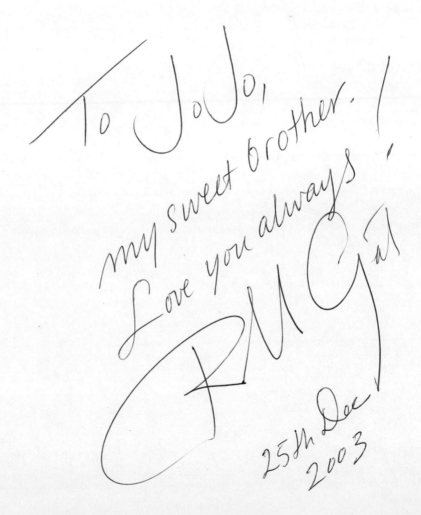

To JoJo,
my sweet brother. !
Love you always !
RM Gal

25th Dec
2003

STICKS & STONES

R.M. GÁL

Writers Club Press

New York Lincoln Shanghai

Sticks & Stones

All Rights Reserved © 2002 by R.M. GÁL

Writers Club Press
an imprint of iUniverse, Inc.

For information address:
iUniverse
2021 Pine Lake Road, Suite 100
Lincoln, NE 68512
www.iuniverse.com

ISBN: 0-595-25576-0 (Pbk)
ISBN: 0-595-65182-8 (Cloth)

Printed in the United States of America

J.O.T. Books by R.M. GÁL

CRUCIFIXION

STICKS & STONES

Non-fiction by R.M. GÁL

FROM TWO FOOLS COMES FORTH A GENIUS
—CHILDHOOD EXPERIENCES OF AN AWARD-WINNING TEENAGE FILMMAKER—

To be published by March 2003

This is dedicated to the one I love
—my number one reader—
John W. Saalfield.

"I was looking back to see if you were looking back at me
to see me looking back at you."

—by g. marshall / a. vowels / r. del naja / w. cobham / s. nelson

ACKNOWLEDGMENTS

Front cover design
Author's photograph
by John W. Saalfield

INSPIRED BY

Rebecca Miracle
—*my sister*—
JP Saalfield
—*my son*—
Heart
Bonnie Tyler

Some of the music I listened to while I wrote this book:

Enigma
Tommy Lee
Massive Attack
Sarah McLachlan
Moby
Remy Zero
Secret Garden
VAS
motion picture music: Queen of the Damned
best-liked songs: Forsaken; Down with the Sickness
favorite voice: David Draiman's of Disturbed

CHAPTER ONE

Georgina Binakas sat alone at her long dining table in her villa, on the east coast of Crete. With her eyes closed, she leaned back against the cushioned chair. She jumped at the sound of an object as it landed on the plate of her unfinished breakfast. Her water and juice glasses crashed onto the stone floor, smashing into glass bits and splattering their fluids. Georgina looked down onto the table to see a glossy News of the Week lying face up in front her and then stared up to see a mask of anger, the face of her husband, David Binakas. She hadn't heard him come in. David's eyes left hers and aimed at the magazine. Georgina looked at it again. She knew the name of the man on the cover and his face, even though twelve years had passed since she had seen him and he had not yet been a man. She also recognised the headline, Crucifixion in America's Heartland. Georgina had heard about it from her friends, who read the International Tribune and watched the news on their television sets, which Georgina abhorred and did not have in her home. The horrible tragedy, world news, had happened last week to a man other than Jud Thorensen but, because Jud had been the central figure of the tragedy, Jud was the one who was featured in the TV news coverage and on the covers of news magazines and tabloids.

Georgina felt as unsettled as the breeze that was picking up force as it passed by her window and headed from north to south. It blew from over the Aegean Sea, which she noticed was a deeper turquoise than was usual on a hot spring day. The American news had been the talk of her friends, a couple of whom had read Jud Thorensen's book, The Crucifixion, a critical success, which had been written under his pseudonym. That Jud Thorensen had written such a book, had then been identified by his real name and become the target of a crucifixion had been unbelievable; that he had escaped from being nailed to the cross had been miraculous.

Georgina, being Greek Orthodox Catholic and preferring to not taint her mind with impure thoughts, had not read his book, considered profane by many Christian readers. Most Cretans had not read it, since it had not been translated into Greek or other languages, although it soon would be. Yet, whether they had or had not read it, those who watched the news considered Jud Thorensen to be a lucky devil to have walked away alive. As the Cretan men, meeting at the tavernas and drinking their coffee underneath the hot sun, talked about the Washburn, Indiana event, they shook their heads and said, *only in America.* Some of them thought that a death by crucifixion would have been too honorable for the man who had tried to disable the reason for Jesus' death by implying that Jesus had not been crucified—if the Son of God had not offered Himself as the Sacrificial Lamb, then who, other than Jesus could die for everyone's sins and become the Savior for all of those who accepted Him into their hearts.

David Binakas had watched the news about the modern-day crucifixion on the television set in his office on the mainland of Greece, earlier this week. The substitution, on a cross, of another man for the now-notorious author had been the talk of his business associates as well as of Constantine Sgouros, once an enemy, now his friend. Although Jud Thorensen's face had been unfamiliar to David, his name had sounded familiar.

Georgina stood up. She wanted to cower. Instead, she looked into the dark eyes of the man she loved but had betrayed with her best intentions. Although David was now sixty-two, he had thick, black hair and a handsome face, lined by the sun's rays rather than by age. He was shorter than

Georgina, who had Minoan blood in her; he had dark good looks and a husky build that showed his pleasure in good food and wine.

David came and stood close to Georgina. He asked, "Am I wrong?" He knew he wasn't but he wanted her to come out with the truth on her own. He continued, "All the way from the airport, I prayed I was wrong. But each time I looked at the face on the magazine cover, I became more sure I was right."

David looked at his wife's long, shining hair wrapped as a glorious crown about her head, her classically-beautiful face, and her figure, as opulent as the gentler hills of Crete. He had come home from Athens today to reassure himself that, despite his evidence to the contrary, his wife had not cheated on him. At age forty-four, she was as attractive to him as she had been at age fifteen when she had married him, by arrangement between her family and his. He had been forty-one and a widower. His first wife and son had been killed in a car accident by a drunken tourist. He had not expected to marry again until his family had told him that they wished to arrange a marriage for him with a pretty young woman who, although she came with a small dowry, could provide him with sons.

Everything about Georgina spoke fertility—she was a goddess. David's mother, Athína Binakas, had insisted that David meet Georgina instead of blindly throwing away the chance at having another happy marriage. But, upon his mother's death two years ago, his family lawyer had given a letter to David in which Mrs. Binakas had stated that Georgina had broken the sacred marriage vow of faithfulness but Mrs. Binakas had not stated when. Yet, David, knowing how much Georgina loved him, would have bet his life on the impossibility of her allowing another man to make love to her—the day Georgina would allow that was the day the Aegean Sea would swallow Crete as it had once sated its hunger with Thíra's volcano, whose eruption had blown the land to bits and left a broken ring in blue water.

Thus, David had discounted the letter as the rambling of an ill woman—Mrs. Binakas had never recovered from an influenza two and a half years ago, when she had given the letter to the lawyer, who had dated his receipt of it, with the instruction to give it to David upon her death. Six months later, pneumonia had set in and taken Mrs. Binakas's life. David had received the letter. And, despite its contents, he had safeguarded it because it contained the only words his mother had ever written to him.

The words included a name which David had recalled this morning when he had seen Jud's face—not in motion on the television but on a magazine cover with a clear photograph—and had realised that Jud's face was familiar to him after all and that Jud's name was the one in his mother's letter. Today, David had removed from the letter from his office safe and read it anew. Mrs. Binakas, not knowing the roman alphabet, had used Greek letters to phonetically spell the name of Jud Thorensen, whom she named as Georgina's lover.

"Am I wrong," David whispered. He was rough when he put his hands on Georgina's arms and pulled Georgina to him, even though he had never before been anything but gentle with her. David added, "You probably don't know I'm a jealous man. You've never given me a reason to be one—certainly, I had never thought so. And I am not only jealous, I have pride. I am proud of my wealth and position, of you, of—"

Just as Leesa entered the room to remove breakfast plates, Georgina pulled away from David and picked up the magazine. Leesa saw the faces of her employers and the broken glass. With no facial change, Leesa left the room to give them privacy and to get a broom, dustpan, and mop.

Georgina did not want to tell David anything. She thought that he was making assumptions out of the blue—even though they were correct. Her arms throbbed with the pain from the red marks inflicted by the grip of his fingers. His short, sharp nails had drawn lines of blood on her bare skin.

With great disappointment that she had not made a confession, David pulled the envelop containing his mother's letter from out of the breast pocket of his suit jacket and threw it down upon the top of the magazine. When Georgina looked at him, he said, "Go on. Open it."

Georgina read the letter to herself and, in an instant, knew she was in trouble. The letter described that Georgina had compromised herself. Although Jud Thorensen's name was poorly represented in Greek letters, it was evident that Mrs. Binakas had been trying to spell the unusual name. An undated letter with a direct accusation proved nothing but, since it had been written by her mother-in-law, it carried weight. Georgina felt terrified by what David might do now that her adultery had come to light. She asked, "When did you first read this?"

"Two years ago. But I disregarded it. I didn't believe it, Georgina." David kept his hands off her, this time. He added, "But I do believe it now."

Georgina asked, "Why would you now, if you didn't then?"

"I think you know why," he said as he looked at the face on the magazine he had thrown down. David's jaw tightened. His head was pounding from his anger.

She said, "David, take me someplace and we'll talk."

David took her elbow and led her outside to his BMW, its engine still warm from the drive that David had made from Irakleío's airport to his villa, near the village of Istron, only a short while ago. Now, with Georgina beside him, he drove fast along the narrow winding road in the car that was like the one his first wife and son, Cynthia and Nicholas, had been killed in. Because he had always worried that a speeding bus coming around a curve would force their car off the road during one of their excursions, he had instilled that fear into Cynthia; he had not thought that the car of a tourist who had been drinking early in the day would travel at a high speed from the opposite direction of his wife's car and tap its front, enough to send the vehicle with his wife and son spinning, until it dropped over the edge of a mountainside. David had loved Nicholas and regretted his death, until the day he had met Georgina. Although still pained by the tragedy, David knew that if his wife and son had survived, he could never have married and made love to Georgina, who made him feel as a virile lover—even when he sometimes wasn't. Georgina was like the fountain of youth for him and he loved her, even though she had borne no sons for him. But today, his feelings were changing.

David and Georgina had almost reached Pherma on the south coastline of Crete. During the hot summer months, many tourists from Europe and the USA came to the island. But Crete's springtime held few tourists and gave them privacy. After the recent Easter Sunday celebrations, most Cretans had resumed their daily bucolic and urban business: fishing, farming—produce or animal, and white collar professions. David Binakas, owner of a pharmaceutical company, Alpha-Omega Pharmakon, with its own research and development as well as manufacturing plant, could do whatever he wanted to, whenever he wanted to.

Now, David's main goal was to find out if he had a personal problem that he would have to solve. He parked along a rugged road, mainly used by farmers with their burros or by shepherds with their sheep and goats. He opened the car door for Georgina and led the way to an ugly beach with rocks that looked barren but had live barnacles suctioned to them and crabs sidling over them. Across the Libyan Sea lay Africa, three hundred miles away. In a dark suit, David sat on the warm sand and pulled Georgina, in a white cotton dress, down beside him. He asked her to remove her sunglasses. He wanted to see her eyes as she spoke. He left his own glasses on so that she could see herself in their reflection as he was seeing her. A large rock gave them shadow, a relief from the sun.

But Georgina was unable to keep her eyes on David because, as she spoke, she relived what had happened twelve years ago on the day she had turned thirty-two. She began to tell David the bare facts with embellishments that slanted the story in her favor and omitted telling him about her pleasure, which was not in her favor to apprise him of. As the scenes became real again, filling her eyes and mind, she became blind to her surroundings.

§

Twelve years earlier, on the morning of December twenty-ninth, Georgina called David. He wished her a happy birthday; he told her that he had not received the approval he had expected to have early this morning of a new drug developed by Pharmakon so he would stay in Athens and gather the additional data that the government agency had asked him to provide before the next national holiday on January first. Because Georgina knew that she would enjoy celebrating her birthday with David at any time, she didn't mind. David told her that he would be home in a few days and asked her to give his love to his mother, who had arrived on Crete this morning from her Athens home—without David, who had been expected to be her traveling companion—to celebrate her daughter-in-law's birthday.

Athína Binakas sent Leesa home at noon and began preparing a birthday meal for Georgina, who had been promising seventeen years earlier as a young woman who would give birth to many sons for David— Georgina's parents each had several brothers and, together, they had given birth to five boys and only one girl, Georgina. So, Mrs. Binakas had encouraged her son to take Georgina as his second wife, although with a poor dowry yet with great potential to provide him with male Binakas heirs. Now, with no male or female grandchildren, Mrs. Binakas still cared for Georgina—even though Georgina was a reminder of the lack she felt in herself because she had given her husband just one child, David.

As usual, Mrs. Binakas had prepared more dishes than she needed to. She chose a few of them to serve Georgina for her birthday meal: grilled fresh fish, young potatoes, souvlaki, and a cucumber salad, followed by baklava; then, she and Georgina took a walk. It was winter in Crete, with sunshine on one day out of four, usually. Because it was particularly windy during that afternoon, Mrs. Binakas and Georgina kept their walk short. When they returned to the villa, Mrs. Binakas went to her guest bedroom and lit the fire that Leesa had prepared before leaving—Leesa had also put kindling and logs in the living room fireplace and Georgina's bedroom one. Mrs. Binakas invited Georgina to sit with her in front of the fireplace while they sipped wine and listened to music. They laughed as they played cards and board-games. By early evening, the sky lost the moon and stars to storm clouds, the wind blew stronger, and hail mixed with rain came down. Mrs. Binakas grew tired and asked Georgina to excuse her.

Because Georgina's own family was in the United States, she had no one to celebrate with—except her husband, who was not here, and her friends, who thought she was with her husband. Georgina called up her best friend, Ariadne, and asked if she would come to the Binakas villa for a visit but Ariadne did not want to leave her home and family tonight. Thus, Georgina drove into Ágios Nikólaos to see her. At Ariadne's house, Georgina felt none of her usual pleasure there, where Ariadne's children, who considered her to be their aunt even though she was not a blood relation, liked to play games with her. Yet, tonight, Ariadne's two boys and one girl wanted only their mother's attention, leaving Ariadne's husband a chance to pay admiring attention to Georgina with a subtle but unmistakable message of desire for her. Georgina felt neglected by Ariadne and her offspring and offended by her husband. Yet, she felt aroused and wished David were home. Feeling she'd rather spend the evening alone, after all, Georgina left Ariadne's home an hour after her arrival.

Driving away from the seaport, Georgina sat in her warm Mercedes and listened to a CD of her favorite American rock group. The wind whipped at her car, causing it to weave. She drove fast as she felt exhilarated by the music. She would see David in a few days; they would be happy to see each other and enjoy a belated birthday celebration together; he would treat her as a queen and lavish her with gifts, including the coveted crucifix she wanted, its cross made of diamonds and its image of Jesus cast in solid gold. As Georgina continued driving along the dark narrow roads with no streetlamps, rain threw sheets of water on her windshield and white beads of hail hurled themselves against the glass. As lightning lit the sky once again, she saw two dark shapes walking ahead along the roadside and, as another blast of thunder caused the earth to shudder, she swerved to miss the shapes. But she had been going too fast. She put on the brakes, pressing them intermittently, and came to a stop as the car skidded slowly into a person, who then disappeared. Only seconds had passed. She was frightened. She got out of her car. With her headlights on, she could not see anyone in the blackness around the car. Georgina jumped when she felt a tap on her shoulder and heard a young man's voice shout through the storm.

He asked, "Would you give us a ride into Ágios Nikólaos?"

Although Georgina's car was facing in the opposite direction from the small city, she turned to face the young man to say that she would take them to Ágios Nikólaos but, upon noticing the other person on his feet again, she instead asked him, the one she still faced, "Have I hurt your friend?"

He said, "No, I don't think you touched him—he probably slipped."

Jud had been knocked down by Georgina's car but he felt all right. He didn't want to worry the driver, who had a Greek flavor in an American accent, so he said, "I'm fine. Please don't feel you have to give us a ride." He stood behind Bill.

Georgina tried to see the faces of the young men, whose voices sounded disarming. The first one had a clear tenor. The second one had a deeper voice, provocative and slightly gritty. The storm was worsening. Georgina changed her mind about taking the young men to Ágios Nikólaos but did not want to leave them stranded. So, she said, "Let me take you to my home." Because the howling wind was loud, she didn't wait for their response. Instead, she pulled them toward her car and opened the doors.

As Jud put their tent roll on the back floor and his backpack on top of it, Bill put his backpack on the back seat and climbed inside. Jud walked to the front passenger side and sat in. A smell of wetness and fresh air entered the dry, stuffy car; rainwater beaded on the leather seats.

Georgina glanced at Jud. She felt sorry for both of them. With the car doors open, before the interior lights had shut off upon closing the doors, she had caught sight of their tired faces and drenched clothes. She asked, "What are you doing here?"

Jud answered, "We wanted to practice our Greek but many of you speak English and won't let us ruin your language."

Georgina laughed—she couldn't imagine his voice ruining any language—and said, "I mean, why are you here at this time of the year—and what happened to you?"

"Bill and I wanted to see Crete while its not crowded with tourists. So we're using our Christmas vacation to see your island while its quiet, cool, and green. We knew we would be here during the wet season but we hadn't counted on this much rain. We've been camping every night but, tonight, the storm blew down our tent and almost washed it away. We were just heading into town to look for lodging."

Bill's intrinsic reason for coming to Crete was because he had Greek heritage and wanted to learn about his culture. Being the beginning of Greek civilisation, Crete was Bill's starting place. It was the island that some scholars had said was called Atlantis, before the tidal waves from Thíra's eruption had wiped out the Minoan culture.

Jud's purpose on Crete was to visit caves and monasteries, some of them isolated and almost impossible to reach because of the harsh terrain they stood on; Jud was contemplating becoming a monk. Being interested in Eastern philosophy, he also wanted to visit ashrams in India and consider living in a cave somewhere in the Himalayas for a few years. His desire was to become enlightened. He thought that isolation and self-denial were, perhaps, the best ways to do that.

Georgina asked, "Are you here with family?"

Bill said, "No." His family was disappointed about his absence from home during the holidays but had known that nothing could have restrained him or Jud from a trip they had been planning for a few months. Jud's father was vexed while his mother, although preferring Jud to be home for the season, didn't mind.

Georgina began forming a plan. She looked to her right at Jud and said, "I'm Georgina. And you are?"

"Jud Thorensen. This is Bill Harcourt."

Bill leaned forward, "We appreciate what you're doing for us, although we don't want to impose."

Georgina was silent. They had arrived at the villa. Georgina stopped the car in front of the gates and used a remote control to open them. She drove up the driveway to the underground garage tucked into a hill and connected to the house—built on higher ground—by a shallow stairway; she used the middle switch of another remote on the middle door and drove the Mercedes inside.

Jud, one of the two sons of the illustrious author, Ogden Thorensen, and Bill, son of Bertram Harcourt, a renowned publisher, were accustomed to wealth so their surprise lay not in the opulence of the villa but in the surprise of the circumstances of the night that had led them from the reality of a collapsed wet tent to the likelihood of sleeping in a modest hotel room to the actuality of resting their tired bodies in a luxurious home.

As Jud and Bill pulled their tent roll and backpacks from the car, Georgina pulled her wedding ring from off her finger and put it inside her coat pocket. She led Jud and Bill up the steps of a passageway and into the foyer. They all removed their shoes. Georgina led Jud to the master bathroom, with its granite interior, on the ground floor. He brought his backpack containing dry clothes with him.

Georgina led Bill upstairs to a guest bedroom with its own bath. Downstairs again, in the master bedroom, she knocked on the bathroom door. Jud partly opened it. He had finished his shower and had a towel around his waist. Georgina asked for his wet clothes, including the wool sweater and down vest. As he quickly stooped down to pick up the mound of clothes, his towel slid higher, allowing Georgina to glimpse a bruise, darkening on his right thigh—she realised she had hit him with her car. Jud blushed as he handed her his clothes. She offered to get an ice-pack for his injury. He refused.

Georgina returned upstairs to collect Bill's clothes. She brought them downstairs and tossed them, along with Jud's, into the dryer in a laundry room next to the kitchen, which she then entered. She warmed up untouched dishes of food and grilled up more fresh fish. Jud and Bill appeared in the kitchen looking revived in their dry clothes. Georgina thought they were both very good-looking boys. She set the dishes on the kitchen table, upon which she had laid out two place settings. She poured two glasses of red wine and set them on the table. She invited the boys to sit down and eat. She left them to go into the living room, where she lit the kindling in the fireplace, a deep inset, its top arc wide and high. A large woven rug with resplendent geometric designs lay a short distance from the fire.

Georgina went to her cold bedroom and lit the fire across from the end of her marriage bed. Although she had been wearing a trench-coat and not been out in the storm long enough to become drenched, she had long hair that was more than damp but less than wet and so she felt a chill. While she had a hot shower, she reconsidered what she was thinking of doing. She was hot and nervous. Her throat was dry and her hands were sweating. She was unsure if she should go through with this impulse.

Georgina was in early thirties and well past the average child-bearing years in her culture. During the first two years of her marriage to David, when he and she had wanted time together without children, they had used birth control methods, although out of accordance with their religious beliefs. Yet, once they had stopped using birth control, Georgina had still not become pregnant. Because David had fathered a child before, he was sure that he was not the reason for the lack and he had told Georgina, in answer to her unasked but implied question, that his first wife had been faithful. So, for several years, Georgina had assumed that she was infertile.

Yet, against David's wishes and, so, in secrecy, she had undergone tests on the mainland of Greece and learned that her reproductive system was healthy. Upon receiving that result, she had asked her doctor if a fertile man could become infertile. He had said that radiation could cause infertility. Old age could cause a low sperm count, as could an illness with high fever. But David was not old and Georgina did not know how to approach him about his health history. Or how to tell him that she was able to bear children. Eventually, she had decided that it would be best to let him continue to think that their lack of children was due to her. She knew his sense of pride—he would be ashamed if he could not father another child. But he also refused to adopt. And Georgina wanted at least one child. And, now, in her house, in the palms of her hands, she had two virile young men to choose from to help fulfill her desire.

She couldn't think of a better gift to give her husband than a child. After years of longing for one, on both their parts, it had come to matter less to her whose loins the child came from. She had begun to fantasize about taking a lover but had never seriously considered doing so—she was a Catholic who would not commit adultery, a loving wife who would not even look at another man, and a woman who was unlikely to get away with a deed from which exposure of wrongdoing would, thus, brand her as an adulteress. Yet, she had continued to fantasize. The fantasy, as a mature flower, in full bloom and fragrant, seemed no more likely to materialise than it had seemed likely to do so when it had been a seedling, fresh and tender—until tonight, when she felt wild and impulsive. And found herself attracted to both young men.

After her shower, with a towel around her, Georgina blow-dried her hair, long below her waist. She compared Bill and Jud with her husband and each other. Bill could pass for being Greek with his black hair, dark brown eyes, and olive skin. He was handsome like David, with a slightly convex nose and a jaw, stronger than David's but similar in its roundedness. His wide mouth was well-shaped like her own. Bill's voice was the pitch of her husband's, only sweeter. He was taller and stronger than David but had a similar bone structure. The odds of Georgina having a child that would have traits similar to those of the Binakas family if she were to seduce Bill were in her favor. Yet, she rationalised that no one would suspect that a child she gave birth to would not be David's, even if there were physical dissimilarities—her friend, Ariadne, found it difficult to explain the variances from herself in the looks of her children, although genetically attuned to both her and her husband: her two boys looked like her husband, while her daughter looked nothing like him and, instead, looked like his parents, whom he faintly resembled. But with Jud, the odds of having a child who would resemble a Binakas were poor—although Jud's eyes were fringed with thick dark lashes and his eyebrows were dark, his hair was a mucky color of dark blond, almost brown, not dark enough; his brow was too fine, his nose too straight, his jawline too strong, and his lips were more sensual than her husband's or her own. And his voice held a vibrant tone that was dissimilar to her husband's hard, contained one. Jud's physique, with almost no body fat, differed from her husband's—Jud was tall, broad-shouldered, and narrow at the waist and hips; his arms and legs were lean, with muscles that became thick when in motion, such as when he had stooped to pick up his clothes from her bathroom floor.

Georgina loosely wove her dried hair and put a clasp to hold it behind her back. In her bedroom, she put on a wine-red dressing gown. While drying her hair, her dilemma had changed from whether or not to commit adultery with no guarantee of a pregnancy to choosing which boy she would commit the sinful act with. Although Bill was an enticing prospect, it was Jud—whose voice, looks, and presence had inspired her to make her fantasy become a reality, in the first place—whom she wanted.

She went into the kitchen. She noticed that one wine glass was empty and the other was half full. Jud had his shirtsleeves rolled up and was doing the dishes. Bill was covering up leftovers and putting them into the refrigerator. They thanked her for the meal. Georgina brought the wine glasses to the sink and tidied up the kitchen; she thanked Jud and Bill for their help and then invited them into the living room.

It was eleven p.m. and, for Georgina, the moment was now or never. She told Jud and Bill that they should all retire. She said nothing more to Jud; she summoned Bill to follow her upstairs. She opened the door to his room. Because there was no fireplace, she turned on the zoned heat and then left. Bill brushed his teeth. He thought that it was odd that Georgina had not given Jud a guest room upstairs or told Jud to share Bill's room, which had two beds and a private bathroom. When he heard a knock at the door, he was not surprised. He opened it. Georgina walked in and placed an extra blanket on his bed. When she left again, he was surprised—he had thought she was going to seduce him. He began removing his clothes as he heard Georgina's footsteps go down the hall and downstairs again. In the silence Georgina had left behind, he climbed into bed. He had a feeling that he and Jud should leave the house tonight because some kind of trouble was brewing, more than seduction. But, since he had recently become confused about his own sexuality and, while still attracted to girls, had become attracted to guys, even to his best friend, he was unsure if he really believed that Jud was in trouble or if he was simply experiencing jealousy. Or, perhaps, possessiveness. So, he disregarded his concerns.

Downstairs, Jud stood waiting for Georgina. As she saw him watch her walk down the stairs, she knew she had a chance with him. She switched off the lamps in the room and said, "Come and sit by the fire for a moment." She sat on the woven carpet and waited.

Jud remained standing. For someone who wanted to become a monk, who must practice celibacy, he was feeling weak. His most recent girlfriend, now an ex-girlfriend, eighteen years old and not a virgin, had left him when he had reneged on an agreement to unite in sex with her on his sixteenth birthday, last February fourteenth, a date he was embarrassed to have as a birthday because his male peers thought St. Valentine's Day was a girlish day to have a birthday on and because his female peers showered him with flowers, candy, and requests for dates.

Georgina summoned Jud, again, but he remained standing. Georgina began to think she was attempting the impossible. Then, she started to feel a sense of fun. If her seducement didn't work, then she would have committed no sin; if it did work, she might have a child—either way, she won, as she saw it. As she relaxed, she saw that Jud felt a release of tension. As she smoothed her hair, her clasp fell out and her hair fell down her back as a sheet of black satin. She reached for the clasp. And as she sat on her hip with her legs to the side and raised her arms above her head to re-weave her hair and clasp it again, she looked at Jud from the corners of her eyes. He looked away from her. Many men would have been hard-pressed to resist her beauty and sexuality. But Jud remained where he was.

Georgina pulled the robe over her legs and said, "Jud, I'm very tired. Will you please sit with me. Conversation relaxes me before I go to bed."

Noticing that she seemed to have no family, he said, "You must not relax often then."

Georgina was irritated. She said, "We don't have to talk if you don't want to."

"I just mean that you don't seem to have anyone to talk to at night. And yet, I would think you would." Jud stopped talking. His conversation was awkward. Georgina's sexiness was stimulating his senses. All he could feel was her presence. The sound of the storm seemed distant from within the cover of a warm, dark room with a woman whose voice and movements sent out waves of sensuality that clung to him and caressed him.

As Georgina looked at Jud's face with desire coming from it, she realised that Jud was afraid of his own attraction to her, enough that he was too blind to see that she was trying to seduce him, which might have struck him with fear, if he had realised it. Georgina changed her tactic and said, "Tell me about yourself. I don't mind if you prefer to stay standing."

"I'm a high school student. That's all there is to say."

"There must be more."

He moved closer and said, "I like to write. About anything. And I read during any spare time I have."

"What do you read?"

"Shakespeare—his comedies, mostly. I don't care for his tragedies. I like classic literature mostly. Sometimes I read mysteries as a contrast to the philosophy books I enjoy. And I read Greek Mythology. Do you enjoy reading?"

"Not much. Unless it's art history and, of course, mythology. I love paintings, sculpture, and textile design." Georgina also read the Bible everyday and enjoyed Christian literature but she didn't want to remind herself of the Ten Commandments at this moment.

"Really?"

Georgina said, "Really. I have a problem with the Italian sculptors, though."

As he said, "How can that be?—the Renaissance sculptures are classical and beautiful," Jud walked to the fireplace and sat down, cross-legged, in front of her.

Subduing her pleasure at his nearness, Georgina said, "For example, Michelangelo's statue of David is magnificent. He is a fine specimen of a man but he has no manhood."

"What do you mean?"

"His penis is too small. One would think that Michelangelo had run out of his fine marble or that he had no experience of seeing a man with something larger. And all those other sculptors' male statues with fig leaves, put on by the Church, covering such small areas. They're absurd."

Jud was red in the face again but, feeling he should say something and try to seem unembarrassed, he said, "I guess there could have been some variations in size—but not to the extent seen in Far Eastern art."

Georgina laughed. "The huge, erect private parts would have ruined the statue of David for me far more than Michelangelo's meager showing." Georgina placed a hand over Jud's as he leaned on one arm.

Jud looked down. He wanted to stand up but was afraid to pull his hand from underneath hers. He asked, "What about paintings and sculptures of women?"

"From the Italian Renaissance?"

'Yes."

Georgina said, "Their stomachs are too big and their breasts are too small. They're too similar, I think. I would have painted thin women, fat ones—a variety." Her hand was still on Jud's. She looked into his eyes. She told herself she had nothing to lose. She said, "Jud, would you lie with me?"

Despite her perfect English, Jud was unsure if she knew the English language well enough to know what she had said but, regardless of what she meant, he wouldn't lie with her or lie down with her, so he said, "I can't."

"May I kiss you? On the cheek."

The firelight illuminated her smile and the cleavage of her breasts. Jud tried not to swallow in the silence—he was sure she would hear him.

Georgina leaned toward Jud and kissed his cheek. She said, "I must go to bed now. Will you undo my hair for me?"

Jud knelt in front of her. He felt the silkiness of her hair as he put his hands around the back of her head and undid the clasp. He struggled with the catch, at first, and apologised as he pulled on her hair. Then, once again, Georgina's hair tumbled down, sweeping over his hands. He would have handed the clasp to Georgina but, while his arms had been upraised, she had put her arms about his waist. He felt a sensation in his chest. He dropped the clasp and put his hands on her shoulders. His heart began to pound.

Georgina smiled and whispered, "Thanks." As she raised herself from sitting to kneeling, she moved closer to him than before and put her face close to his. She asked, "May I kiss you? On the lips, just once—I promise, that's all."

Jud moved his face close to hers and closed his eyes. Georgina took a deep breath. She held her lips to his and felt sensations rise through her gut as she felt the thrill of the forbidden. And the sweetness of his mouth. She was sure he was a virgin, as she had been when David had taken her. Other than her husband, she had never touched a man. Or boy. Tonight, on her birthday, she had expected her husband to make love to her on their bed, king-size and luxurious. Now, she intended to make love to another man on a woven rug barely distinct from the cold, hard stone. She was aware of a motion somewhere nearby but ignored it.

From the top of the dark stairwell, Bill turned away. He went back to his room without being able to speak a word about leaving, after all. He removed his clothes again and climbed into bed.

Disturbed by the sound of the guest room door and wondering who was in the house, Mrs. Binakas put on her slippers, left her room, and walked down the cold hall to the top of the stairs. Downstairs, darkness surrounded the firelight that cast its golden gleam on Georgina as she kissed a man, gilded by the light and less distinct. Mrs. Binakas squinted. Her eyesight was poor. But she knew that the physique belonged to someone other than David. The two figures were as a frontispiece, the frontal area in shadow, the edges around their figures were rimmed by light that gradated into indistinct light until disappearing into shadow.

Georgina thought she heard a sound. She took Jud's hand as she stood up and led him to her bedroom, now warmed up by the blaze in its fireplace. Georgina said again, "Lie with me."

No longer in doubt that she knew what she meant, Jud sat on an edge of the bed. Georgina gently pushed him back on the bed. He lay on his back. She lay beside him. Jud closed his eyes. He didn't know what to do. He wanted the whole scene to go away so that he wouldn't have to feel this desire to put his arms around Georgina and feel the fear of doing so. Then, he felt her straddle him. He opened his eyes as she pulled his shirt from inside his pants and unbuttoned it from bottom to top. As she pressed her body down on him, she felt the length and hardness of his penis. She kissed his chest. Jud rose onto his elbows, Georgina slowly kissed his lips as she eased his shirt over and off his shoulders, smooth and hard. Jud kissed Georgina back. Then she kissed his chest moving down to his abdomen. Jud could barely stand the erotic feelings he had. Georgina felt his body pulsing with desire in unison with her own. She tore away his shirt.

With one hand, Jud caressed her breasts lightly and, with the other, pulled her closer to him and kissed her harder. Georgina lost the last of her patience. She undid his jeans. He had no underwear. Jud removed his jeans as Georgina stripped off her dressing gown. He stood before her. She put her hands all over him, pulled him onto her bed, and then lay on top of him. They rolled over. And he was on top of her. Then, his words sliced into the fabric of their passion, bringing in an unwanted cold. He said, "I don't want to get you pregnant." He knew he was almost too late to say that.

Georgina went still. Jud felt her pause. He started to pull away. She put her arms around his shoulders and put her lips to his ear and kissed him there. An exquisite thrill rode down his long body. Georgina whispered, "It's okay. I can't have children." She held his buttocks. He thrust his penis inside her vagina. He was too fast, he climaxed—she had nowhere near begun. But those few moments with him had been enthralling. So this is what a younger man was like. As Jud lay on top of her, she felt his heart beating wildly. She caressed his back and thighs. He leaned on one hand and ran his other one down her side, along her right hip and thigh. Then, he touched her hip bone and massaged it. They kissed again and then their tongues touched. He kissed her breasts and her stomach. He was ready again.

They took a slower pace. He was a fast learner. And as he thrust in and out, she felt the friction on the sides of her vagina and had an orgasm like none she'd had before. The insides of her body pounded, slow and heavy, for a long time. He felt her body's heavy pulse; she felt his as he came with her. And then it was over. But, as he kissed her breasts and was ready again, she put her arms around him and held him tightly.

After their third time, they showered together. They returned to the bed: he with the intention to sleep, she with the intention of experiencing fellatio cunnilingus with him. It was after her intention was fulfilled that they made love again as they sat up, their legs around each other's hips. Then, they went to sleep. One hour later, before dawn, Georgina woke up from a dream that her husband would be home earlier than he had planned. She didn't believe in dreams as messages but she didn't want to take any chances. She woke up Jud. He kissed her. She wanted to make love with him again but didn't dare. Instead, she pulled away from his warm arms and told him that he and Bill had to leave after breakfast. Jud felt her brusqueness. He left her bed to have a shower. A cold one. But not as cold as Georgina's brusqueness.

Georgina lay waiting for Jud to come out. She would never see him again after today. Her husband would be home from business before New Year's Day. Within a few weeks, she might be able to tell him they were expecting a baby. She had much to look forward to.

After Jud showered, dressed, and left her room—all the while with Georgina's back to him—Georgina did the same, as quickly as he had. But Mrs. Binakas had been up earlier than usual. She was in the kitchen. Georgina ran to the foyer closet and reached into her coat pocket for her ring, which she hadn't wanted to wear while she made love to a man other than her husband and which she thought might deter a teenage boy from making love, although that was unlikely from what she had heard from friends more experienced than herself with men. Yet, she still didn't want Jud to see the ring this morning. But worse, she didn't want Mrs. Binakas to see her without it. So she put the ring on and ran to the laundry room where she pulled Bill's and Jud's clothes out of the dryer. She threw them on top of the boys' backpacks and tent roll, which they had put in the foyer, earlier. She ran to the dining room and saw Jud and Bill sitting on either side of Mrs. Binakas at the head of the table, David's place. In front of them lay a breakfast of boiled eggs, fresh greens and tomatoes, goat's milk cheese, olives, and toasted bread. Georgina looked at her mother-in-law's placid face.

Mrs. Binakas had decided to make the best of a bad situation by serving the boys, who had introduced themselves with foreign names unfamiliar to her ears, a good meal and hoping in her heart for the best. Mrs. Binakas did not agree with Georgina's tactics to have a child but it was too late now to change what she knew must have happened—she could see it in Jud's face and, now, in Georgina's. Mrs. Binakas thought that if a grandson came out of this, then the sacrilegious union just might be justifiable. With her eyeglasses on, she admired the good looks of the two young men at her side but with her inside feeling, she feared what could happen to her family if David ever found out about Georgina's adultery. Her first hope was that David never would find out. Second to that, she hoped she would die before he found out. Yet, she thought he should know. Thus, that morning, she had written a letter to give to the family lawyer. It was to opened by David upon her death.

Jud noticed Georgina's wedding ring. Although his family was Christian, he was not. And, even though he was not Christian or of any other religion, he was shocked that he had made love to another man's wife. Yet, rather than feeling more inclined to pursuing a monastic life, he knew now that he couldn't. Despite the techniques he knew he could use to avoid the temptation of sex, he had no wish to forego the pleasure of sex and the feeling of joy it gave him. Jud lowered his eyes. He could not look at the woman next to him who had introduced herself as Mrs. Binakas and was Georgina's mother-in-law and not her mother, as he had first thought when he had assumed that Binakas was Georgina's maiden name. If Georgina had been a widow, she would have been unlikely to have thought to have drawn the ring from her finger. Why Georgina had made love to him last night, Jud could not comprehend.

Georgina read Jud's face and was sorry for the pain he was feeling. With Mrs. Binakas in the room, she could not reassure him that he had no fault in having slept with her, a married woman. Georgina nodded to her mother-in-law and wished she could read her thoughts. She saw reproach in Bill's eyes. Sunshine and fresh air came in through the dining room window, framing rainbows that seemed to begin and end on Crete. The boys would have a warm, dry day for hiking and then re-pitching their tent. Georgina decided not to have breakfast with them. Without saying good bye, she turned around and left the room. Somewhere inside her, a modest sadness began to grow. Whom would she be hurting if a child came from all of this. Certainly not Jud.

§

David Binakas watched his wife's eyes begin to focus on his face and her present-day surroundings again. Georgina had been far away from him while she had told her story, an abridged one but full with what she had left unsaid and full with the emotions that had transformed her face during her story. Her fingers were holding the diamond and gold crucifix he had given her the year she had cuckolded him. Although he still loved her, he couldn't live with what she had done—he almost wanted to kill her and then himself. He could not accept that another man had known his wife in the most intimate way and that she had known the carnality of another man. He wanted someone to pay—to take away his pain.

As he had listened to Georgina, he had felt a swelling anguish and the quick birth of a desire to seek revenge on Jud for having touched his wife and for having given her a child—a daughter that he, David, had thought was his own. And for the impending damage that would be done to the marriage arrangement he had made eighteen months ago between his daughter—apparently Jud Thorensen's—and Stephen, son of Constantine Sgouros, the Greek City Planner, now David's friend but, at one time, an enemy.

Diana Binakas was to wed Stephen Sgouros in five years, once she turned sixteen. Stephen, now age thirty-one, had been forced by Constantine, per David's persuasion, to give up his engagement with a woman who had a modest dowry in order to accept the bid to marry into the influential Binakas family. Thus, Stephen had done as his father had wished: he had relinquished his lover—with a heartache that, because he had enameled it with indifference, reflected callousness to her—and he had become betrothed to Diana. Later, his ex-lover had married another man. David had felt guilty about his influence in helping to bring about Stephen's sorrow but hoped that Stephen's heart would mend.

Now, on the beach in Pherma, with Georgina sitting beside him and waiting for him to make the first move, David tried to piece everything together. He wondered why Athína Binakas, his mother, had given her letter to the lawyer only two and half years ago when she had known of Georgina's adultery for the last twelve years—she had either written the letter back then and simply waited to give it to the lawyer or had written it years later and then given it to him. Either way, she had known from the beginning about Georgina's sin. And, although she could not have known that Diana's father would become famous and impossible to remain unknown to David, David thought she should have revealed the circumstances of Diana's conception to him—at least once Georgina had revealed her pregnancy. And his mother should have told him of Georgina's adultery, regardless of whether or not Georgina had become pregnant.

David saw how odd it was that Georgina had not become pregnant during the first seventeen years of their marriage and, then, had never become so during the years that had passed after Diana's birth. He had hoped for more children after Diana. Now he knew why they had not come, before or after Diana's birth—he, not Georgina, was the one who had been unable to have children.

That Diana, age eleven as of last September thirtieth, bore no resemblance to him had not caused him to be suspicious of the authenticity of his fatherhood. Even Georgina, whom David had been with during childbirth, barely passed as the biological parent of Diana. When Diana had been a toddler, her face had seemed to lean toward the looks of Georgina or himself, but, now, as Diana approached the teens, her features had become more distinctive and unlike his or Georgina's, her slender figure grew tall—at age eleven and standing at five feet, seven inches, she stood face to face with her mother—and her hair remained fair.

David had even imagined Diana's resemblance to himself and, looking for it, had seen it. Yet, now that he knew she was not his child, he saw none. And anyone who had met Diana and then seen a photograph of Jud might awaken to an awareness of the pair's resemblance but Constantine Sgouros had likely recognised it as certain, since he knew of the possibility that Georgina had cheated on David, who, with his mother's letter tucked in his mind, had told Constantine of the fantastic notion that Georgina had slept with another man and that, of course, he didn't believe it—David and Constantine had been telling secrets only three months ago, while celebrating the January Second festival, as they had drunk raki all night. Then, still awake and beginning to sober during the morning, David had felt that no harm had been done to the arranged marriage because Georgina really had not betrayed him and, if she had, she could have done so after Diana's birth. But everything was different now—she had cheated on him; Diana was not his child, and he, David, had planted the seed of that possibility in Constantine's mind.

If it could have been that Jud Thorensen had remained anonymous, Mrs. Binakas's accusation had been left unwritten, and Diana remained known as David's child, then, when Diana reached sixteen, she would marry Stephen Sgouros and, eventually, bear his children. Then, once she had borne his children, if her biological heritage of being Jud Thorensen's daughter would come to light, a rage would rise that would know no bounds—David did not want to think of what Constantine would do if he were to discover that his grandchildren were also those of the man he thought of as the Antichrist, Jud Thorensen, author of The Crucifixion, a book Constantine had read and then burned. *Jesus Christ,* thought David, *he would probably kill them all.*

Thus, this morning, after David had bought the News of the Week, he had sat in his Athens office with Jud's image in front of him and when his secretary had told him that Constantine Sgouros was on the line, David had not taken the call that he feared. He knew he would have to speak with him soon. And when he did, he would let Constantine lead the conversation, just in case Constantine was not calling about Diana's real father.

Had David paid heed to his mother's letter two years ago, he would not have arranged a marriage that had been damned from the beginning. What marveled David was that Georgina had certainly remembered well the face of the man she taken as a lover and had recognised Diana's likeness to him for these many years. And, yet, she had said nothing.

David stood up. The air had cooled. The beach was overcast by a fog coming in. He offered his hand to his wife and pulled her up. He spoke to her, "I want you to do something for me." Georgina nodded her head. The terror she had felt earlier at home had laid a mantle of ice around her shoulders. She wondered what David was thinking about Diana. And about herself.

§

In bed that night, David lay awake. Georgina lay asleep beside him but far away, on the other side of the king-size bed, almost on the edge. He had made love to her but she had been passive. And he had been frustrated.

David felt like an idiot; he had raised Diana, someone else's child, as his own for eleven years. And, worse, Diana was to have played an important role in his life. David had built a small empire with Alpha-Omega Pharmakon and, through Diana's future marriage to Stephen Sgouros, he was to enjoy the power and prestige that would come from his family alliance with the Greek City Planner, Constantine—a planner of cities and a wielder of political influence. Diana's marriage would have united two families whose wealthy and impoverished relatives had feuded for generations until the feud had ended a generation ago; it would have been the first actual Binakas-Sgouros marriage, signifying a healing of emotional wounds that had come from the onset of a physical feud, which had begun when a Sgouros man had killed a Binakas woman, his future wife, in a fit of jealous rage over a man supposed to be her lover, who upon the girl's death, confessed that he had lied about her promiscuity and, in shame of what he had done, in grief over her death, had slain himself. But because of Georgina's sin, now visited on Diana, the marriage and the acquisitions that David had anticipated were disintegrating.

Georgina's fate was unknown to him. Georgina had fallen only once from the pedestal he had placed her upon. Her method of providing an heir, although not of his blood, could have succeeded—Diana could have looked like him. If Diana had looked like him, perhaps Athína Binakas would not have given a tell-tale letter to the lawyer because, although she would still have been sure of Georgina's infidelity, she would have been unsure of the child's biological heritage. And wanting a grandchild as she had and an heir for her branch of the Binakas family, Mrs. Binakas might have foregone her moral beliefs and let everything be. Yes, it was too bad that Jud Thorensen had not given Georgina a child that had traits indiscernible from those of the Binakases.

That all family members, Binakas and Sgouros, could have ignored the illegitimacy of Diana—legitimate by birth because it had occurred within wedlock but illegitimate by her conception—would have been improbable yet not impossible if Jud had stayed anonymous. They might have assumed that Diana exemplified Binakas traits from past generations that David did not.

David knew that Diana had seen Jud Thorensen on the news and he wondered what she was thinking because, of all people, she would be the one to look upon Jud's face and know it as her own. It was as if, one day, for some reason, she would want to show the world who her father really was and, at her conception, had chosen all of the genetic codes that would manifest her resemblance to him and prove her biological history.

David thought that he would, after he had carried out his revenge, exile Diana to a boarding school in a foreign country. He would miss her. Although his love for her was waning, almost as if it had never been, it still existed.

Yes, after David had proof beyond doubt that Diana was Jud's child, he would have his revenge. The plan had come easily to him, long before Georgina had finished her story in Pherma today. His plan to cause Jud's death would place no blame on his own shoulders, no blood on his own hands, and no suspicious looks to be cast his way.

§

The next day, David conversed on the telephone with Constantine about the ill-fated union of their two children for the first time. As David had expected, Constantine remarked upon the drunken night during which David had joked about Georgina's one night of lust with a stranger, when Diana must have been conceived.

And then Constantine said, "Jud Thorensen is, of course, Diana's father. And, of course, there will be no marriage between his daughter and my son."

David felt the anger that underlay Constantine's words and, as he had during the drunken night, David remained silent about his mother's letter, because Constantine would become enraged to learn that David had disregarded what Constantine would consider to be substantive evidence of Georgina's adultery.

Constantine added, "We will talk more about all of this when we meet."

CHAPTER TWO

Within a week of the Washburn crucifixion in March, Jud had arrived at his parents' home in Clinton, a rural town forty-five minutes outside of Ocean City, Massachusetts. News media had followed him there and joined with other television, magazine, and newspaper reporters who had already staked out the Thorensen home, as they had his apartment in Ocean City and Mara Sylvan's house, also there. Mara had refused to come to his parents' estate and, instead, had gone to her own place. Jud had jeopardised his relationship with her to the degree that he could lose her completely. Mara had not blamed him for making love to Angela Wynne, who would turn eighteen in April, but she hoped that his first instance of being unfaithful would be his last. So, when he had told her that he had asked Angela to come to Ocean City, Mara had told him that she needed time to think, by herself, and to understand her emotions.

In the meantime, Angela Wynne was caring for her mother, Doris, at their Washburn home, also staked out by the news media. Mrs. Wynne had recently been released from Washburn's only hospital after being diagnosed with hemophilia. Their small town was crowded with visitors wanting to see Golgotha Hill, where three crosses had once stood and two men had died. A third one was in a hospital in critical condition.

At the Thorensen household, the atmosphere was tense. Helen had wanted Jud to come to his childhood home against the wishes of her husband, Ogden, who was spending more time away from the house with his writer friends.

Lisbeth, Jud's teenage sister, was glad to have him home, even though some of her friends were no longer allowed to visit her while Jud was there because of the rumors, publicly unconfirmed, that he had made love to a teenager, Angela Wynne—rumors that she had seduced him were also circulating from Washburn. Privately, Jud had admitted his liaison with Angela to his family. Ryan Wallace, Jud's attorney, had told him that he was lucky that she had not been sixteen or younger—otherwise, the Steward County District Attorney would have charged him with statutory rape.

Jud's older brother, Pastor Jared Thorensen, in Maine, was unsure if he would be able to hold onto his ministry or his fiancée because of the notoriety that Jud had brought to the family name and had not yet come to see Jud since his return home.

Jud had told Helen that he should leave but she'd asked him to stay. She felt that he was misunderstood; she didn't care about what others thought that he had done or caused—she loved him. In fact, he was a hero—he had saved two lives. The ones who had committed crimes had each participated in his own way and had used Jud as an excuse for his own wrongs to others and, in particular, to Jud.

Helen knew that Bill Harcourt, as Jud's publisher, was receiving even more mail about Jud's book, The Crucifixion, since the Washburn tragedy. She wondered if the sacks of mail equaled the number that she had rerouted from her home to an office, complete with staff, she had rented in Ocean City. Helen had changed their home telephone and facsimile numbers to new and unlisted ones. She wished she could change their address as easily. Yet, the news media vehicles were beginning to reduce in number.

Helen was also concerned about her mother, Margit Kis, who was ill with no specific ailment—she was old and living alone in her large home, in Transylvania. When Mrs. Kis had been ill a few years ago one summer, Helen had taken Jud and Lisbeth with her while she cared for their grandmother; Jared had stayed at home with Ogden. Helen hoped she did not have to go to her mother's home now—she didn't want to leave Jud this soon after his ordeal. Also, she knew that, although Jud was not in a state to go anywhere yet, he would want to go with her to see his grandmother and visit, once again, the house in which he had been born—when Helen had separated from Ogden after an argument, she had, in her pregnant state, taken Jared with her to live with her mother and father, now dead. It was ironic that she, Helen, had been born in the USA while her parents had been staying in their American home—sold since her father had died—and, yet, had given birth to one of her three children in Transylvania.

Helen picked up the box that Jud had addressed to Angela on a pre-printed form with Ogden Thorensen's residence information on it from the side table in the lobby. She knew what was in it—a birthday gift. On Jud's first day back in Ocean City, on behalf of Angela, Jud had contacted the Bentilee College of Music to find out if they were still accepting applications—they were, even though the college had already sent out acceptance letters to many of their prospective students, not all of whom had responded. Thus, at Jud's request, Bentilee had shipped application forms with a catalog to Angela, who had completed them within a week and, along with her high school transcripts and written documentation about her formal training from her guitar and vocal teachers, shipped them via overnight delivery to the school. So, the birthday box contained a dress for Angela's audition at Bentilee in late May.

Lisbeth had volunteered to shop for the dress. Although her taste in clothes was wild and colorful, unlike anyone else's in the family, she had, in Helen's company, followed Jud's suggestion to choose a simple blue dress, a size four. And though Lisbeth preferred rock music and trendy shops, she had enjoyed being in an elegant shop with soft rock—yet, she had not revealed her pleasure to her mother, who would then have encouraged her to shop there for herself. Yet, Lisbeth had told Helen that she was looking forward to meeting Angela, only a year older than herself, and confided that she nor her friends cared that her brother had slept with

Angela. Most of her friends drooled over Jud. And, if the truth were known, so did most of their mothers who, while prohibiting their daughters from going to the Thorensen home, had continued to visit Helen and still smiled at Jud—if they caught a glimpse of him.

Helen sighed and took the boxed dress to the door where a man in an Air Express uniform waited. She greeted him, thanked him, gave him the box, and accepted the Sender's Copy. In the distance, down the tree-lined drive, through the iron gates, she glimpsed a parked luxury car, different from any of the news media vehicles with their station names or reporters' personal cars, dusty and well-ridden. This one looked clean and new. The tinted car windows looked black as the sunlight bounced against them.

Helen lay down the Air Express form on the side table, turned around and faced Jud who had just come downstairs. She knew he was hurting, physically and emotionally. But so was Mara, emotionally. She looked at the cuts around his neck and the rope burns around his wrists. Rather than his usual dress trousers and long-sleeve shirt, he wore jeans and a sleeveless tee shirt. His hair was wet from the shower after a workout that had taxed his tolerance for the pain caused by his injuries and intensified by any body movement. Helen could smell the medication he had put on his back. She said, "Turn around, sweetie." Jud sighed and turned. She gently lifted up his shirt and looked at the lashes on his back. She said, "The lacerations are looking less nasty. Did you take the painkiller pills?"

"No."

"I wish you would."

Jud said, "Mom, you know I won't take them. It's just something I don't do."

Helen herself didn't take aspirin or medicine of any kind for any reason but felt sure that she would if she had the kind of severe pain that her family doctor had said that Jud's wounds were likely causing him. Ogden had all kinds of medicines in the bathroom cabinet. Helen had started to substitute placeboes in some of the bottles—Ogden's only comment was that his sleeping pills were more potent. But sleep was one thing and pain another. She said, "Jud, you'll feel better if you get some relief from the pain."

The intercom buzzed. Helen pressed a button and said "Hello."

The person at the other end said, "I'm looking for Jud Thorensen."

"May I have your name?"

"Georgina Binakas."

Jud felt a wave of surprise flood through his body.

Helen said to Georgina, "Would you hold for just a moment, please?" She asked Jud, "Do you know her?" As she looked at his flushed face, she realised that he did.

Jud took a deep breath and wondered what was next in his life. He wanted to rest, to have no more input from the world. He was writing two thousand to five thousand words a day on the book, Desire; Sex & Spirituality, that he had started in Indiana. He had found it difficult to resume the book after a two-week lapse, caused by his abduction and imprisonment—and then their aftermath. He was used to the continuity of working on the first draft of a book every day without fail, until completion. So, he had no intention of dropping this project again for any reason—even for Georgina Binakas.

Although to Jud, the length of his pause had felt endless, to Helen, Jud's pause had been imperceptible and, in the moment Jud said he knew Georgina Binakas, Helen went to the intercom and pressed the button to open the gate. Security guards would ensure that no news media vehicles would follow. Helen opened the front double-doors and, without surprise, saw the black luxury car approach the circular fountain in front of her home. Although Helen was anxious to consult with the kitchen staff about the dinner arrangements for tonight—Bill Harcourt and his wife, Linda, were coming to dine with the family—at the moment, she wanted to meet the woman with the faint foreign accent.

Wearing a white chiffon scarf, black sunglasses, black suit, and black shoes, Georgina stepped out of the car. The water spurting from the sunlit fountain behind her lent no lightness to the solemnity of her manner or walk. Photo-journalists with their telescopic lenses took photographs. Jud stayed within the cool darkness of the lobby as Georgina climbed the steps to the open door.

Helen opened the door wider and said, "Welcome. I'm Helen Thorensen. Is it Mrs. Binakas?" Helen offered her hand.

"Georgina." As she stepped inside, she removed her dark glasses and shook hands with Helen. She looked at Jud. He was taller and more filled out—although, she observed from the looseness of his jeans at his waist, he must have been slightly heavier before the Washburn incident. He had become a gorgeous man.

Jud had lost his manners. He said nothing nor did he move. He recalled the day that Georgina had walked away from him. He had held no illusion that they would continue a love affair while he and Bill were on Crete or that she had any feelings for him. But he had felt hurt that they had not exchanged another word, as if she had gotten what she wanted and could cast him off as if he were an object rather than a human being. He had started to fall in love with her as they had sat in front of the fireplace before they had gone to the bedroom and made love all night—by morning, he had been sure he was in love. But she had pushed him out of bed. Then, when she had entered the dining room, she had looked as cold and hard as the wedding ring that had appeared on her finger, sometime between leaving her bed and then turning her back on him. One look of acknowledgment or one word from her would have dismantled his anxiety. But Jud had let that hurt go a long time ago. Then, as now, she had a life he knew nothing about and he had his own. Their pleasurable time had ended. He had moved on, as she had. It was surprise more than anything else that kept him tongue-tied.

Georgina said, "Hello, Jud."

He nodded.

Georgina came closer; she kissed his left cheek and then his right one. In the mirror above the marble table with the vase of lively flowers throwing color and fragrance into the room, she saw Helen's stare. She knew that her presence was exotic despite her dark clothes. It was provocative as she had intended. She wore nothing under the jacket. Her diamond and gold crucifix lay glistening on her bosom. And she wore a hint of eastern spice.

Jud asked, "What may I do for you?"

Georgina heard with a thrill the voice, now fuller, that had seduced her fantasy into reality on that wild, windy night on Crete when the storm had pounded at her home but had still been no rival for the night of passion she had spent with Jud. Her dark eyes stared into his.

Helen realised that her own presence was superfluous and impeding whatever exchange Georgina would have with her son. She said she had household duties to tend to and excused herself.

Jud took Georgina to the conservatory, its glass-paned roof peaked at eighteen feet. Cool, humid, and brick-floored, it stood toward the back of the house and was private. Potted trees bordered a dining table at one end. Exotic orchids bloomed in ceramic vases on side tables. A water spray came from a wall fountain. At the end wall, opposite the fountain, were Jud's desk and powerbook. Tucked in an alcove was a rolled-up sleeping bag. Jud slept in the conservatory every night so that he could fall asleep staring at the night sky with its galaxies. These days, he awoke just before dawn every morning. He disliked morning and afternoon, as bright to his eyes as daily life was intrusive to his thoughts. His pleasure was in the remains of the day leading to the peace of night and sleep. And, once awake, the privacy of pre-dawn. Sometimes, he would fall back asleep but most of the time, he would get up to write at his desk or walk outside.

Although the world of worry, politics, religion, careers, and consumerism bored him, he continued to care about people—not about their disagreements with each other or criticisms and judgments of each other but about their essence of beauty, love, and compassion—and he had been moved by the many letters of support that he was receiving. He wished that he could help whoever did not feel joy in his life to feel it and that he could help others to enjoy what made them happy—and to understand that they could be happy, regardless of their circumstances, good or bad.

He hoped for the best with his relationship with Mara. He would rather make love to her than worry about their future together. He would rather help Angela become independent and so risk Mrs. Wynne's misunderstanding of his motives than to leave Angela languishing under the rule of her mother, who saw a small world full of obstacles. He hoped that his brother Jared would be happy in his own life and not continue to use him, Jud, and the past events as reasons to be miserable, even if he would be unable to retain his ministry. And, Jud wished that his father, if never to speak with him again, would reclaim his own happiness—he was still the esteemed Ogden Thorensen, still had his friends, and still had a wife who loved him very much and could use his attention.

Jud knew that his family thought that he was suffering because of the abuse he had taken during in Washburn. They disbelieved that he was looking at it as history. He had learned from the Cretans twelve years ago that the past was the past. As it was, the Washburn experience had been exhilarating, even though he had known pain—and fear, especially on Mara's behalf and then Angela's. Now, he had a new sense of the eternity of his consciousness, regardless of physical hardship or physical death. He wanted to make the most of each moment rather than lose it to unhappiness about the past or to striving to make some future moment better—because the present one was not good enough. And thereby neglecting the present one, the only one he had.

Thus, Jud was ready to accommodate Georgina, if he could. He offered her a seat on a wicker settee with cushions. He pulled the cane chair from his desk, put its back toward her, sat upon it to face her, leaned his arms on the chair back, and said, "So, what can I do for you?" He smiled at her.

At first full of persuasion because she had expected resistance, Georgina had submerged her concern for Jud's well-being in the drama she was to lure him into. But, now, without the need to fill her mind and emotions with the art of heavy enticement, she was free to feel her fear for his life, which, after seeing him again, had intensified. But Diana was in Athens and would have no chance to live if Georgina did not return to Crete with a promise from Jud that he would follow. Or best yet, go to Crete with her now—yet, Georgina knew, as David did, that the Harper trial in Washburn might affect Jud's willingness to leave the United States before the trial would begin and then end. She suspected that David might not mind a delay till winter arrived because most of the tourists would be gone and rural Crete would be solitary again, better conditions for his plan. Georgina knew that the only way Jud would not be involved in the tragedy that her husband had planned for him was if she told Jud nothing and left. Yet, for Diana's sake, she could not do that. And David had told her that he had other means he could use any time he wished to bring Jud to Crete if she failed to. Georgina removed the scarf from her hair, pinned into a Psyche knot. She said, "I told you a lie, Jud."

Jud felt his heart rise in his chest. He felt his breathing quicken because he knew that there was only one thing that she had told him. He asked, "You mean that you could have children?" Without waiting for her answer, he stood up. And then he waited.

"Yes." Georgina held her crucifix as if it could save her from all that was to come. She could see in Jud's face that he knew what she was about to say and that he cared. The course was set. Blood would be shed. Yet, Georgina was relieved, because if Jud had not cared and would not go to Crete—and if David's other means should fail—then Diana would be sacrificed. If Georgina could have taken Diana out her Athens school without David's knowledge and brought her to her own family in California, she would have. But David had ensured that Georgina would be unable to do so by instructing the private school that he alone could remove his daughter from their tutelage and by his keeping a watch on every move Georgina made as he tended business from his house rather than from his Athens office. Georgina continued, "You and I have a daughter."

Jud felt overwhelmed. Because of that, he laughed. Then, he said, "You will excuse me. This is funny."

"I'm serious."

Jud stopped laughing. He said, "I know. But this is crazy—what am I to think or feel after all these years? And how can you be sure that your daughter is mine? Besides, your husband has been her father for eleven or so years." Jud paused and added, "Or is he no longer living?"

Georgina said, "He is alive." She pulled a photograph from a small, flat bag that hung from one shoulder. She handed it to him and said, "This is Diana."

Jud sat down beside her, took the photograph from her hand and looked at it. He passed it back to her and said, "I can see a similarity—if I want to look for it."

"She was younger in that one. This is what she looks like now." She gave him another photo.

Jud looked at it and then back at Georgina. As he handed her the photo, he asked, "What does your husband look like?"

"Nothing like you."

Jud stopped playing games. He said, "Diana hardly looks like you. I can see that she looks too much like me to not be mine." Slowly, a small feeling of kinship for the girl was forming. Jud resisted it. He asked with disinterest, "Why do you want me to know about her?"

"My husband, David, has a letter from his mother, whom you met in my home, that states my affair with you—she wrote your name, although poorly. David had disbelieved the letter, until he saw you on television and in magazines and then saw how much you and Diana look alike. He read the letter again and when he spoke aloud the written name in it, he heard the sound of the name he had been hearing on the news—yours. David didn't know how it could be possible for Diana to be your child—or how you and I could have met, in the first place. I had no choice but to tell him our story because Diana bears no resemblance to him. He is being very good about it and has sent me to invite you to our home to meet her. He had thought that a letter, even by courier, would be a poor way to break the news to you.

To give you an idea of my history: my family immigrated to this country from Crete before I was born. After my parents had begun to do well financially in this country, they could afford to take vacations in their homeland. So, my teenage summers were spent on Crete. My parents arranged my marriage to David Binakas with his mother. Mrs. Binakas has since passed away."

Jud said, "I'm sorry."

"Thank you." Georgina continued, "My mother-in-law loved Diana, even though she had wanted a grandson. Diana was born in California because I went there to stay with my family during my pregnancy—David agreed to this because he anticipated that I would get the best pre-natal care in the States. He wanted everything to go right. But my reason was that I wanted Diana to be born here so that she could have American citizenship, since that is what I have. Yet, because of David, Diana is a Greek citizen—Greece recognises Diana's dual nationality even though it is unrecognised by the US. Except for vacations in California, Diana has spent her life in Greece. She is a happy child. David feels that, because Diana was born here in the States, she should know her American father."

"It seems to me that your daughter would be better off by knowing nothing about me."

"Diana has a right to know about you. She will find out anyway."

Jud ignored what she had said and asked, "Georgina, why me?"

She rose, stood close to him and said, "Do you expect me to explain in a few sentences my history with David and all the reasons for my decisions that led up to the night that you and I spent together?"

"No. I know I couldn't explain my life. I'm just asking, why me?"

"You were in the right place at the right time, even though you, obviously, were not the perfect choice. Your friend would have been a better one."

"I want to feel bitter about this. You used me. You kept someone you call my daughter away from me. She and I know nothing about each other. And now, after these lost years, you want us to meet. If she should find out about me, just tell her I don't matter. Your husband is the one who loves her and has raised for all of these years." Jud left unsaid that he felt a strong urge to meet Diana.

"Jud, you are tiring me. Will you come to see her?"

Her tone reminded him again of that night when she had commanded him to come to her side. Now, he sat on the cane chair and put his head in his hands. His head was starting to hurt. He didn't want to forsake a little girl or her mother but what could he ever say to Mara that would not be the last straw to break the camel's back. That she had been taxed emotionally by his recent exploits might seem as nothing to her when compared with his having a child—with another man's wife. He rubbed his temples and said, "I will have to let you know. I cannot make a decision right now."

Georgina was disappointed. She put a hand on his hard bare arm and slid it around his scarred wrist, near his face. Her knuckles brushed his cheek. She said, "Please."

Jud raised his head, put his hands down, and looked into her eyes as he said, "I want a DNA test before I make a decision."

Georgina was taken aback even though she knew that David wanted this also. She said, "But surely you can see that she looks like you. I've been with two men in my life, my husband and you. Diana is yours."

"I want a DNA test and to see a copy of the results for myself. I do believe you. And I have a gut feeling about this—I don't need scientific evidence to know that Diana is of my blood. But I want the test—more for her sake because, if I do come to visit, I think that everyone should be sure that I'm her father."

"Very well."

"Isn't your husband upset about all of this? I still don't understand why you want to disrupt your family life."

"Diana is looking more and more like you. She has told me that there are whispers at her school that she seems different from her father and even from me. It's not just the looks. It's her mannerisms. Even her thinking.

She's more relaxed about life—as you are. David is not. Diana's told me at times that she would think she had been adopted if she and I didn't share a similar voice and have common interests. We also get along well. She and David love each other but they don't get along well. He won't accept her as she is. He is very religious, as I am; he likes a system and controls, as I do. Yet, Diana is free-spirited. But while I allow her freedom, David scolds and restricts her. Then, she cries. Don't get me wrong—she is happy. David is a good father but he and I both think that it would be good for her to relate with a kindred spirit. And that would be you." Georgina was telling truths and lies. Either way, she was revealing more than she had wanted to. Yet, she needed Jud to come to Crete, the sooner the better, because, then, Georgina wouldn't have to live with the dread of what was to happen— once it had happened, it would be in the past and she could then look ahead to happier moments.

Jud absorbed what Georgina had told him. He was sure that he would go to Crete to meet Diana. But not yet. He said, "Let's take this one step at a time."

"All right. My husband has a pharmaceutical company through which we can send your blood sample to a lab that tests DNA and compare it with Diana's." With one movement, Georgina leaned over Jud's forearm, turned it to the underside, and, without touching a vein, pressed hard as she cut into his skin with her crucifix. Georgina blotted his blood with her chiffon scarf. She folded the scarf so that the blood was in the inmost part and put it inside her small bag.

He said, "I would have given you a strand of my hair."

She said, "It's easier for the lab we use to test blood." David had told her that he wanted a blood sample from Jud. Then, the same lab, lab technicians, and testing method could be used for Jud's and Diana's DNA. And his own.

Jud looked down. Blood still oozed. He grabbed a rag lying near a watering can on the ground. He held the rag to his arm and then tossed it down. He had been cut by diamonds twice—Angela had cut him with her engagement ring in Washburn, by mistake, and now Georgina had sliced his forearm with a diamond crucifix, on purpose.

Georgina handed Jud the latest photo of Diana and said, "You may keep this one."

Jud took it. He walked to his desk and put it down.

Georgina said, "There's one more thing. David has requested that you not tell anyone about your coming to Crete—for now." She continued, "Diana has not been told about you, yet. And we don't need you to bring the news media to Crete. With your fame, any news about you will be splashed all over the world. Here's my address and phone number—but don't call unless you have to. How should I get in touch with you—other than by courier?"

Still standing by his desk, Jud wrote down his new e-mail address on a piece of paper and gave it to her as she came near him—she put it inside her bag without looking at it. Jud saw Georgina's eyes water and tension cross her brow—he wondered why. He admired her face and figure, constant reminders to him of their night together. He thought he should inquire where she was staying and invite her to stay for dinner. He did neither. Instead, he walked her to the front door. "By the way," he asked, "do you have other children?"

"No. My husband had a son during a previous marriage but his son, along with his first wife, died in a car accident."

Jud realised that Georgina must have believed, prior to the time he had met her, that she could not have children. And, somehow, found out that she could while it was her husband who could not.

Georgina looked into Jud's face, covered by a mask of indifference, and hoped he would come to Crete soon, for Diana's sake—one night, while Diana had lain asleep, David had led her into Diana's room and held a dagger close to Diana's face. Then, he had led Georgina into the hallway and whispered that she had best do whatever it took to get Jud Thorensen to Crete, even if she had to make love to him, or he would kill Diana. Although lesser than her fear for Diana's life, she had felt a shiver of fear for her own life, which could be in danger if David had no care if she slept with Jud again—unless it was David's test to see if she would cheat on him anew. Yet, unsure of what could come to pass, she had gone to her gynecologist in Athens and been fitted with a diaphragm.

But, now, as she stood at Jud's door, ready to be ushered out, she saw that she had gone to the trouble for nothing. And she did not have the definite commitment from Jud that David wanted. So, as Georgina put on her dark glasses, she asked, "Will I see you again before I return to Crete in a couple of days?"

"I don't mean to be unkind Georgina—but for what purpose? I promise I'll let you know—one way or another." Because he didn't want her to feel rejected, because he still cared for her, and because she was the mother of his child, he put his arms around her and held her for one moment. Then, he opened the door and watched her walk to her car.

He went upstairs to his room to change for dinner. Then, he returned to the conservatory to get Diana's photograph and put it in his shirt pocket, next to his heart.

CHAPTER THREE

Before dinner with the Harcourts, Jud asked his mother to say nothing about Georgina Binakas's visit. When Helen asked him why, Jud said that it was not social conversation. When she asked him what the nature of the business had been, Jud paused. He thought of telling his mother about her granddaughter and then decided against it because he knew that she would persuade him to see the child, regardless of whatever his own desire was, and, if he were allowed, to bring her home with him, which he was disinclined to do, even to visit her grandparents. He wondered what game Georgina and David were playing with him. While sincerity had infused much of what Georgina had said, deception had nudged around it. Yet, Diana was real and honest. But he wanted to make up his own mind about a commitment to go to Crete without his mother's strong influence. Also, he recalled Georgina's request that he tell no one about his fatherhood. But there was one person that he was going to tell. In the meantime, he told his mother that the nature of business was unimportant.

During dinner with Bill and Linda, Jud paid partial attention. His thoughts about Diana were running rampant. Even without Diana, his attention to his dinner companions would have been sparse because, when he was in the process of writing a book, he would pay full attention to someone and then lose awareness of him as new ideas for his book rose up and occupied him. Several moments would pass before he would realise his lack of attention and then bring his mind back to focus on his present company. Tonight, rather than his book, Diana's face filled his eyes and her existence filled his thoughts. Parenthood was something he did not desire—as it was so with marriage. But he was not faced with either, yet. Visiting Diana was not the equivalent of being a father to her. And Mara, who was the only woman he would propose to if he ever wanted to wed, had said she had no interest in marriage or children. Jud knew from Gail, Mara's work associate, that Mara and Ryan Wallace had once had a relationship. At the time that Jud had retained Ryan as his lawyer, he had been unaware of that. Later, Gail had told Jud that Mara and Ryan had gone through hell together—about what, she was unaware of. Jud wondered if Ryan could be the reason that Mara discounted marriage—and perhaps children—for herself. And he wondered how Mara would regard Diana.

After Jud said good night to Bill and Linda, who had their own young daughter, safe at home, Jud had a word with his mother, grabbed his overcoat and was about to leave the house when his father walked through the front door. Jud stood aside and looked at Ogden with the hope that he would acknowledge him or speak to him but Ogden, with pale hair and ice-blue eyes, brushed by Jud with a silence that blasted as the howl of a Norwegian wind would on a winter night. Jud felt a shaft in his heart but ignored it. In back of him, he heard Ogden call out to Helen.

Jud pulled his sports car out of the garage and drove down the long driveway. As the gates opened, camera flashes blinded his eyes. He stopped the car, got out, and became surrounded by the media.

Questions came from all directions. Where are you going. Whom are you seeing. Tell us about the upcoming trial with Rev. Jon Harper. Are you going to Washburn soon. Are you going to write a book about your abduction and near-crucifixion. How do you feel about Jesse Redmond and the Farnhams after what they did to you. Do you think they deserved what they got. Did you sleep with Angela Wynne. What happened to your relationship with Mara Sylvan—is she giving you the cold shoulder. Who was the woman in the black suit at your home today. Are you going to pose in the nude for Flirt. How does your father feel now that your work is being critically acclaimed. Is your next book controversial. Why didn't you shoot Rev. Harper. Are you afraid for your life. Did you know that—.

Jud said, "I can only repeat what you learned today—the trial is scheduled for September first. I will be there to testify during its beginning." This was his first statement in two days. "I mainly just want to thank you for your restraint. I know you have your jobs to do but I can't answer any more questions right now. My mother feels badly for you all and wants to know if she can send any refreshments out to you. I can call her on my cell phone, if you do."

The news media crowd laughed. That was just like Helen Thorensen. She was always gracious and kind, even when some of their members asked questions that trespassed the border of nicety. Ogden was polite but preoccupied. Lisbeth always smiled and waved at them—all of the members went easy on her with questions, even though she told them some things that they might not have dared to ask about. In fact, it behooved them to just listen to her.

Tonight was a bonus for the news media because Jud had been rarely glimpsed once he had disappeared into the Thorensen estate upon his return from Washburn. They liked him because, unlike his older brother, Pastor Jared Thorensen, who was reserved and economical with his time, Jud often gave them the time of day, once he emerged into the public eye. And, like his mother, he was kind. They had seen that when, standing without defenses, he had faced them inside the large auditorium of Triunity University in Washburn. They had been ready to verbally crucify him but, instead, once seeing him in person, many of them had simply asked questions and listened to his answers. Some press members, though, were getting tired of Jud's evasiveness about his personal life. One of them asked again about Mara Sylvan and how she felt about his cheating on her.

Although the question was an effective way to cut down on Jud's time with them, Jud was simply anxious to reach his destination. So, he said, "If you don't mind, call my office number to set up a another time for questions." He laughed and added, "Come up with some new ones."

Someone said, "What do you think of rape?"

Jud looked into the eyes of the only photographer who had infiltrated Washburn's hospital, under security from the news media, on the night of Good Friday and said, "Why do you ask?"

The photo-journalist had found out about the blood on Jud's bed-linen and, having heard from a private source that Rev. Jon Harper had made implications regarding Jud and Angela, had begun speculating. He had seen Jud with Angela and didn't think that Jud had raped her, or was capable of such an act with anyone, but it would make a good story, if he had. Jim Brandtem said, "I just wondered. And it is a new question, isn't it?"

Jud said, "Yes, well, ask me again another time." He climbed into his car and waved as he drove off. Mara had told him to be polite to the news media. As an investigative reporter, as well as someone also pursued by reporters, Mara knew and understood both sides of the experience. But Jud hadn't needed her advice. Yet, he knew his quietness could be mistaken for coldness. Thus, he made it a point to overcome his innate reserve with his innate friendliness.

§

Jud reached Mara's home. Mara didn't know he was coming. The interior lights were out, unusual even at eleven o'clock for her. Jud realised that, in his anxiousness to see her, he had been reckless in action. He sat in his car. The lights around her home contrasted with the darkness of her windows. He felt embarrassed. It was obvious to the reporters at Mara Sylvan's home that she didn't know that Jud Thorensen had been coming to see her or, if she had known, she didn't want to see him. It occurred to Jud that Mara might not even be home. He got out of the car and was deluged by questions and camera flashes again. The hitherto unknown author of The Crucifixion and his own close call with being crucified would be big news for a while. Jud said good evening to everyone and knocked on Mara's door. As he stood there, he turned to face the news media and said, "You've caught me with egg on my face. I didn't call her first."

The reporters laughed and would have persisted with questions but Jud told them what he had told the reporters around his home—to call his office. And then, the door opened.

Mara had just woken up from hearing voices outside and come to the door. Questions and camera flashes stopped abruptly after Mara gave a brief smile, pulled Jud inside, and shut the door. She wanted to talk to him. She took his coat. Jud tried to kiss her lips, she turned away. When he started to speak, she held up her hand. Although Mara was exhausted, she hadn't been able to sleep until she had taken half a sleeping pill. It had caused grogginess. Every sound around her was intensified. It was like a hangover, something she'd experienced once and hadn't liked. She ground coffee beans in the all-in-one coffee maker and winced from the noise. She added water and started the percolation. Her head hurt. But she still wanted to wake up.

Jud stood waiting and looked at Mara's tousled gold hair and her short cotton robe. He knew she had nothing on underneath. Suddenly, he didn't feel like talking at all. In the low light of her kitchen, Mara saw the look in Jud's eyes. She poured the coffee into bone china beakers and placed them on the counter in the middle of the kitchen. Then, she left, went upstairs, and returned in a sweater and jeans. Jud was sitting on a stool and holding his coffee.

Mara said, "I imagine that you have something to tell me judging by the way you came here late tonight without calling first. And I have something to tell you. You can start, though, if you want to."

Mara seemed inaccessible to him and unlikely to be receptive to anything he might say. Jud's heart ached. He said, "Mara, I made a mistake. It's late and this isn't the time or place for what I was going to say. I'm sorry." Because Mara was still standing, Jud stood up again; he put down his coffee. He looked down as he waited for her to tell him her news.

Mara sensed his hurt and said, "Jud, I do want to hear what you have to say."

He looked up. She didn't sound sincere. He said, "Not now."

If she hadn't been anxious to tell him her news, she would have coaxed him to tell her what was on his mind. Instead, she said, "Well, all right. I spoke with my mother—"

"And while we're on this subject, Mara, just who is your mother? The first time I heard that you have alive-and-well parents was on Good Friday in Washburn."

"Let me tell you a few things first. My parents have never claimed me. I don't have either one's last name. At my mother's sister's home, my parents visited me, until I was seventeen, when I got tired of their secrecy about me and left. I confess my parents paid for my education and supported my career. I do love them—very, very much. But it's painful to be unacknowledged by your own parents in public. When I was born, my mother was single and my father was married to someone else. Did you notice how Sheriff Bledsoe, in Washburn, sometimes stared at me,?—I look very much like my mother who, in recent years, has become well-known and makes television appearances. My father was famous before I was born. He recently divorced. That's why I'm able to tell you this now. His affair with my mother has become a moot point. He just married her—after many years of being apart, other than to come together to see me. They eloped right after his divorce became final. Apparently they were trying to reach me while I was locked up with you in Washburn and, when they couldn't, left for a honeymoon in Europe. When they got there, they saw me in the news with you. They decided that since I was all right they would have their honeymoon. They've been making their own headlines since their return today. They're upstairs right now."

Jud hung on every word Mara spoke. He waited for more.

"You can imagine the reporters' reactions to their arrival. They were almost as amazed as I was—in a different way, though—they were amazed at who my parents are while I was amazed that my parents had started up their relationship again and gotten married. The three of us have been answering reporters' questions all afternoon."

"Mara, who are your parents?" She was driving him crazy with her cat-and-mouse game. While Mara elicited information from subjects under investigation with silence and a few well-timed questions, she meted out her own information in her own chosen sequence and timing, regardless of the torture to the listener, straining from unquenched curiosity.

Knowing Jud was entrenched in wanting to know, Mara continued, "We spent all evening trying to catch up on each others lives—I hadn't seen either of them for months."

"Mara. Please."

She breathed out, "My father is Van Silverman, the lead singer for Romeo, and my mother is Dr. Sherry Hall, psychologist and feminist." Mara felt awed by her own words.

Jud was blown away. At last, he said, "I am very happy for you, Mara, and your parents."

She looked at Jud and appreciated his sentiment. She hadn't meant to prolong her story. It was an overwhelming emotion for her to be able to admit who her father and mother were. She had trained herself for her entire life to never speak of them as her parents and she felt that she had just told a secret that should still be untold. She said, "I'm happy for them. But it's been difficult for me to live my life without being able to say who my parents are. Most of my childhood was spent with my mother's sister and her husband. And they have a son, older than I, so, in a way, I have a sibling. When I think of it, over all, perhaps it wasn't as difficult as I had sometimes thought it was."

"I hope I will meet your parents." Right now, he planned to leave and let Mara go back to sleep—she looked tired.

Mara said, "I'm not sure."

"You mean, they don't want to meet me?"

"I mean that you might not want to meet my mother. Tonight, I told her about us. And, I'm sorry to say now, about Angela and you. I should have known Sherry would go into a tirade. She told me that while we had relationship problems, we should abstain from sex."

"And is that all that you were going to tell me if I hadn't asked about your parents?"

"Actually, I was going to tell you only about my parents." She paused and then continued, "My mother didn't think that I should tell you of the idea of abstinence from sex and that I should just refuse your advances."

"And what do you think?" Jud had no idea what she would say now.

He was caught off-guard when Mara said, "I think that if we abstained without my telling you why would cause more problems—you would think that I didn't find you attractive in that way any more. We can't have that." Mara put her arms around him and kissed him hard. He lost his balance and backed into a wall. His body wrenched from the pain that seared through his wounded back upon the impact. Mara held his shoulders and, with her lips against his, whispered she was sorry. Then, she gently unbuttoned his shirt, pulled it from his arms, and threw it down on the kitchen floor—all the while she was kissing him. Jud pulled off her sweater. They went into the dark living room. She took off his belt; she undid his trousers, pulled down on them and let them fall. He pulled off her jeans. Jud and Mara knocked a small table over as they fell onto the couch. They made love. As Jud was unable to distinguish between the feel of extremes in hot and cold, he was unable to differentiate between the physical sensations of pain from his wounds and the ecstasy from Mara's lovemaking. Later, Mara opened a window to let in fresh air and pulled a sheet over them. They fell asleep wrapped in each other's arms.

Jud woke up and saw a faint light start to brighten through the curtains. He fell asleep again and dreamed. He saw Diana's face but it kept changing. When he awoke again, Mara was just opening her eyes, a sliver of sunlight running across them. Through the entry that led to the upstairs and the kitchen, he caught a glimpse of Van Silverman, in black leather, making fresh coffee and Dr. Sherry Hall just picking up Jud's shirt off the floor. A paper fell to the floor. Outside, he heard the voices of reporters and photographers; inside, he heard the ring of the telephone. Jud kissed Mara's shoulder as she moved her arm from his hip to his chest. He closed his eyes. He opened them again when Van Silverman, his long brown hair framing a good-looking face with faint lines, stooped down in front of him and said, "You have a call."

Jud took the cordless phone from Van who, embarrassed by seeing his only child in the arms of a man, left the room immediately. Mara kissed Jud but said nothing. She reached for her clothes from the floor, dressed, and left so that he could have privacy.

Jud said, "Hello."

Helen said, "Good morning, sweetie."

Because his mother had seemed unable to prevent herself from calling him that name, Jud had long ago stopped asking her not to. When she said nothing further, he asked, "Are you going to tell me why you called?"

Helen was wondering who had just answered Mara's telephone with an English accent. She said, "Angela Wynne telephoned. I told her you would probably be home later. She was very sweet and said she would call back. But I wasn't sure if you would be coming home today, so I just wanted to let you know that she had called. I sensed that she was concerned about something."

"Thanks, Mom. I will be home later."

"Love you."

"I love you, too. Bye." Jud pulled on his trousers and everything else, except for his shirt, which dangled enticingly on a stool next to the one that was occupied by Dr. Sherry Hall. He took a deep breath, walked through the entry, and swiftly grabbed his shirt as he said good morning to the doctor. He held the shirt to his chest.

Sherry said, "Good morning. May I call you Jud?"

"Of course." Jud pulled on his shirt and buttoned it.

Rather than tell him what he could call her, she said, "You don't have to call me Dr. Hall." She observed his dishevelment and felt the sexuality of his energy. She was disturbed by her daughter's blatant disregard of her advice and continued, "These are not favorable conditions for us to meet in but they will have to do. I can't tell you or Mara what to do but I would advise you to see a psychologist together—and perhaps separately as well. You need to work things out with each other."

Jud said, "Thank you for the advice. But with all due respect, Sherry, no one knows Mara better than she knows herself. I'm sure someone could tell me something I don't know about myself but I'm not planning, now or in the future, to lay my life experiences in the mind of a stranger who, unfamiliar with them, and having no basis of understanding of my nature will dissect them and then offer me advice from a perspective that comes from his own set of beliefs and his own experiences in life, which have small or no similarity to my own." Jud was surprised at himself. He was making a bad start with Mara's parents, especially her mother. He added, "I respect your profession. I believe it helps many people. But it's not for me. It's up to Mara regarding herself."

Sherry stared at Jud. No one had said anything like that to her before. And, although she disagreed with him, she felt a smile inside, a smile she withheld from her lips. Jud was independent and, perhaps, wild. She had the feeling that no one could shake his self-reliance.

Jud smiled at Sherry. He liked her. She had the same gold hair that Mara had and the same glow of mischief in her eyes. But he knew she was a very different person.

Mara entered the kitchen. She was followed by Van, who offered to make breakfast for them all. He had expected to find an awkward atmosphere. Instead, his wife and Jud Thorensen were relaxed with each other.

Jud excused himself and ran upstairs to Mara's bathroom to wash in the claw-footed bathtub, recently vacated by Mara, and then went into her bedroom closet to don the fresh clothes he kept there for overnight sojourns. When he came down again, he had Diana's photograph in the pocket of a clean white shirt. When he had first put it in a shirt pocket yesterday, he had put Diana's face toward his heart. When he had pulled the photograph out of that same shirt this morning, her face had been in the opposite direction. Then, he had known that the wisp of paper that had flown out of his shirt pocket and had been picked up by Sherry had been real, not imagined. If Sherry had looked at Diana's photographic likeness to himself before putting it back in the pocket, it was no wonder that she had spoken to him as she had. Now, he knew that he could not back out of telling Mara about Diana. He had considered backing out because Georgina had emphasized that he not tell anyone and because, whenever he thought about the act of telling Mara, he felt nervousness rush through his body. But the main reason was that he thought that Mara would grow tired, once and for all, of his secrets, which, since most of them had been by his own choice to have kept, were unlike hers which she had been bidden by her parents to keep.

As soon as Jud had entered the dining room and then sat down in front of hot tea and an English breakfast of oatcakes, a Midlands food with a secret recipe that Van had guessed at, and treacle syrup, Van said to Jud, "I hear that you've found a singer with a big voice. What is it that she wants to do with all her talent?" Contrary to his wife's feelings about Angela Wynne, he doubted that Angela could come in-between Jud and Mara and, now, even though he was still enjoying popularity as what people referred to as an aging rock star, he was interested in finding and developing new talent. And he wanted to know about Angela Wynne.

But Van looked at his daughter's face and decided to pursue his quest when he and Jud were alone. Sherry's face clearly showed that he had been more than insensitive.

§

After spending the day with her parents and dining with them in the evening, Mara decided that her newly-wedded parents should have privacy in her home, from which even Jewels, the golden retriever whose owner, a jewel thief, sent to jail by Mara's hand was gone—the thief, out on parole, had come to Mara's house and re-claimed his dog two days ago.

Mara also decided she wanted to be alone with Jud. So she suggested that he and she go to his family home, which offered more privacy than her own did.

Once at the Thorensen estate, they saw Ogden, who was just on his way out. Mara greeted him and kissed his cheek. After he kissed hers, he said good night. As was usual, while Jud looked for signs that his father was feeling less harshness toward him, Ogden ignored him.

Mara entered the conservatory while Jud went to the kitchen to make a phone call. It was to Angela. Mara turned from her view of the night sky as Jud entered the room and closed the double-doors behind him. She took the glass of water he handed her; she walked to his desk where her bag was and pulled out a birth control pill, which she swallowed with a sip of water. As usual, she double-checked that she had not missed taking one. She had never missed before, nor had she now. She couldn't go through another abortion again—the emotional upheaval she had put herself through had been too much. Ryan had been using condoms and then said that he didn't want to anymore; when he had told her to get a diaphragm, she had done so. But, one night, feeling half-hearted about their relation-ship, she had inserted it incorrectly and become pregnant. Until that time, she had not wanted children but she had wanted that child more than anything else in the world. Yet, Ryan had not wanted it. What had tran-spired after their disagreement had brought hell into her life. When she had told Jud that she didn't want marriage or children, she had meant it. And still did. But she also knew that, if she were to become pregnant again, she would keep the baby, not based on moral issue but based on her heart. In the meantime, she preferred to stay single and childless.

Jud asked, "Are you sure you wouldn't be more comfortable if we went upstairs to my bedroom?"

Mara said nothing and pushed a button on a stereo that sat on a table in the alcove holding Jud's sleeping bag. A serenade played. She put her arms around his neck and when he put his arms low around her hips, they slow-danced as they had less than two weeks ago by Lost Lake. Jud started kissing her. Outside, the trees allowed the winds to play their games and responded with sways and whispers. Dark clouds moved aside for the moon and let a few stars glisten through. Mara's and Jud's hearts beat together in a faster rhythm. Jud kissed her neck and shoulders. Mara kissed his hair and caressed his body. It seemed as if hours passed. After he let her go, he unrolled the sleeping bag and lay it near the glass-paned wall overlooking a garden that slipped into the distant lawn. The dark garden lay with budding spring flowers and brimmed with summer's promise of a wild array of roses. Hedgerows lined either side of the garden, the field, and ended at the copse. Mara lay down in her clothes; Jud lay down in his. They embraced. Slowly he removed her clothes and offered her pleasures that she could not name. Later, she made love to him. And then, cocooned in the sleeping bag, they slept.

Mara woke before dawn to see that Jud's eyes were open. A soft lamp-light lit gleams in his eyes. The brick floor's hardness had seemed to press through the sleeping bag. But its coldness had not. Leaving the warmth, Jud and Mara dressed, put on coats, and went outside into the cold and dark. Jud closed the conservatory door behind them and led the way down the stone path under the arbor, along the right hedgerow of boxwood.

Mara took his hand as they walked. She asked, "Jud, are you troubled by what happened in Washburn?"

"No."

"You hardly sleep anymore."

"I feel restless. I have dreams. But no nightmares—I'm not troubled. All that you and I went through is over." He added after a pause, "But, there may be more to come."

"What do you mean?"

"There is something I have to tell you. But you can't tell anyone. Your mother might have already guessed at part of it."

When he didn't continue, Mara stayed silent. They were nearing the field and would soon be in the dark copse.

The sky was becoming lighter. Mara said, "Jud, you don't have to tell me anything." She meant what she said but she also was aware that what she had said would likely create in Jud what it had created in many people who heard it: an irresistible urge to spill out their guts. Especially, the way she said it because she had never been anything but sincere during each instance of saying it.

Yet, before Mara's verbal relinquishment of hearing him out, Jud's urge to tell her about Diana already existed. He just didn't know how to begin.

Mara waited. Then, she said, "What does it have to do with?"

"A little girl."

"Whose little girl?" She thought about Blossom Harcourt, Bill and Linda's daughter.

"A girl who belongs to a woman on Crete." Jud felt as if he were learning to think, as if he had to consciously think of one sentence and then the next, as with learning to walk again, he supposed, placing one foot forward and then the other. And so, being afraid to take the next step, he was afraid to state the next sentence.

When Jud said nothing more, Mara asked, "What does this girl have to do with you—have you met her?"

"No."

Mara waited.

Jud said, "But I think I will meet her."

Mara hardly recognised Jud—although he could be silent when he preferred to enjoy stillness or his own thoughts, he was rarely silent from experiencing a loss of words, as he was now. She said, "You act as if you're afraid to tell me who she is."

"I am." He stopped walking.

Mara stopped. She still held his hand.

"Mara, the girl is my daughter."

Mara steadied her own pulsing senses. She released his hand and put her hands in her coat pockets. In the dimness, she could see more clearly than she could have if they had stood in brightness because, rather than being distracted by vision, she could sense vibrations of thought and emotion that she might otherwise have missed. She cognised that many past and future events surrounded his admission. She said, "Tell me about her."

"She's eleven years old. Her name is Diana. Her parents are Georgina and David Binakas. Only, I'm the one who fathered her.

"Bill Harcourt and I were backpacking on Crete when we were sixteen. There were many storms. During one of them, we were picked up by Georgina and brought to her home. She and I made love. Bill and I left the next morning.

"Georgina came to my parents' home two days ago and told me about Diana. And about the letter her mother-in-law had left for her son, David, to read upon her death. It told about Georgina and me—it gave my name. I don't know just when he read the letter but he did nothing about it until he saw me in the news and noticed that Diana looks like me. Georgina thinks it's inevitable that Diana will find out about all of this so she and David want to be the ones to tell her. They want me to meet her. I don't know why. Nor do I know when they plan to tell Diana about me."

Mara asked, "What happened that night on Crete?"

Jud didn't want to tell any more than he had. He left unsaid: Georgina's seduction, which implied a one-sided responsibility—it had been any-thing but that as the night had gone on; Georgina's thin lie of being unable to bear children; the bareness of her ring finger—the disguise of her marriage; his and Bill's breakfast with Mrs. Athína Binakas and the brilliant rainbows in the sky, contrasting with his bleak feeling that had ensued when Georgina had turned her back on him. Jud said, "It was just a one-night stand."

Mara felt the wealth of Jud's experience that sat in his pretense of an emotionless interaction but left it alone. Instead, she asked, "Does she have other children?"

"No."

It was clear to Mara that Georgina had wanted a child under any cir-cumstances and that her husband had been unable to give her one. It was also clear that Jud wanted to meet his daughter. Because, if he didn't, he could just forget about all of this—and that was something he just wasn't doing. Mara asked, "Did you tell Georgina you would go to Crete?"

"I told her I would consider it and let her know. I want to meet Diana. But I don't want to commit to what will be an intrusion into her life without thinking about it first. And I won't go if it turns out that she does not want to meet me."

"If you do go, when would you?"

"Georgina asked me to come this summer but I want to finish the first draft of this book and, then, its second. After that, it will be nearly time to go to Washburn. I suppose Ryan has told you what he told me—Angela, you, and I will be asked to take the witness stand during the early days of the trial, expected to end at September's end. So, I would expect to go to Crete in October. David and Georgina don't want reporters to find out that Diana is my child so I'm supposed to keep secret my kinship to her and my visit to see her. From everyone."

Mara asked, "How would my mother know any of this?"

"She may have seen this photograph." Jud reached inside his coat. The newly-risen sun poured light through the trees just as he pulled out Diana's picture.

Mara breathed deeply. It was a clear picture. The girl was Jud's child. She even had a few small moles in her complexion, similar to Helen Thorensen's. But her eyes and mouth were the giveaways—they were identical to Jud's. Mara couldn't help herself as she said, "Jud, this is a wild ride through life with you. I don't think you can stay out of trouble."

§

When Jud and Mara returned to the estate, Mara went upstairs to take a shower in the private bathroom of Jud's room. Jud went to the kitchen to make breakfast for both of them. No one else in the house was awake.

When the phone rang, Jud picked it up and said hello. Then, he heard a click.

Georgina had called him from her hotel room in Ocean City. She had memorised his parents' phone number from an Air Express form, just in case she needed it. She was returning to Crete tonight and had thought that she would tell him to forget everything she had said. She had been thinking that maybe she would find a way to keep Diana safe without endangering Jud's life but when she had called and heard Jud's voice, she had realised that she wanted to see him again and that, maybe, she could find a way to keep him safe while he was on Crete.

CHAPTER FOUR

While Georgina was in the States, David sat with Constantine in David's Athens office, to which David had not been since he had begun keeping an eye on Georgina. While she was away, he was transferring much of his work to Crete where he would continue to keep an eye on her once she returned home—so that she could not run away with Diana before Jud's death, which would be perpetrated with Georgina's necessary assistance. If Georgina ran away with Diana after Jud's death—well, he couldn't allow that either. She was his wife and Diana was, legally and emotionally, still his daughter.

David said, "Constantine, don't you think that before we break the marriage arrangement between Diana and Stephen, we should see what the results of the DNA tests are? Georgina will bring a sample of Jud Thorensen's blood with her when she returns from the States." David did not tell Constantine that he had already submitted samples of Diana's and his own blood to Pharmakon to send out to a lab for testing their DNA before Georgina had left Crete because, if Jud were not the father, he prayed that, somehow, he himself was—even though, as Jud sensed that Diana was his child, David sensed that she was not. Yet, David was inclined to being sure about this matter and wanted proof beyond all doubt.

David continued, "Then, since you insist, certainly as I would have expected you to, I will be the one to dissolve our arrangement so that you are not seen to be at any fault in the dissolution—for which I'm sure that I can come up with a reason which will not cause you humiliation or bring you questions."

Constantine thought that David was dreaming—there was no graceful way to dissolve what everyone had thought of as perfect union, one that had been highly publicised by the two families—a large party had been held to announce and celebrate it, one of the most anticipated marriages in Athens society. But Constantine said, "We all know what the DNA results will be but go ahead with the tests anyway. You are sure that Georgina will go along with your plan for Diana's natural father?"

"Of course."

"Really. Does she know the details of this plan?"

David said, "Yes. At first, it had seemed unfortunate that I had told her about it before I had thought it out. Yet, nothing else would have coerced her to go to the States to entice Thorensen here—she has told me that Diana must never know who her biological father is. My plan will take care of that."

"But David, Georgina has agreed to help you with a revengeful death? She is the one who has been instrumental in smoothing out the differences between our family members. She is the one who has made them aware of how good this marriage would be for everyone and how we should all forgive and forget. And now you are telling me that she is going along with your scheme? I don't believe you. I'd like to. But I don't."

Constantine was right. Although Georgina had agreed to help David with Jud as they had left Pherma after her confession, she had backed out after hearing what it entailed. David's threats to her life to induce her help had meant nothing to her. And David, a civilised man, would not and could not torture her. He wondered if another admission to Constantine would be a good idea. While the first one he had made regarding Georgina's adultery had been thought to have no substance, this one truly had none—so he said, "I had to give Georgina the only reason that would motivate her to agree to bring Thorensen here: I told her that I would kill Diana if she did not help me."

Constantine thought about his own plan to kill Diana, a simple way to end the marriage arrangement—his son couldn't marry a dead girl. And everyone would feel sorry for Stephen's and his family's loss. And it would be a death that would not reveal the murderer. The Sgouros family would save face. Didn't David see that it was only a matter of time before relatives of both families would question Diana's physical traits, unlike David's and too like those of a famous man. If Jud and Diana continued to live and the marriage was simply dissolved, Constantine would end up with far-reaching, long-standing embarrassment and possibly the loss of his esteemed position. If Jud died while Diana continued to live, Diana's traits would still be speculated upon, the marriage plans would still have to be canceled and then the ensuing scrutiny that Constantine wanted to avoid would occur.

Constantine was unsure whether to act on his plan for Diana now or to wait until David took his revenge on Jud. If he acted now, then David would not have Diana as his bait to lure Jud to Crete. It would be a shame if that didn't happen because Constantine knew that he would enjoy the demise of a man who had demoralised Christianity and was the reason for a child that had been born not only in original sin but had been born as an originator of sin, for what else could she be, since coming from a father who was some kind of devil. Constantine would not deny that he was a superstitious man—he felt his own morality threatened by having associated his son with Diana Binakas. Constantine asked David, "When do you expect to carry out your plan?"

"I hope that Georgina will bring Thorensen with her this week. If not, I imagine he will come some time after the Washburn trials, perhaps October." David had continued to monitor the American news.

Constantine said, "David, this marriage between our children can never take place. But I will defer to your wish to see the DNA reports, even though I'm already sure of their results. I will say nothing about any of this to Stephen, yet. You have until the first of the New Year—if Mr. Thorensen is not taken care of by then, you and I will have another talk about Stephen and Diana. *And I will do what I need to do,* he thought.

David was pleased by the length of time that would occur before he would have to make a public announcement regarding the dissolution of the arranged marriage between Stephen Sgouros and Diana Binakas.

Constantine asked, "I was thinking, David. Would you mind introducing me to Mr. Thorensen?" Constantine decided he would take care of Diana soon after David took care of Jud Thorensen.

David was surprised by the request but said, "Not at all, Constantine. Once I know when he is coming, I will let you know."

"Are you sure he will be here?"

"Georgina will ensure it. She will do whatever it takes. I'm sure that if she is unsuccessful with her mission during this trip to the States, she will develop a campaign. I don't know what Thorensen is like but, judging from what I've heard, he is compassionate. I think he will want to meet a child he has fathered. Of course, once he is here, he will never meet Diana—I cannot allow her to form an emotional attachment to him. He will be a dead man and she is still my daughter."

Constantine couldn't help but notice that, despite David's wish to wait for the DNA results, he spoke as if he already knew, as he himself believed, that Diana was Jud's child.

§

David was at home when Georgina arrived from the States. She told David that Jud had agreed to visit Diana; she hoped that her lie would become a truth. Georgina gave him the chiffon scarf, stained with Jud's blood, and told him that she had not had to suggest a DNA test—Jud had insisted upon it. David was pleased about that. He asked her why the blood was on her scarf. When she told him that she had cut Jud's arm with her crucifix and then pressed her scarf on his wound, David was stunned.

David had used an elaborate method to acquire a sample of Diana's blood. He had taken Diana to his doctor's office to have her blood drawn. He could have inflicted Diana with a cut but he was unable to bring himself to hurt her. Sometimes, he wondered how Georgina could believe, despite his display with the dagger, that he would really do harm to Diana. Yet, he had needed to be convincing. And Georgina's belief served his purpose—to ensure her co-operation regarding Jud's demise.

As Georgina left his office to change from her travel suit, David put the bloodied scarf inside a plastic bag. He had to be positive that Jud was the father before took the revenge he had formulated because, despite his mother's letter naming Jud as the co-adulterer, despite Georgina's confirmation of the letter, despite the mismatch of his own DNA with Diana's, and despite the resemblance between Diana and Jud, David thought that there was still a remote possibility that Georgina could have slept with yet another man, if she had been that desperate to have a child.

That Georgina had not brought Jud with her had been disappointing to David—although expected. Yet, David had plenty of time for what he wanted to do—being unaware of Constantine's plan regarding Diana, he assumed that the timing for his revenge on Jud was not critical to Constantine. And, besides, they had more than four years to dissolve the marriage.

§

The DNA test results came back—Diana was the daughter of the American author. Now, David had only to wait for Jud to call Georgina to tell her when he would arrive on Crete.

David continued to allow Georgina to think that Diana's life was, without question, in danger. He watched Georgina read the Bible every day, saw her hold her crucifix, and, sometimes, he went into her studio to watch her paint. Jesus was her favorite subject, always shown healing people and never shown suffering on the cross. She had done oil paintings of various saints including Basil, a flying Francis of Assisi, and Paul. But her most recent one showed none of the peace of the others. It was of Saint Sebastian, tied to a column and dying from arrow shafts piercing his body. Although absorbed in her work, Georgina still often noticed David's presence. Whether she did or didn't, he stared at her graceful form, with her black shining hair tied back and hanging down below her waist.

While many of Georgina's portraits of Diana were on the walls of their villa, David's favorite one hung on a studio wall: grinning from ear to ear, Diana, stood on a large rock in front of the Aegean Sea; she wore a cotton frock and was barefoot; in the crook of one arm, she held a large conch shell; with her other arm she was reaching out and petting a goat with a square bell. Whenever David saw the painting these days, he was reminded of her real father and then he would remember that Diana must not actually meet Jud. David did not want to see her cry when he was dead and gone.

§

At St. Mary's School for Girls in Athens, Diana sat alone in her dormitory room. Her parents had visited her today, per David's request for permission from the school to take Diana to lunch. Over the years, Diana had seen David and Georgina together or separately, frequently. These days, if they came at all, they came together. When she had asked them why, David had said that he was working at home on Crete, with no given reason for it, and that her mother was busy in her studio. Today, Georgina again had been anxious to see her but Diana didn't know why. And she was unaware that Georgina had just returned from the USA.

Diana wiped away her tears with her sleeve. There was no one to comfort her. The other school girls teased because she was tall, for a Greek girl, and because she was often writing stories or drawing pictures. Diana liked the other girls and wanted to join in with their talk about music and cute boys. But some of the girls were snide to her—as well as to each other. So, she spent more time than she might have making her own children's books. Diana had a best friend, Julia, also her roommate But, due to illness, Julia was confined to an infirmary bed and disallowed visitors.

Diana looked forward to going home this summer, even though poppies and other wild flowers would not be blooming as they did during her winter vacation from school. But she could still follow the sheep and goats to the ocean shore every morning at eight and watch them go to the water's edge for a few moments, for no apparent reason, before soon returning to graze upon the grassy hills and sparse crags; then she could run alongside the goats as they ran toward the shepherd, while being herded by the running to and fro of a shepherd's dog, barking, playful yet serious. Diana loved the musty smell of the sheep and goats, the sound of their voices and bells, and their frolics. Lambs would run back and forth in races with each other while their mothers watched. Near the trees, some of the goats would look like satyrs when they stood up on their hind legs to reach the tender leaves.

Later in the morning, Diana would meander with her mother or go with her to a cave where they would light candles and pray at the altar within. They didn't go into caves during the winter because water flooded them, including the huge and yawning Cave Dikti, dark home of Zeus, deep in descent and length. Late in the afternoon, if Diana didn't spend time in her mother's studio at her own table with watercolors and handmade papers, she went to the shore again and walked barefoot along the rocks to the tidal pools, where orange or purple starfish lay in the water, held by hollowed rock and heated by the sun. Sea urchins sat as if dead but with wavering thorns. Gray sand-dollars lay flat and heavy. Happy in their easy pace, speckled brown sea cucumbers drifted in the water.

Sometimes Diana ran with the wind over Cretan hills. As a goat would, she skirted nimbly around the rocks, strewn everywhere. The sun lightened the top layer of her hair to pale blonde, unlike either of her parents' in its fairness, and put a honey tone in her white skin. Her gray eyes sparkled as the Aegean's sunlit waves did and, when she bent down to pick up miniatures of conches, whelks, wentletraps, and periwinkles, her eyes reflected and held some of the violet of the sea that was mostly aqua in color and yet reflected other blues along with greens and purples, depending on the light in the sky and the depth of the tide.

Longing to go home, Diana gazed outside at Athens streets lit by street-lamps and commercial lights, bright in the dark night. She wiped her eyes again. The teasing had been worse today. During the last year or two, the other girls had starting telling her that she was adopted because she didn't like look her parents. She didn't have their black hair or dark eyes. And she was already taller than her father. But, today, out of cruelty rather than belief, they had said that she resembled the devil, the man on the covers of the magazines. Diana thought of the Sisters—they had stopped the girls from teasing her today.

The Sisters liked Diana because she was good-natured and did well with her school subjects. Diana was obedient—she saw no reason to be otherwise. She did her in-class academic work because, if she didn't, she would become more bored than she already was. And she looked forward to finishing her homework so that she could create her own worlds with stories and drawings.

But, tonight, she couldn't focus on those. Instead, she pulled out the magazine that she had bought at a newsstand, then put into her school bag and brought to her room. Her parents had not seen her buy it while they had browsed on the opposite side of a kiosk in Constitution Square. Diana stared at the face on the cover. It was her face. Yet, she would not have wondered if this man were her father if it were not for two incidents.

The first one had occurred when she and her parents had sat in a restaurant for lunch. Diana had pulled out a sketch-book from her school bag and found that her pencil box was missing. Her mother had invited her to get a pen out of her handbag. Then, Diana had seen a notepaper with two American addresses, written in her mother's hand, with Jud Thorensen's name, which she had seen and heard often since Good Friday, even though the Sisters forbade talk about him. Paper-clipped to the notepaper was another sheet, slightly larger. Diana had glanced at it. Printed in a bold hand, unfamiliar to her, was an e-mail address: iota@jot-works.com. Diana had released the papers and dug deeper for a pen. If she had been alone with her mother, she would have asked her why she knew the addresses of a famous American man who looked like Diana herself. Instead, she had eaten her lunch and felt glad she had bought the magazine. When her parents had brought her back to school, David had kissed Diana's cheeks, as usual, but had given her a weak hug, while Georgina had hugged her as if she would never let her go.

The second incident had occurred a few days ago when David had taken her out of school to go to a doctor's appointment. He had told the doctor to examine her for anemia. The nurse had stuck a needle in her arm, drawn blood, put a gauze pad over the punctured vein, and told Diana to hold it there. As the nurse had turned around, her father had taken the gauze and pretended to throw it away while he'd asked for a fresh one. But Diana had seen him with sleight-of-hand put the bloodied gauze inside his jacket pocket which, unknown to her, was lined with plastic wrap. Diana knew she didn't have anemia and she wondered why David had wanted her blood. She had thought that he might be testing the DNA in it. She had learned about such things from American news. And she had later inferred that David was questioning her origin.

Now, sitting in pajamas, loose and comfortable after the formal school uniform, Diana turned from the window pane and faced the computer screen on the right side of her desk. She could hear girls outside her door talking. The room curfew was still an hour away. Diana logged onto her computer, brought up the Ethernet, and signed into her e-mail account. With her breath held and her fingers shaking, she typed in the e-mail address that she had seen in her mother's handbag into her Address Book. Then, she logged off. That was all she could handle for tonight. Or for a long while, perhaps.

CHAPTER FIVE

Jud had walked the streets of Ocean City and smoked a cigar. Now, among the floor-to-ceiling bookcases along three walls and a fourth wall of glass, he sat in the small office of his apartment, which his housekeeper, Mrs. Wilkins, had prepared for his return from the Thorensen estate. The house plants were alive and well; fresh air filled the rooms. It was five thirty a.m. He was ready to write and looking forward to it.

A week ago, he had finished the first draft of Desire; Sex & Spirituality. A few days before finishing it, he had started to feel disappointed as he had sensed the approach of the end of the book, as a vacation, winding down—anticipated and seeming as if it would last forever, until the middle days arrived and slid into final days, enjoyed yet full with the awareness of upcoming closure. Jud had taken pleasure during the upward part of writing the book to the feeling that he was in its middle and, as he had felt it finishing, had savored every moment up to its completion. Then, with a letdown feeling, he had set aside the manuscript for a few days, after which he had reviewed and edited it.

Today, he looked forward to starting the second draft, which would occupy most of the day and each day thereafter until complete. Fresh material would take him ninety minutes, if words flowed well—but a second draft sometimes occupied more hours a day and more days. He played a new composer's music on the stereo, in a window corner opposite to the jade tree. With dictionary and thesaurus next to him, he turned on his computer, into which he had transferred the manuscript from his powerbook, put on the Remote Access for the Internet, and then logged onto his e-mail account. He opened up the In-Box and caught the name Binakas and the symbol for Greece, gr, after the e-mail address. This would be Georgina's first e-mail. But rather than Georgina's name, he saw the name Diana. It took his breath away. He thought about Diana every day.

She had sent the message last evening:

Dear Mr. Thorensen:
    I'm Diana Binakas. My parents are David and Georgina Binakas. I believe my mother knows you. Is this true? Please tell me the truth. I go to a private school and don't see her often. When I do, she is always with my father and I feel uncomfortable asking her questions about you in front of him. She doesn't use a computer so I cannot send e-mails to her to ask her things. I know you are busy but I hope that you will have time to write to me. Thank you for your attention.
    Sincerely,
    Diana Ellen Binakas

After he read her note, Jud stood up and opened up his file cabinet, to the left of his desk. From the top drawer, he pulled out the Air Express package from Georgina. He had left it unopened when he had received it a month earlier—it was now late May. He tore it open and, as he had expected, saw DNA reports and a note from Georgina:

Jud:
    For privacy's sake, names were not sent to the lab: Subject II is Diana; Subject III is you. David is Subject I but his report is superfluous and has been excluded—he had his DNA tested, just in case he was Diana's father, rather than you. Or, if neither of you were, then he could wonder who else might be. But, as you will see, there are no question marks. For your information, great

care was taken to identify the blood samples accurately and conduct the tests
precisely. We look forward to hearing from you soon.
    Best regards,
    Georgina Binakas

Jud could feel Georgina's acerbic bluntness. He read the two reports
and their summary. Then, he sat down again, stunned, even though he
already knew that Diana was his daughter—yet, now, he had scientific
proof that would be irrefutable in the eyes of the world. Although the
proof did not increase Jud's desire to meet Diana, which he ever felt,
Diana's e-mail did. It was a simple one and had touched his heart.

He returned to the computer and wrote:

Hello Diana,
    Yes, I know your mother. You said you hadn't asked her anything about
me but, since you have my e-mail address, I am guessing that your mother
must have told you something. Yet, it seems that she doesn't know you are
writing to me. I'm sure that you could tell your parents that you are. I look
forward to hearing from you again.
    Warm regards,
    Jud

It seemed to Jud as if Diana still knew nothing about him but had been
able to acquire his new e-mail address, difficult to discover by anyone.
That Georgina would have given it to Diana without an explanation was
unlikely. That Diana would have found it and sent an e-mail to him without knowing of her connection to him was just as unlikely. Thus, until he
found out more, he had kept his response to her simple and generic.

Jud returned to his manuscript, broke for breakfast, and then dressed
for an event which he had anticipated: Angela's audition. He had finally
convinced Doris Wynne that he was not trying to separate her from her
daughter and that he would do anything he could to help them both set-
tle in Ocean City if Angela attended the Bentilee College of Music, an
exceptional conservatorium. That Mrs. Wynne thought he was treating

Angela as he would a prostitute by offering to pay for her music education and treating her as a concubine by offering her a home—although not with himself but with his parents, per his mother's consent, should Mrs. Wynne prefer to stay in her Midwest town—were of a reasoning that had no existence within Jud's realm of thought. Yet, via his three-way telephone discussions with Mrs. Wynne and Angela, Mrs. Wynne had agreed that she would accept Jud's offer to help her find employment, if she were to come to Ocean City. During this time, Angela had been accepted into Bentilee but, because she was applying for a scholarship rather than allowing Jud to fund her tuition, she was to have an audition. She could have sent in a taped cassette but had chosen to try out in person, in order to strengthen her ability to gain a scholarship.

§

That Angela would be the last to perform at Bentilee College of Music was working out well. She would have been too ill to be one of the first ones to do so—she was nervous, she had thrown up twice, and her hands were like ice cubes. She sipped her water. Her stage fright was well-known in Washburn. Most of the time it had consisted of fear, dealt with by her co-stars' blocking of exits and, then, by Angela, herself, walking onto the stage, where fear had no access to her. But Angela's experience at Triunity University in front of the hordes of news media members and the general public had been different—she had been nervous throughout the pelting of questions to Jud, primarily, and then Mara, Bill, and herself about their roles in the modern-day crucifixion. Yet, even so, she had looked forward to a live audition until she had found out about Van Silverman, who had contacted the college administration and gained permission to attend her performance.

At the moment her name was called, Angela walked onto center stage with her guitar and saw, sitting in the front row, Bentilee department heads and a few faculty members. In the middle of them sat Van Silverman and Van's guest, Jud Thorensen. Even though she had spoken many times with Jud on the telephone during the last few weeks, she felt as if she would faint when she met his eyes. She had dreamed about seeing him again and touching him. That Romeo's Van Silverman was sitting there was almost beyond belief.

Then, the heat of the lights on stage reminded her of the thrill of doing what she loved to do. Fear deserted her. She leaned her acoustic guitar against a stool. Her hair was long, loose, and blue-black; her skin was whiter than white; her blue eyes were wide open. In the slender, sleeveless blue dress Jud had sent for her birthday, she relaxed into position, her hands lightly over each other, palms together, and sang, a cappella, an excerpt of an aria from an Italian opera with a clear full voice. She understated her movements and focused on the emotion of the song. Midway through her allotted five minutes, she stopped singing and pulled her guitar over her head with its black leather shoulder-strap, silver-studded. Then, she played and sang a portion of a rock song she had composed: she picked a few introduction notes on her guitar, strummed it as she sang one verse, and then ripped into the song's lead guitar solo. As she bowed her head, she heard applause.

When she looked up, she saw everyone on his feet. She could feel her mouth start to wobble as she felt the urge to cry. But that would be poor showmanship. She forced a big smile although her lips were almost out of her control. She bowed again and, as she left the stage, waved—because everyone was still on their feet clapping. She leaned her guitar on a wall and ran to the ladies' room. Her energy-buildup had hardly been released and was too much for her body but she savored the thrill she felt from having performed well, regardless of what would come next for her.

When her body stopped shaking, she picked up her guitar and returned to the auditorium. One of the department heads had stayed around. He said to Angela, "None of our freshman has hit every note perfectly in a piece like that aria. But you did. Congratulations." She thanked him. He left. She lay her guitar on top of its case, at one end of the front row, and then walked up the two men waiting for her.

Angela took a deep breath and said, "Hello, Jud." His hair was longer. He still looked thinner than he had when she had first met him but his face showed no signs of suffering. He looked tired but every part of his face seemed to be smiling at her. She went into his arms and held him as tightly as he held her. It felt good. She released him.

Jud said, "Angela Wynne, I'd like you to meet Van Silverman."

Van put an arm around Angela and, for a brief moment, squeezed her shoulders before removing his arm. He said, "There's something about you. Besides major talent, that is. I would like to talk with you about a few things. Find out what direction you're headed in—I hope it's my favorite music, rock and roll."

"It is. It's wonderful to meet you Mr. Silverman."

"Van."

Angela continued, "I'm awed that you came to see me. I can't thank you enough just for being here." Angela looked into his green eyes, like his daughter's. Angela said, "Congratulations on your wedding. I'm glad for Mara, too."

"Thank you. Jud and I would like to take you out for dinner as a belated celebration for getting into Bentilee and for what I think will be a full scholarship."

Angela knew that Jud would again offer to pay for her education if the scholarship were denied but she hoped she would get the scholarship. Angela said, "Thanks, I would love to go to dinner with you." She put her guitar into its case, which she snapped shut and then placed next to her small suitcase. She would be flying back to Washburn tomorrow morning. Knowing that her audition would be in the afternoon, she had booked a flight that had brought her to Ocean City in the morning of the same day and taken a taxi to the college.

Jud asked, "Is your mother here? She had told me that she was coming with you."

"She was feeling unwell, once again, so she canceled her ticket."

"I'm sorry to hear that." He was also surprised that anything could have kept Mrs. Wynne from coming to Ocean City, not because she was particularly interested in Angela's audition but because she and Angela had been invited by Helen to stay at the Thorensen estate, something she would have enjoyed. And because she would have wanted to play chaperone for her daughter. It was ironic that an illness of Mrs. Wynne's had been the reason that Jud had met Angela on his first day in Washburn, setting into motion the tragedy that had turned the anonymous quiet town into a notorious one.

Van said, "Well, let's go shall we?" His mind was taking in much information—he saw danger in leaving Angela and Jud alone together. His wife's intuition seemed to be better than his own, in this case. Yet, there was nothing he could do about it. Mara was out of town. And he couldn't, out of the blue, invite a stranger to his wife's home in Bridgeford, just outside of Ocean City. It was not that he saw Angela and Jud as animals who couldn't control their impulses, it was that he saw an attraction that crackled between them drawing them closer together until, when too close, they snapped tightly to each other. He remembered, as a child, playing with a magnet and a small metal bar. At first holding them apart, he had moved them closer and closer to each other to see how close he could get them and still keep them from touching. When he had felt too much pull between them, he had pulled them farther apart and then attempted moving them closer together again without letting them touch until, in one instant, they suddenly snapped hard together.

Van didn't think it was love as it was when he watched Mara and Jud together. But with Angela and Jud, there seemed to be a rush of adrenaline and a wildness, which must necessarily include some feeling of love, even if not of the intensity he sensed Jud had with Mara. So, although he, himself, couldn't control tonight's circumstances, he hoped that Jud would drop off Angela at the Thorensen home and then go right home to his own apartment. If Angela had been going to any place but a Thorensen home, he, Van, would have found it easy to offer her a ride after dinner to a hotel, rather than allow Jud to do so, without raising suspicions that he was trying to keep the two of them apart.

§

It was after midnight when Jud brought Angela to his parents' home in Clinton. It was a warm spring night. The photo-journalists took photographs through the open car windows as Jud opened the gates to the estate and drove through. Inside the house, he took Angela to the door of a guest bedroom. He told her he would be back in the morning to take her to the airport.

Angela said, "Thanks for telling Mara's father about me. I like him very much. It's funny—I've listened to Romeo's music, their lyrics, often—it's odd to me to think of Van as a parent. Jud, thank you for everything you've done for me. You cannot imagine how much I appreciate this. It's a dream come true."

"Angela, I appreciate your thanks. But you don't need me. You've done this all on your own—you are amazing. In fact, I want you to have something." He carried her suitcase and guitar case into the bedroom and said, "I'll be right back."

While he went to his bedroom, on the same floor, Angela took her clothes from her suitcase for the next day. She opened the door when she heard Jud's knock.

He walked in with a guitar case. He lay it on top of her bed and opened it up. He pulled out a Fender electric guitar. He said, "This is for you. I don't think you'll want to carry it with you on the plane so I'll save it here for you, until you come back."

She asked, "Is it yours?"

"Yes."

"You play the guitar?"

"Sometimes. Usually my acoustic one these days. I used to have a rock band while I was at Ocean City University."

Angela hadn't taken the guitar from him yet so he said, "You don't have to take it if you don't like it."

"I'm honored, Jud. I would love to have it. Thank you." She took the guitar from him; she felt the closeness of the strings against the neck and the smoothness of the flat, heavy body. She felt embarrassed—it was such a personal gift. She thanked him again and lay it in its case on the bed.

Jud said, "I'll see you tomorrow morning."

"Don't leave."

"Angela, I have to—I can't do this. You know I love Mara."

"And you love me?"

"Yes."

"Kiss me."

"Angela, you tempt me." Inside, he also struggled. He wanted to stay, he wanted to go. He wanted to make love to Angela, he wanted to be faithful to Mara. He didn't want to be torn apart. Angela would rather not share him, Mara did not want to, and he, himself, would find his life to be simpler if he loved just one woman. He said, "I can't stay."

But, then, he pulled her into his arms and kissed her. She kissed him back, passionately. He pulled away from her. She watched his back as he walked out of her door. Jud left the estate for his apartment—but he felt as if he'd left part of himself behind.

§

Early in the morning, Jud was in the conservatory when Angela came downstairs in her faded torn jeans. Through the open double doors, he heard her in the foyer and immediately went to her side. He saw that her face was white and her eyes were red. She asked if he would take her to a place where they could speak privately. He took her into the conservatory. They stood by the wall fountain and faced each other. The day was overcast and cast a gray light through the glass panes that made the faces of Jud and Angela appear ashen.

"Jud, how could you leave me like that last night?"

"I'm sorry, Angela."

"We mean something to each other—I feel it all the time. I've missed you these last few weeks and I've dreamed of seeing you. Do you think that all I care about in my life is music and a career? I may be only eighteen but I'm not a child and never have been one. You're pushing me away—and you seem to think that giving me things will take the place of showing how you feel about me. When you left Washburn, I cried. You know what we felt together and what we went through—and the things we said before you left. I could never expect you to part with Mara. But I love you. Just how could you leave me like that last night—as if I have no feelings?"

"Angela, I don't know where to begin. I do love you. I love many people in my life. But Mara and I have been together for over a year—you and I hardly know each other—"

"That isn't true, Jud. Time makes no difference to knowing what someone's like. I may not know your favorite color but I know you care about people."

"I'm trying to be faithful to Mara."

"Why? You're not married, you're not even engaged."

"We have an unspoken agreement," Jud said. Yet, since he had slept with Angela, he had tried to quell his feeling of having done nothing wrong and his knowing that, given the same circumstances, he would repeat his actions. Jud asked, "Would you give me time?"

"To decide between us?"

"No. Time to see what unfolds. Although I cannot foresee how each of us will fare in the future, together or apart, I don't see our disagreement as a reason to take the place of caring about each other, to spoil our times together, or cause us to separate, when all we want to do is be together. But you are free to go out with other guys—you are only eighteen. Despite what you've said before, you might enjoy going out with someone your own——." He stopped because Angela's expression told him to say no more.

Angela said, "Please—don't give me any conventional talk—I've heard it all before—I would not have expected it from you. I can give you time. But would you would treat me as you did before?"

"I need to keep our relationship platonic."

"I don't think that's fair. But, for now, I'll let this be. You can still kiss and hold me." When he said nothing, she added, "Are you thinking you can't do that—without making love to me?"

"I don't know. How about you—can you be with me and not feel anything that way?"

In that instant, Angela realised that she had her answer. She also knew that he was as lost as she was in their mutual attraction. She asked, "You won't send me home without giving me a kiss? It's safe to—we can't make love right now."

Lisbeth stood in the doorway. This was the first time she had seen Angela, other than on the TV news. Lisbeth saw self-assurance with shyness and a young face with a mature beauty. She felt passion in the discussion between Angela and her brother. Lisbeth cleared her throat and said, "We're waiting for you. But take your time."

Jud smiled at Lisbeth and said, "Thanks, Lis, we'll be right there." As Lisbeth left, he turned back to Angela, shy and forthright, gentle and determined, and asked, "What was your father like? You're not much like your mother in looks or personality—or interests."

"He was charming, intelligent, and loving—I loved him very much and, even though it's been years since he passed away, I still feel very close to him. Sometime, I will tell you more." Angela didn't want to tell Jud that her father had exuded some of the qualities Jud did, such as a wild independence yet with a quiet manner, that had often become rife with humor.

Jud put his arms around Angela. He kissed her lips. He looked into her eyes, still like blue flames, and then kissed her again. Angela let his lips tease hers until she pressed onto his a final kiss.

Then, Jud escorted Angela to the kitchen where his father, mother, and Lisbeth were having breakfast. There were three other place settings. Jud introduced Angela to everyone and, as he explained that Angela's mother had been unable to accompany her daughter due to illness, Helen removed the place setting that had been set for Mrs. Wynne.

Because Angela was shy, Jud was the one to tell his family of her talent and her successful audition. Angela blushed, his family congratulated her. Lisbeth liked Angela. She noticed that, even though Angela was not much more than a year older than herself, Angela behaved older than she or any of her friends did. But she worried—because of all the girlfriends that Jud had dated, Mara was her favorite.

Conversation was general, pleasant and, as was usual since Jud's return to Clinton, without verbal exchanges between Ogden and Jud. Thus, everyone was surprised, except for Angela who was unaware of the rift between father and son, when Ogden looked at Jud and spoke to him directly. He asked, "Where is Mara?" Ogden hadn't seen her for days. Helen had stopped answering his questions that were regarding Jud's business. And Ogden didn't want to draw Lisbeth into his dissension with Jud by asking her his questions. Thus, unless he asked Jud directly, he had no way of knowing where Mara was.

Jud looked at his father. He said, "She's in California."

"Why is she there?"

"She's investigating Omni-Drug, a pharmaceutical company that, while unable to obtain a patent in the US for an asthma drug, is trying to distribute it through a Greek drug manufacturing and distribution company. The problem is that the drug can't do what Omni-Drug claims it can do. Mara thinks that the California-based company is falsifying the reports it's showing to the Greek company." What he didn't tell them was that Mara had chosen this assignment because the Greek company was Alpha-Omega Pharmakon, belonging to George Binakas, a major stockholder, the father of Diana.

Jud had received another e-mail from Diana last night. In it, she had said that her parents had not mentioned him but that she knew of him from the news stories. She had found his e-mail address in her mother's handbag. And that, since he was a friend of her mother's, would he mind writing to her. Jud hadn't answered yet because he didn't know what to say. He thought that he should not correspond with Diana under these extraordinary circumstances, unless her parents knew about it. Yet, he didn't want to reject her.

Ogden had just said something.

Jud said, "I'm sorry. Would you please repeat that?"

Ogden said, "Would you please tell Mara that I send her my love? And tell her to be careful." Ogden had wanted to know about Mara but also to remind Jud of her, now. Ogden disliked Angela—she had the kind of beauty his friends wrote about and the kind of self-confidence, despite her shyness, that they, with their self-doubt about their own talents, envied.

Jud told Ogden that he would be calling Mara tonight and give her his message. Then, he excused Angela and himself—it was time to drive her to Ocean City. Angela thanked the Thorensen family. Helen hugged her; Ogden wished her well; Lisbeth invited Angela to meet her friends, once she moved to the East Coast. While Lisbeth helped her mother to clean up the kitchen and as Ogden went to his study to write, Jud ran upstairs to get Angela's suitcase. And Angela mused on how her own mother hadn't hugged her once she had turned thirteen—when her mother had lost interest in her and her father had died.

Jud escorted Angela to his car and drove her to the airport. Jim Brandtem was ready with his camera when Jud kissed Angela good bye. The weekly tabloids were paying him well for photographs of Jud because, each time he was on their covers, especially with Mara or Angela, their sales increased.

§

When Diana received Jud's response to the first e-mail she had sent to him, she was delighted. But she was afraid to act on his suggestion that she tell her parents about their correspondence. She realised that Jud could not know what she believed—that he was the cause of the rift between her parents. In fact, he could not know of the rift. So, Diana responded to him by stating that she was her own person and had a right to communicate with whomever she wanted to. And that she would like to be his pen-pal.

She checked her e-mail the next day and received no reply. After a few days had passed, still with no reply, she sent him another note, telling him a few generalities about her life. She received nothing back. This time, she waited only two days to send him another e-mail. When there was no response the next day to that one, she sent him an e-mail every day for the next week—still with no responses. The day after her last e-mail to Jud, during mid-June, Diana left St. Mary's to return to Crete for her summer vacation and observed that the alienation between David and Georgina was more noticeable in the home environment than it had been during their last visit to her in Athens.

Although, Diana loved David, she often felt awkward with him and supposed it was because of his frequent absences due to business trips. Yet, she realised that whenever she visited her grandparents in California, she felt an immediate ease in their company, as if she had never been apart from them. Diana wondered if David ever sensed her discomfort with him; perhaps, he had his own discomfort with her. She knew not how to talk to him nor he to her, even though each tried to communicate with the other.

Diana knew that David was proud of her writing and drawing abilities. She thought that he loved her. But he was strict. And if she did anything that he deemed wrong, he was cool toward her for days—even when she apologised. The last time that Diana had mustered up the courage to offer an apology, David had used it as an opening to scold her further. Yet, he was finding less to scold her about and seemed to barely notice her.

Diana had noticed the changes in her parents' behavior around the time she had found Jud Thorensen's e-mail address. The changes had continued; they were also increasing in number. David no longer kissed Georgina or held her close. He gave her no surprise gifts and, instead of speaking to her in a loving voice and behaving as if he would do anything she would ask of him, he treated her with polite disinterest. And she treated him the same way. They seemed uncaring about Diana's observation of their different treatment regarding each other.

Regarding Diana, David was aloof while Georgina was as loving as ever. Yet, Georgina had become as protective of and restrictive to Diana as David already was to her and he had since become such to Georgina—when David had gone to his Athens office two days ago, he had taken Georgina with him, leaving Diana at home with Leesa. At the time, Diana had not realised that this would become a pattern. Yet, even so, she had begun to feel like a prisoner.

Diana tried to feel good despite her parents' miserableness and despite Jud's neglect. She had stopped looking out for an e-mail from him because her disappointment at not receiving one was too great. She thought that, although he must know he was her father, he did not care about her. Yet, this night, a week after being home, she saw an e-mail from Jud among her other new ones. He seemed genuine when he apologised for having not responded to her e-mails. She wrote back to him. Thereafter, he replied to every e-mail she sent him. She dared not ask him how he could be her father. But she enjoyed writing to him—about anything—and sending him drawings from her own books by scanning them and sending them as e-mail attachments.

CHAPTER SIX

Constantine Sgouros had four children: three girls and one son, his youngest child. Unlike many other Greek men who took wives around age thirty, he had taken one at age twenty-one. Since his son, Stephen, had become an adult, Constantine had not been on his native Crete to visit his past, until today, even though he had been on Crete a few times during the last two years as a guest of David and Georgina Binakas and would be again, after he had spent a couple of days alone. He wanted a clear mind after the hustle of Athens, the arguments at home with his wife, and the problem of Diana Binakas.

It was a hot day in late June. Having brought his car on the ferry, Constantine drove southwest from the port of Irakleío to Anapoli and then parked near the long Ravine of Aradaina. He wore a black crocheted head covering with dripping crocheted tears, reminders of the battles with the Turks and the loss of Cretan men. He wore a cotton shirt, khaki pants, and hiking boots. He carried a knapsack with water bottles.

Despite the bands of steel-gray in his black hair and deep lines in his sharp face, Constantine was a few years younger than David and in strong shape due to his daily exercise in a gym. Yet, the descending of the thousand-foot gorge needed his careful attention. The path of packed-together round stones formed zigzags down the steep side. When he reached the gorge's bottom, buried by oversized pebbles and rocks, Constantine walked by a burro's dry bones and a splintered saddle. A goat skull lay nearby—as did a shepherd's staff, split into sticks.

When he reached the other side of the gorge, he climbed up the zigzag path—the only way to get to the tiny ancient village of Aradin, home of the impoverished ancestors of the Sgouros and Binakas families. The sun baked him. Once he reached the top, he drank a bottle of water and returned it empty to his knapsack. He took a few more steps to reach the deserted village and stood in the midst of the yellowed stone houses, with eroded mud roofs, doorways with no doors, and gaping holes for windows. It was here that the feud had begun between the Sgouroses and the Binakases, when a Sgouros man had killed a Binakas woman. After that, the manifesto between the two families had been: an eye for an eye. Thus, there had been many deaths and much suffering. At last, the police had come and dispersed the families, warned never to return.

As a young adult, Constantine had been glad when the feud had ended, even though his immediate family had not been directly involved. Now, as a man who had adult children with grandchildren, he had been pleased that Stephen, age thirty-one, his last child to be married, would marry into the wealth of the Binakas family. David Binakas had followed a masterful course to power and money, begun before his birth, when Nicholas Binakas had married Athína Stavrós, the daughter of a rich family—Athína's parents, unable to prevent their willful marriage, had forgiven the couple, who conceived but one child, David. After David had grown up, he had built up a pharmaceutical company, married Cynthia, and sired a son, the young Nicholas. Constantine would not have wished harm on the boy but, when young Nicholas had died with his mother in the car accident, Constantine had not been sorry. But, then, David had found new joy when he had married Georgina and, several years later, been blessed with another baby, albeit only a daughter. Constantine picked up a stick and snapped it into two. *Yes,* he thought, *a daughter who had turned out to be the daughter of the Antichrist, who was bringing foul ideas into the world about Christianity.*

Constantine's entire life was built on the Bible—his interpretation of it. And he could not allow his son to marry an ill-conceived girl with defiled blood. But if he and David dissolved the marriage arrangement for their children, many questions would be asked by family and friends. The prevention of what seemed to others to be a perfect union would be the source of curiosity and the cause of scrutiny, which would have dissipated with time had not Diana's father become famous and been damnable. Thus, the tearing-asunder of the marriage plans for Stephen and Diana would lead to the revelation of a scandal. And a new feud between the families could begin. Constantine thought about all that he had said to David in their recent conversations. And about all that he had not said, such as how Stephen was faring.

The family of the girl that Constantine had dissuaded Stephen from marrying had not argued with the Sgouroses because he, Constantine, had paid them off. But Stephen had become depressed when the girl had married another man. Constantine knew that Stephen took comfort from the thought of marrying into the wealth of the Binakas family but, over all, Stephen's heartache remained unassuaged. Thus, Constantine did not know how he was going to tell Stephen that his marriage to Diana could not be allowed to occur. Stephen's reason for relinquishing the girl he loved had become void. He might commit suicide.

Constantine watched a shepherd walk toward him from around trees bordering a curved path with a shallow incline. The man beckoned him. Once inside a roofed house, matted here and there with green moss, Constantine saw dried olive branches in the corner fireplace, a bed made of branches and blankets along a wall, and a wine barrel at the bed's end. Hypodermic needles lay on the ground—Constantine guessed that the shepherd used opium. The man was shy and didn't speak. He offered Constantine wine, cooled in the dark interior. Constantine sipped it. It was the strongest wine he had ever had. Yet, before he thanked the man and left, he had a second glass.

This time, Constantine easily descended the gorge and climbed back up the other side. Because of the heady effect from the wine, he didn't care if he fell. If he did, all of his problems would no longer be his and, because of Jesus's sacrifice on the cross, he would go to Heaven, despite his sins. Yet, in safety, he reached his car and drove to a shore just east of Anapoli. That night, while sitting on a rock, well past sunset, he watched the glow of lanterns from the fishermen's boats and smoked a cigar. Then, once inside his tent, he slept well.

On his second day on Crete, after breaking his camp, he was invited by a fisherman to his house for breakfast. There, he ate fresh fish, wild horta, and slices of bread. Constantine thanked the fisherman and promised to bring or send him a new set of guitar strings from the mainland—the fisherman's old beaten guitar stood in a dark corner and bore the disappointment of two broken strings.

Constantine took a drive north to Triados. He drove along a dirt road lined by stone walls that had cypress trees on either side. He parked his dusty car and walked past the Osios Monastery, silent and austere. He walked several yards away from the road leading to it and, as he descended on an uneven hard path, he passed the older monastery in ruins. An intact, small church and large cave were nearby. Yet, Constantine continued downward among the cliff-faces, mottled with green growth, until he came to a bridge of green carpet above a gorge's base. Afar, lay the ocean. The monks had become too old to climb back up and so did not come this way; there were no new, young monks. Even tourists rarely came here—the descent and then the return ascent were too hot for summer tourists and too treacherous for the few winter tourists. Constantine crossed the bridge to another cave, a small one with small stalactites and stalagmites. As he entered, he picked up two of the many thin orange candles littering the ground and one of the few strings, which he followed through the light sifting into darkness until he reached the end of the passage, punctuated by a small altar. With his cigar lighter, like a small blowtorch, he lit candles and placed them on either side of the portrait of Jesus.

The candles cast rivulets of wavering light. Constantine got down on his knees, made the sign of the cross, and prayed to God. Then, he confessed his sins—past and future.

§

On his third day on Crete, Constantine sat in David's office, which, through one window, overlooked the inner courtyard where Diana, on summer vacation from school, was sketching at a stone table while Georgina, her own hair recently cropped short to her jawline, combed Diana's long hair and dressed it with blue ribbons. In back of Constantine, the other window revealed hills.

Constantine said, "I've been looking forward to this meeting, David. I hadn't expected my business trip to Italy to be extended. But I'm pleased to hear that you have everything still under control." He had been assured by David that Georgina was sure that Jud would come to Crete before January first of the New Year. Constantine continued, "As you know— there can be no marriage—I have not changed my mind about that. But I still will say nothing to Stephen, yet." He gazed at Diana through the window. When a union between her and Stephen had been proposed by David, he had not jumped at the idea for several reasons: he knew that his son wanted to be married by age thirty—instead, he was thirty-one and would still have had another five years to wait if all had been going according to plan; Georgina allowed Diana to run wild and do anything she wanted, which would make Diana poor wife material; the ill feelings between the two families still simmered beneath the surface of amicability, despite Georgina's efforts to soothe; he had foreseen that Diana would be taller than Stephen, something that Stephen wouldn't like.

Constantine again continued, "Let me see the DNA tests, David." He took the papers from David's hands and examined them. As he had been told, the reports matched up the DNA of Subject II and Subject III, Diana and Jud. Although Constantine had thought the tests were unnecessary, now that their results existed, he was surprised to be anxious to see them—because he could hardly believe that scientific methods could prove a person's genetic make-up rather than because he doubted who Diana's father was. Yet, he asked, "You are sure that no mistakes were made?"

"I'm positive. I had the DNA in my blood and Diana's tested before I received a sample of Thorensen's blood. Diana's DNA did not match mine."

"Then, follow through with your revenge on Mr. Thorensen, since you must. But you will announce the dissolution of the marriage arrangement so that I am blameless—only when I say so, though." Constantine looked at David. David still seemed to be ignorant of the only real way to end the marriage agreement with no questions from anyone about the reason why: the sacrifice of Diana. Constantine hoped Stephen survived all of this. He had only one other worry—he asked, "You are ensuring that Georgina will not take Diana away from here?"

"Of course. Georgina is obeying me. She still thinks there is a reason to fear for Diana's life. Thorensen will come here to see Diana." David wondered if Constantine wanted Jud dead as much as he himself did and if that was why, therefore, underneath his calm, Constantine seemed anxious that Diana wouldn't disappear.

Constantine said, "Good, very good."

"I have an idea how Georgina can pay—" David heard a knock at the door and was glad because he suddenly decided there was no need to tell Constantine of the small but poignant twist for Georgina's role in his revenge on Jud. She would pay well for her adultery. David said, "Come in."

Georgina walked in with Diana. Georgina had heard David's sentence, although it had been muted, but she made no reference to it. Instead, she and Diana welcomed Constantine Sgouros to their home and Georgina told them what time dinner would be.

§

After dinner with her parents and Constantine, Diana was excused by Georgina. She ran to her room, pulled the ribbons out of her hair, and had a bath. She put on her pajamas, turned on a low light after turning off the bright overhead one, and put a chair in front of the door so that she would hear a scrape if anyone pushed open the door, which was at her back when she sat in front of her computer—she sat there now and switched it on. She savored reading Jud's latest e-mail. Jud had sent one each day this week and each one had been a highlight for her. She read the one she had pulled up on her computer screen:

Dear Diana,
You were quite a humorist in your last story. I liked your drawings for it. Do you sketch from life or from memory?
You wouldn't be interested in my life, right now. I am still working on the second draft of a book, from morning till night. I follow an exercise routine and walk every evening. That's it. That's all I do.
Yeah, it's cool that Mara returned from California yesterday. We had supper with her parents in Bridgeford. Her dad made bangers (sausages), mashed potatoes, and mushy peas. Then, we had hot custard over treacle pudding. I think you would have liked it.
About three weeks ago, I wrote to your mother to ask if our writing to each other is okay. I suppose I will hear from her soon but I don't receive all of my personal mail anymore. And so, in case she didn't get my letter, would you please pass along these numbers to her so that she can call my apartment or send a fax at her convenience: 555-555-0108 / 555-555-0109.
By the way, you have a beautiful name. Did your parents name you after someone in your family or for the Roman mythological Diana?
Love,
Jud

Diana copied down Jud's numbers on a piece of paper, which she folded up. She realised that Jud must have been waiting for her mother's reply during his long pause in sending e-mails and then, after giving up waiting, had resumed doing so. And he likely had the Binakas telephone number—yet would not call their residence. Diana wrote:

Dear Jud,

I saw Mara's parents on the news, via the Internet. I guess Van Silverman is starting a world tour with Romeo this fall and Dr. Hall is going to join him when she can—that's wild. There's a rumor in the entertainment industry that you're getting offers for making a movie about what happened in Washburn.

I sketch from life—but I try to interpret what I see and not just put it down mechanically. I learned that from Mama—she has been painting for a long time. A few days ago, she put aside a painting of a saint with arrows in his body. I was relieved. It was horrible. I don't think she's going to finish it. Instead, she's painting another portrait of me. She gets carried away sometimes—she's already done too many paintings of me. Come to think of it—she chopped off her hair—it's very short—on the day she put away the saint painting. I was already in the studio when she came in. I was shocked but I think she looks good.

I was named for my grandmama in California but I think she was named after the huntress, Diana. I took archery lessons last year but I didn't enjoy them. So my bow and arrows sit somewhere behind a canvas in Mama's studio.

I will give your numbers to my mother. Do you speak Greek? Tell me more about your English meals when you have them! I think I eat too many vegetables. Mama and Papa make me. Even when I'm at school, I try to do as they say. I say my prayers every night, too. You probably don't pray?

Love,

Diana

Diana shut down her computer, picked up Jud's numbers, and jumped into bed. As she had during times when she had been particularly tired and climbed into her comfortable bed and felt thrilled to have attained what had seemed far away—comfort and sleep—she grinned and then tightened up her body and relaxed it, this time from the thrill of having heard from Jud again. She dreamed about meeting him one day.

Diana was almost asleep when Georgina entered the room; she heard the scrape of the chair she had forgotten to remove from the door. She turned to face her mother who now sat on the side of the bed. The lamplight caught the love on their faces. This was one of the few evenings that her mother seemed to be at peace.

Georgina wondered about Diana's chair but said nothing about it. Instead, she said, "Good night, sweet stuff." She stroked Diana's forehead. Diana took her mother's hand and put a warm, damp, wrinkled paper into it. Georgina unfolded it and saw Jud's name with two telephone numbers. She asked, "Where did you get these from?"

"From Jud Thorensen. I found his e-mail address and sent him notes. He asked me to give you these numbers." Diana felt her mother's tension. She sat up. She said, "Mama, didn't you get a letter from him asking if we could communicate?"

"Yes, I haven't answered it yet. I wasn't aware that he had said you were already corresponding. Why are you?"

"He's been in the news—I was curious about him."

Georgina took a deep breath. The one thing she and David agreed on was that while Diana was the drawing-card to attract Jud to Crete, she was never to meet the man for whom David had planned a mortal death. Georgina's heart sank and then rose to her throat. She wanted to cry. She didn't want to be a party to David's plan. But if she had to choose one life over any other. It was Diana's. She said, "I forbid you to write to him any more. Is he writing back to you?"

"Yes." Diana mused on what her mother was thinking.

"Promise me that you will no longer write to him."

Because Diana had been used to few restrictions from her mother, she was unused to disagreeing with her. So, she did not argue with her. In fact, she said nothing.

Georgina said, "Diana, you must promise me what I ask or I will have to remove your computer and your phone line. You didn't keep his phone number, did you?"

Diana felt her hope of speaking with Jud on the telephone fade. She had not lied to her mother before and did not now as she said, "I promise I won't send any more e-mails to him. I do have his phone number but I won't use it." Nor could she use it—any calls to his number would be listed on the phone bill, something she had been shown by her father a few times when he had told her that she called California too often. Diana didn't want any of her freedoms removed

"Thank you, Diana." Georgina quickly added, "You are not to communicate with Mr. Thorensen in any way." She put her arms around Diana and kissed her.

After Georgina left, Diana switched on her computer and logged onto her e-mail account. Although her mother did not use a computer, her father did. So, she changed her e-mail password—her father knew it and could decide to access the e-mails she had saved. If her mother was adamant against her correspondence with Jud, then her father would be more so.

§

Because Jud had a set-up that enabled him to take telephone calls while he was on-line, he was just scanning the In-box for his latest e-mails, looking for one from Diana, when his telephone rang. He screened the call but, as soon as he recognised the voice, he picked up the phone and said, "Georgina."

"Hello, Jud. I think it would be best if you didn't correspond with Diana anymore. There is no reason for it." She could hardly speak to him. Her emotions had unsettled her insides. She had just left Diana's room. It was nine-thirty p.m. in Greece. She knew it was four-thirty a.m. in Massachusetts but she had heard from Ariadne, who read the tabloids, that the crucifixion author had a strange sleeping habit—he awoke before daylight hours started—an apparent truth, on this morning.

Jud took in the abruptness.

Georgina asked, "Are you still there?"

He said, "Yes, I'm here."

She said, "Why didn't you telephone me about writing to Diana? I told you not to call unless necessary—but you should have called about this."

"Perhaps."

"I had thought that once you received the DNA test results, you would let me know what your plans are regarding coming to Crete."

"I'm sorry. I thought I had plenty of time to think about this."

Georgina said, "Of course—there is no hurry. But why would you delay?"

"Will I get the privilege of writing to Diana once I make a commitment to a visit?"

"When would you be making this commitment?"

"What if I made one now?"

"Would you make one now? Even if I deny you the writing privilege."

"Georgina, you give me nothing. You want me to say yes to you and all you want to do is say no to me. I'll let you know my decision once I'm sure about it." He took Diana's photo out of his shirt pocket. He had a feeling that the e-mail he had on his screen right now would be the last one he would receive from Diana. He said to Georgina, "I have your phone number. I'll call you." He hung up.

Georgina had felt his disappointment in the outcome of their conversation and knew she could assure David, if he asked her again, that Jud would be coming to Crete and just hadn't decided when.

She had denied Jud the knowing of his own daughter and soon she would have a role in denying him his life. She couldn't feel any worse. It was ironic that her payment to him for giving her a child was the promise of an early death. She went to her room and cried.

CHAPTER SEVEN

During July, as Jud sat at his mahogany desk and prepared Desire; Sex & Spirituality for publication, Mara came into his office, the only small room in his Ocean City home. She had just finished reading the final draft for the book, different from the first draft she had read. Jud saw that she was upset. Mara sat in the window seat, framed by long drapes and over-looking the harbor. The late afternoon sun was bright over the Atlantic Ocean and lanced Jud's eyes as he looked at her, now in silhouette, and asked, "What's wrong?"

She opened up his manuscript and said, "I see you've revised and added. How does this sound to you," *Many eastern gurus teach that enlight-enment comes to one who loses all desire and, thus, frees himself of the karmic cycle of birth and re-birth; he is then absorbed into All-That-Is or God. Yet, karmic justice does not keep us in the cycle of physical life because karmic jus-tice is nonexistent. Karma means action, nothing more. Karma is neither good or bad. There is no separate power or supreme being, imbued with any quali-ties we care to give him, that is judging our behavior and then rewarding us— or punishing us, only to send us back into physical life until we get it right. It is our own desire to experience the physical that keeps us coming back for more.*

One could say that the guru is farther from becoming enlightened than many other people because he, himself, has great desires, such as the one to teach and influence. He designs systems of living to hasten one's enlightenment:

*best hours for sleep; proper foods to eat; types of medicine, exercise, and medi-
tation; best architecture; astrology charts—how to live one's life according to
the planets' influence; appropriate behavior and dress; the list is endless. These
systems are valuable when offered as possible ways to live rather than as the best
or only ways.*

*Indeed, the guru is not farther than anyone else from enlightenment—by
his own definition or another's. Yet, nor is he closer. There are no levels to
attain, distances to travel, or lessons to learn. According to one concept of
enlightenment—understanding and witnessing the eternal nature of Creative
Intelligence, its silence and dynamism, equal to the unmanifest and its inherent desires—enlightenment can be instant. Since dynamism permeates silence,
sending forth desire, then elimination of desire must be impossible—even the
desire to have no desires is a desire; the desire to not be re-born is a desire.*

*Life is a process of becoming. Many people are being, doing, and having
what they want and wanting more. Our thoughts are expanding as the uni-
verse is. Everyone and everything is in an endless process of becoming. Our
spiritual selves, which are individual expressions of God, create and sustain
our physical bodies. The body is not separate from the spiritual—God, the
Gap, All-That-Is, or Whatever permeates all of creation, known and unknown
to us. Desires from the unmanifest create the manifest.*

Mara said, "Aren't some people going to think you are saying that gurus
are ignorant? That you think you know more than they—who are considered holy and firmly established in consciousness?"

Jud moved so that he could see Mara without the sun in his eyes and
said, "Some might think that but that is not what I mean. How can consciousness be measured—how can enlightenment, if you believe in it,
which I do, be determined. And who decides what is holy. Everything
non-created and created must be holy or nothing is. Gurus, priests, and
saints are no more holy than any other living being—no one is superior or
inferior to another. Just different. Each life is to be respected—regardless
of how it is lived. It's true that we learn from others as well as from our
own experiences but teachers come in all forms—not necessarily packaged

as spiritual or religious leaders but as musicians, homeless persons, politicians, children, artisans, and so on."

"I understand but there is room for misinterpretation." She looked at him, knew his thought, and said, "I know—there's always room for that. But you go on with," *A guru tells you, as Jesus Christ and other great spiritual leaders taught, that your power is within but then, as most religious and philosophical organisations do, he often tells you to subjugate your preferences to those ways of thinking and living that he says are right. Yet, who is to say what is right. And right for whom—surely not for everyone. The adage 'one man's food is another man's poison' is true: one man's joy can be another man's sorrow. Each person learns what is good for himself, a process of personal experience, which a guru can assist with but need not vanquish by insisting he is right.*

Thus, a guru who teaches his listeners to look within and then tells them to think as he does rather than to listen to their inner selves is unaware of his hypocrisy. He encourages each person to express his own nature and then helps him bury it under a new set of constraining beliefs which often cause a distrust of one's self. A person truly following his nature, which is all good, is happy. Yet, despite our welcome individual diversity, we are not that different from each other because our true natures come from the same place—the field of all possibilities, the stream of consciousness, Creative Intelligence, God. Yet, each nature holds a different set of desires and preferences.

Therefore, each man's experience is valid—whether he is a monk or a prostitute. One is not better than the other. Just contrasting. Each has chosen his own experience. Mara said, "I'm going to stop here. You are criticising certain spiritual leaders."

Jud said, "Mara, I'm simply sharing a few ideas, perhaps not widespread but are known by others. In this book, I suggest that each person live his own life and make his own decisions. If following a guru and then belonging to his organisation or any other type of organisation is a desire, that's fine. But if a person is unhappy or feels inferior because he cannot conform to someone else's ideal, impossible for anyone to achieve, then, maybe, he should choose another system or follow his own inner guidance system.

"Organisations can be good for people. They are formed by the beliefs of their constituents. Some constituents change their beliefs. Then, either the organisation changes—if its majority wants a change—or the dissatisfied minority leave. Or the minority stays and suffers from its differences with the organisation.

"The excerpts you read are within an integral context. I'm done with the book and I like it. As for punishment for bad deeds, I have two main points. My first is that many gurus say that All-That-Is or God is Unconditional Love. If so, punishment cannot exist within Unconditional Love, Whose inherent nature is all that is good. My second is that many spiritual leaders know that time is a manifestation. From the unmanifest outlook, where no time exists, all of creation—everything that ever was and ever will be, with their infinite probabilities, yet with no predestination because of free will—exist simultaneously so why are some of the leaders telling people that they are paying for mistakes in past lives when no life is in the past—or future. Who is to say what mistake came first and should be paid for when—presupposing a judgment from who-knows-whom. As they say on our news station, 'It's all happening now.' Pardon me for twisting the meaning to my own ends."

Mara smiled and asked, "What does Bill think?"

"He thinks the book is fine; he's ready to publish it. I'm not trying to change the world—I wouldn't dream of it. I don't care to try to change how people think. I enjoy offering my ideas through books—that's all. Yet, I do care about how people feel and hope that more people come to appreciate themselves, which I believe leads to their greater appreciation of others."

"But doesn't Bill think you are going too far with these ideas?"

"He didn't say so." Jud shaded his eyes with by holding his hand to his brow as he looked at her again and said, "Mara will you please come away from the window?"

She went to him and sat on his lap; she put her arms around him. It was wonderful to be able to hold him tightly now that his back, although scarred, was healed. Mara said, "Jud, I love you. I agree with much of what you say. But after Washburn, I'm afraid of others' reactions. I had used to be fearless. My last investigation that I would call bold was when I was in Iraq interviewing people as they were being arrested for smuggling bibles into the country. When I had started looking for the author of The Crucifixion, I had thought I was doing a lightweight investigation. I didn't know you were the author or that finding you would lead to tragedy. I just can't bear to think of anyone being angry with you for voicing an opinion, something that others do all the time. But many of them have the agreement of the population, which you rarely have—you don't think as many others do." Mara kissed him. She prayed that he would stay safe.

"Everything is fine. It always is. We are all immortal. Only the body dies. Like many, I'd rather live a long, happy, healthy life than die young. But the value of a life doesn't lie in its length. One moment of human life is precious. Almost any parent who has lost a baby will likely tell you that he would rather have had that child for whatever the short duration was rather than not to have had it at all. And that baby has had an experience of human life as no one else has had. It still hurts the parent but I think it helps to understand that the essence of the life, the baby, that experienced physical life for a short duration, during this life experience, exists and always will."

Mara kissed him. She felt better about her own past. It was after she had met Jud that she had begun to heal emotionally from her own loss of an unborn baby.

The phone rang. Jud picked up the receiver and said hello. A man's voice that Jud didn't recognise asked for Mara. He asked, "May I tell her who's calling?"

"I will tell her myself."

Jud handed the phone to Mara. She said, "Hello."

"Miss Sylvan?"

"Yes."

"This is David Binakas. Thank you for your exposé on Omni-Drug's falsification of reports. You saved my company a great deal of money and my reputation. We were close to buying its new asthma drug and distributing it. I apologise for calling you at Mr. Thorensen's but, when I couldn't reach you at home, knowing that you two are—well, close to being engaged,—I hoped you would not mind a call there."

"Not at all. And you are welcome." If she hadn't known that Jud had given his unlisted number to Diana to give to Georgina, she would have wondered how David Binakas could have discovered it.

"Is there any way I can thank you? I would like to do something for you."

"Thank you but there is nothing I need."

"Very well. But I am grateful. If you should think of anything at all, call me. You know where I am."

"Of course. Thank you, Mr. Binakas."

"By the way, I have a favor to ask of you. My daughter likes your father's group, Romeo. Would you mind sending an autographed photograph? It would cheer her up—she is under the weather, as the English say." David presumed that Mara did not know that Diana was Jud's daughter but he anticipated that Mara would tell Jud about Diana's illness, an inducement of Jud's commitment to come to Crete. David avoided using a ruse of Diana being on her deathbed—he wanted to apply pressure to Jud in increments. He and Georgina had been surprised that Jud had not yet called them with an arrival date. If all else that he had in mind failed, David was prepared to go to the US—his desire for revenge, steadily fueled by the loss of the Sgouros alliance with his family and the knowledge that Jud had once touched his wife, knew no boundaries.

Mara said, "I will send a signed photo to your daughter." She distrusted David. He was an honest man but a ruthless one, as she had learned during her investigation. She disbelieved that David, a native of a country where the dishonorable had suffered torture, legal and allowed during early Greek law, would invite Jud into his home to meet his daughter, begotten by Jud rather than by himself. Unlike other Greek citizens, David Binakas likely saw nothing wrong with the early law. That he had allowed his wife to tell Jud that Diana was Jud's child and then invited Jud to his home made no sense, unless, rather than his friendly claim of wanting Diana to know her real father, he wanted revenge.

David asked Mara, "Would you ask the group to write a personal message to my daughter, Diana?"

"Yes, I will."

"Now, I have a greater debt of gratitude to you. Thank you, Miss Sylvan. Good bye."

"Good bye." Mara hung up and said to Jud, "I advise you not go to Crete."

"Why not?"

"He said that Diana is ill. He's lying."

"You can't be sure."

"No. But I distrust David Binakas."

"I'm going to Crete, anyway. I want to see Diana." He still thought about her everyday and missed hearing from her and writing to her—as Diana had obeyed Georgina to stop writing to Jud, so had he stopped writing to Diana. Jud heard footsteps, louder than they needed to be.

A petite and pretty brunette, a young bride, Mrs. Wilkins knocked on the door jamb. Whether a door was open or closed, she always knocked because, sometimes, Jud and Mara didn't notice her approach. She enjoyed working for Jud. He paid her well, treated her as an equal, and had the kind of looks she liked. She loved her husband but, as she made love to him every night, she closed her eyes and fantasized about Jud. She said, "I'm leaving now, Mr. Thorensen. Have a great weekend. You, too, Miss Sylvan." She knew Jud preferred informality but she had requested that they use formality.

Mara said good bye. Jud followed Mrs. Wilkins to the kitchen and said, "Thanks for everything, Mrs. Wilkins. I wish you and your husband a happy first anniversary." He pulled out of the refrigerator a wrapped-up bottle of French champagne and, as he handed it to her with a gift certificate to the newest hot restaurant in the city, he said, "Here's something to extend the celebrations with."

Mrs. Wilkins knew that Mara must have told him. Mrs. Wilkins preferred to have Jud know nothing about her personal life and she, herself, to know as little as she could about his—not easy to do while she worked for him. And now that he was famous, if she didn't read the magazines and the tabloids, her friends read them and gave her reports on her employer. She thanked Jud and left.

Jud scooped up Mara into his arms and took her to his bed. Sunset was still far away. Through the French doors of the bedroom, they could see the sky change from orange to twilight and to navy. But before they fell asleep, as moonlight made patterns on their bodies through the net curtains, Jud remembered the night before his trip to Washburn, when the moonlight had made the same patterns but Mara had not been with him. He held her closer and sank into a place with no thoughts, just awareness. They missed the flush-rose of dawn.

§

During August, Angela brought her mother to Ocean City, Massachusetts. Doris Wynne had already acquired a job at Harcourt Publishing House, thanks to Bill Harcourt. Angela and Mrs. Wynne stayed at the Thorensen estate while searching for their own apartment, in Jud's company. Three blocks from the Bentilee College of Music, a brownstone building sat with five condominiums, two on each of the first two floors and a vacant, newly-renovated one, alone on the entire third floor. Mrs. Wynne didn't want to look at it because of the expense but Jud insisted. And when he realised that Angela liked it, although she did not say so, and heard Mrs. Wynne compliment it, he told the real estate agent that they would take it. He paid the first year's rent in advance and told

the Wynnes that Angela could pay him back when she made her first mil-
lion dollars. Because Mrs. Wynne wanted to keep her house in Washburn
and because her furniture would have been out of place in the brownstone, Jud helped her buy a few pieces of furniture, that day, to have deliv-
ered later. Angela and Mrs. Wynne returned to Washburn to pack their
clothes. Mrs. Wynne rented out her house, furnished, to a young, childless
couple.

When she and Angela returned to their new home in Ocean City a few
days later, they saw the Fender guitar in its open case in the middle of the
drawing room. Next to it was an amplifier. Angela felt overwhelmed. Mrs.
Wynne felt discomfort in accepting Jud's generosity but she nor Angela
could stop its momentum. And Van Silverman was already talking about
getting a recording contract for Angela. He was going to have her make a
demo tape and, because she was a beauty, a music video.

Jared Thorensen had retained his ministry and fiancée, who had given
him a conditional second chance—she would stay engaged to him if his
younger brother stayed out of trouble. Jared visited the Thorensen estate
with her, maintaining separate bedrooms. Jud came there to see him and
meet her. He and Jared got into debates, upgraded from childhood squab-
bles, about any subject that came up between them. Ogden did not
acknowledge Jud. The breakfast with Angela in June had held the last
words he had said to Jud. Helen kept in touch with her relatives in
Transylvania regarding her mother, who was recovering well from her
abstruse malady.

Mara took an assignment that her Ocean City Tribune editor, Bos
Stoughton, persuaded her to take. One of Mara's fellow reporters, in
Central America investigating stories on child smuggling into the US, had
taken ill. Mara agreed to replace him but told Bos that she had to be back
in the US by September. He agreed to send a replacement for her before
then. And, since she would already be in Washburn as a witness for the
prosecution at the Harper trial, she could take over that assignment from

the initial reporter he was sending, once she was no longer required to take the witness stand.

And somewhere in August, on the day that Mrs. Wilkins told Jud she was pregnant and he congratulated her, Jud received a package from Georgina. Inside it was an eight by ten oil painting of Diana, signed by Georgina and dated in March. It depicted Diana, with a grin, sitting on a stone wall with wildflowers on her lap, a sketch-book and paint-box next to her, against a sky of rainbows. It prompted Jud to call Georgina and tell her about his plan to arrive at her home on October twenty-fifth, a date which he thought would be past the time for the end of the Farnham trial, the second one—for which he wanted to be available in case he was called to testify. Georgina told him that the date was fine and that she would send a chauffeur to the Iraklefo airport for him. He asked her how Diana was. Georgina said that Diana was well and would be starting a new school year before August's end but would come home for a few days to become acquainted with Jud, once he was there. She told him that Diana had sent a note to Mara to thank her for the photograph of Romeo and their autographs. She reminded him that he should be discreet about his arrival to their island.

Jud didn't know what David and Georgina thought he would do. He was disinclined to announce his every move to the news media, who had numerous breaking stories to follow, rather than to follow his fading story.

He hid the painting of Diana's likeness in his walk-in closet from Mrs. Wilkins's eyes. Until he could frame it and, one day, display it freely, he hoped.

By August's end, although Jud had not started another book, he had written a pornographic short story for Flirt and an article for Enlightenment magazine. Both pieces would be published in October. And he had done interviews for a couple of news magazines.

CHAPTER EIGHT

In early September, Jud, Mara, and Angela flew to the Midwest. From the Fort Brent Airport, Angela rented a car and drove to Washburn to visit Mrs. Wynne's new tenants, per Mrs. Wynne's request. Jud and Mara drove into Fort Brent where they had lunch and Jud found a birthday present for Diana, whom he knew must have been born in September, if she had been a full term baby. He air mailed it from Fort Brent. He wanted to give her a gift because, although she did not know him as a father, she knew him as a friend. He was unsure that she would receive it and was unaware of what would happen: *Leesa, aware of the tension but unknowing of the unfolding drama in her employers' home, handed the package to Diana, home from school for a weekend; Diana noticed Jud's return address on the label and ran to her room to open the package. Inside, was a small book of prayers in the English language, bound in white leather and embossed on the front with a cross.*

From Fort Brent, Jud and Mara drove forty-five miles north to Washburn. They passed through a town that was booming. Due to the past gruesome events, Washburn was on the map for tourists. More industry was moving in; many stores and restaurants were being built; a new hotel was coming and the secluded Fallbrook Inn, where the three Ocean City residents had reservations, was going to expand its size. Jud and Mara met Angela, at the appointed time, outside Ryan Wallace's temporary office near the courthouse.

Inside his office, Ryan, Jud's lawyer and Mara's ex-lover, exchanged greetings with the three. Ryan was tall and thin; he moved quickly. His hair had thick waves and was dark red. He had a lively face, big smile, and a bass voice—he belonged to a barbershop quartet. He was happy to see Mara again and he beamed a smile at her. He pulled up chairs for all of them.

Jud asked Ryan, "How are Rev. Harper and Carl Farnham holding up?"

Mara and Angela stayed silent and listened. Neither of them wanted to see either of those two men again.

Knowing how he himself would feel in Jud's position, Ryan thought that Jud wanted to gloat over the two prisoners—Carl had progressed from lying in critical condition in a hospital to being well enough to join Rev. Harper in the Howard County Jail, just south of Washburn's center. Ryan said, "They are secure, under lock and key."

Mara noticed Ryan's face and guessed at his thoughts. Ryan knew almost nothing about Jud. She wished that Jud had not chosen him for his lawyer. Ryan could be vindictive in small or large ways. She had seen him get angry about the chipped paint of his car door after someone had tapped it accidentally with his own door; then, Ryan had used his car keys to scrape a long mark along the door of the other driver's parked car. She couldn't have imagined such resentment or retaliation.

Jud said to Ryan, "I feel badly for them. Although neither wants to see me or cares what I think or feel about them, I wish could be of some help, somehow."

"You can't see them, of course. They can have visitors but not anyone who is a witness."

"It's too bad—too many charges have been brought against each of them. Rev. Harper came into the situation after much had already happened."

"That may be." Ryan was beginning to think that his client wasn't for real. Yet, since his meetings with Jud in Ocean City, he had gleaned inklings of Jud's kind of thinking, foreign to himself, although he had observed it in other people. As a private lawyer, one that was biased rather than fair-minded, Ryan believed in crime and punishment with a vengeance—he wanted to see these two men strung up. Then, after it was all over, he would like to get Mara away from Jud, even if he could not get her back for himself.

Ryan continued, "The charges have been made—you nor anyone else has control over them. These men have done wrong. They will each have a fair trial and will be sentenced with the appropriate penalty."

"It sounds as if you think they will both be found guilty."

"At this point, it doesn't matter what I think."

Jud said, "I can't change what's happening but we have enough people in jails. These two trials are expensive, in the ways of time and money—neither of the men could possibly repeat their past actions, extraordinary ones taken under extraordinary circumstances. I'll answer questions as precisely as I can on the witness stand but I won't try to slant things against Rev. Harper or Carl."

Ryan knew what Jud was referring to. He said, "The questions I asked you in my office are indicative of what you will be asked by the prosecuting and defense attorneys."

"I realise that."

"Your concern should lie with the defense attorneys—from what I've heard, they are going to make the three of you look bad." As he observed their sincere faces and Jud's easygoing manner, he added, "As much as they can. But before you answer their questions, think about them first."

Ryan thought that Jud was going to make a poor witness for the prosecution but at least he wouldn't be a hostile one—he had come to Washburn voluntarily—and he would be an honest one. Ryan looked at Mara and Angela—they weren't much better than Jud at pointing fingers. Ryan was glad that the District Attorney office had clear and significant evidence.

He, himself, was in Washburn to take care of things for Jud after Jud returned to Ocean City and for his own added pleasure of assisting the

DA office's prosecuting attorneys, as well as watching them in action. Neither defense lawyer had a leg to stand on. Carl would likely be in jail for the rest of his life and Jon Harper—who had many supporters in town, some of them possibly on the jury—would be declared insane or get the death penalty, a law which Ryan agreed with, although he knew that Jud did not.

Ryan looked at Mara and Angela and wondered why they were quiet. He was unaware that neither one wanted to be in Washburn or to be confined with each other in his small office—the airplane ride with the three of them seated together had lasted long enough and been awkward enough, not to mention the stares from other passengers intentionally passing by.

Ryan gave them the scheduled days to appear in court and invited them to dine with him later that evening. The first of the trials would begin tomorrow.

Soon after the onset of the first trial, Jud, Mara, and Angela were each called to the witness stand during the Harper trial, expected to last for a month. Since the three had given depositions in March, they were excused for the trial's duration and for the subsequent Farnham trial.

The three also met with Sheriff Bledsoe, Deputy Blint, and Lisa Chalmers, a paramedic, who had helped them through the aftermath of their ordeal on Golgotha Hill with the three crosses, no longer there. Lisa was amused to see that Jud had managed to keep both Mara and Angela, so far. Lisa herself was happy—she had started dating the Sheriff, who congratulated Mara on the marriage of her famous parents and told her that he should have guessed who her mother was.

The news media coverage was less than it had been in March during the crucifixion but was still considerable. As before, the mayor called a press conference. As before, Jud, Mara, and Angela, without Bill this time, answered questions. Ryan stood nearby.

That next morning Mara said good bye to Jud as got ready to fly back to Ocean City with Angela. She knew he would be leaving for Crete in a few weeks. And she mused over how he would be spending those few weeks now that his book was done, leaving him with free time on his hands, and she wished she was going home with him. Yet, she had promised Bos, her story editor, that she would stay and cover the Harper trial but had reminded him, again, to replace her for the Farnham one in October.

§

Once in Ocean City, Angela resumed her classes at the music college and made up assignments she had missed during the beginning of school.

And Jud fell more in love with Angela. Yet, he ensured that he was never alone with her because he knew that they would make love. So, he took her out only when her mother could come with them. Or friends were with them. But, because of Angela's request at his parents' home when she had come to Ocean City for her Bentilee audition, he was careful to treat her according to the way he felt—so, he and Angela enjoyed each other's company, even though they shared few kisses. Jud never brought her back to his apartment or any other place where they could make love, which he found difficult to avoid because, the more careful he was about not being alone with Angela, the more he saw ways and places for them to be alone, which was what he wanted but was the opposite of what he thought should be. It might have been easy to succumb to his desire for Angela if his love for Mara had lessened but he loved her more than ever.

By September's end, Jud didn't know what to do with himself. He loved two women and could touch neither: Mara was still away and Angela was, by his self-imposed faithfulness to Mara, as distant as the sun. So, he was starved for sex.

He dreamed about making love to Mara. And, sometimes, to Angela. He missed every aspect of Mara. When he lay awake thinking about her, he could see her smiling face and her lithe body. He almost felt her skin against his. He almost smelled her hair and felt it against his face. When he felt her lips on his, his hand reflexively reached out for her. When he didn't feel her, his sensations filtered into nothingness.

CHAPTER NINE

Jud's disappointment saturated October, whose third week had arrived, because Bos had still not sent a replacement for Mara in Washburn and so Jud was not to see her, even for a moment, before leaving for Crete. Jud spoke with Mara on the telephone every night. She knew his departure date for Crete and that, thereafter, he would be returning in two weeks; she already had the address and phone number of the Binakases, which she would use only in an emergency, since she was not supposed to know about this trip.

Jud had seen Angela only a few times in October: along with doing homework assignments, she had begun work on a demo tape and a music video with the guidance of Van Silverman, whose world tour with Romeo would begin on November first.

On the morning of October twenty-third, a Wednesday, when he was to take Angela out for lunch, he picked up the telephone to hear Dr. Sherry Hall's voice. She congratulated him on his published spiritual article and then she said, "Jud, I'm wondering why you are writing pornographic material."

"You must mean my story for Flirt."

"Yes, you know I do. It's obscene. Why are you doing this? You don't need to."

"The words pornographic and obscene aren't in my personal dictionary and, if left to me, wouldn't be in any dictionary. There's nothing dirty about sex—whether it's done or written about."

"Sex is a private act."

"For most people."

She said, "You don't have to write about it."

He said, "No one has to read it, either." Jud continued, "What you call pornography is just a graphic description of what many men and women do everyday. Sex is a natural act, whether homosexual or heterosexual, like any other natural act. And having sex can lead to children."

Sherry laughed. She had been a feminist for all these years and now had a potential son-in-law who wrote pornographic material. It was ironic. Although not all of her friends thought that porn was anti-feminism. She herself had used to think so.

Jud continued, "While it seems that sex is for the sole purpose of pro-creation, it is not—maybe for animals. But not for human beings—we have no mating season. We need no special condition. We have the free-dom to have sex whenever we want to."

"I agree with you Jud. I just don't see why you have to write about it. What if you have children one day?" Sherry thought about the sweet girl in the photograph she had seen fall from Jud's shirt and had guessed was his daughter—concern for her was the reason why Sherry was calling Jud.

"I enjoy writing about it. And there is nothing about it that needs to be hidden from children—they can learn about sex, when they are ready to, from their parents or school or in other ways. It doesn't harm them to know. And a child can grow up to choose celibacy or sex."

"You didn't pose for Flirt. Don't you think that's hypocritical?" She didn't think so but she wondered what he would say.

"That was a choice. I don't care to pose naked. And I don't care to be in a porn film. But there are those who do. You have to choose whatever suits you."

"Jud, I don't understand you. In some ways you are conservative, I think. But, in many ways, no one can tie down your thoughts or hold you to a moment. Sex is a personal thing. When you write about it for others to read, you are writing about your own experiences. And about the women in your life. Van is not thrilled about your article."

"You are being protective of Mara, I see."

"Not just Mara."

In the silence, Jud realised that this phone call was about Diana.

Sherry wanted to ask him about the girl in the photo—she had tried to bring it up with Mara but had met silence. Instead, she asked, "Does Mara know what you wrote?"

"I didn't mention the story for Flirt or the article for Enlightenment to her. The Flirt story was a piece of fantasy, Sherry. I pulled from my own experiences but it's still a piece of fiction—although, I see your point, fiction is often real or becomes real—after all, fiction and reality come from the same place—thought."

"I enjoy your work, fiction or otherwise. But I advise you to think twice before you do some of the things you do."

"You may not believe this but my life was dull before I wrote The Crucifixion, at least in my terms. I've changed since then. And I could change back but I don't want to. I want to see what's next. I want to bite into life. I want to see what's out there—which for me is adventurous, although certainly tame for others. I'm still a mild kind of guy—I just seem to invite wild experiences these days."

"Yes, you do. I'm having my own new experiences, too, although unlike yours. I've been a respected psychologist for many years. Since Van's and my marriage, which brought into the open our long-term relationship and Mara's illegitimacy, I've continued to be respected by many people but I'm being criticised by others who think that a feminist shouldn't marry a sexy rock star or marry at all." She added, "I'm helping Van get ready for his tour—we hope to see you along the way."

"I would like that very much. I'll check out your itinerary with Mara."

"By the way, Van is very impressed with Angela's guitar work. I heard her voice for the first time yesterday—she is incredible. She should be coming on tour with us. She said she's having lunch with you today?"

"Yes."

"Would you please tell her that she's welcome to stop by our home this evening to meet some of Van's band members? Van has just brought in a new one."

"Of course."

After they said their good byes, Jud picked up his acoustic guitar again and finished roughing out a new song. He had written many since his university days. Then, he left for Bentilee College of Music. He took Angela out for lunch, told her about Sherry's invitation, and then told her that he was going to Europe for two weeks but did not disclose his reason for traveling. Instead, he let her assume that he was taking a vacation.

After lunch, Jud took Angela back to Bentilee; he found himself alone with her when she pulled him into a dark utility closet. As they kissed, she undid his belt and he unbuttoned her jacket. Jud felt as he had last spring, as if he were free falling.

The door opened. A custodial gentleman, very old but with good eyesight through his eyeglass lenses, let Jud and Angela walk out with something that was not grace but, under the circumstances, resembled it, in that the custodian made no comment and pretended that he had seen nothing, even though he was thinking that Jud may look distinguished in magazine photos but, in person, he looked young, libidinous, and unlike what he, himself, thought that a respected author should look like. Or behave like.

Jud pulled his unfastened overcoat around him. Angela walked him to the exit doors and held him for a moment before she kissed him good bye and wished him a safe journey. A group of students stared at Angela, whom they knew, and at Jud Thorensen, whom they recognised, and thought that perhaps, after all, the rumors about their affair were true, not that they cared. But it was interesting gossip.

§

That evening, after finishing a late dinner with the Harcourts, Jud stood in Bill's study near the fireplace mantel. Bill sat in his comfortable leather chair. Ribbons of light played on the dark walls as flames, fed by pine logs, rose and fell.

Jud said, "Bill, you're happy, aren't you?"

"Yes. Very."

"Do you find life simple? Clear cut?"

"No, Jud. Not at all." He knew Jud was aware of his, Bill's, homosexual feelings toward him even though they remained unspoken. "But I suppose to you, my life seems less complex than yours. The fact is that whether your life is simple or complex doesn't matter. It's how you view your life and how you live it that matters. Sometimes you just have to accept things you don't understand and let them be. I wouldn't beat myself up over my own sometimes-displeasing thoughts and emotions the way you beat yourself up over your feelings for Mara and Angela."

"I don't feel as badly as I look to be feeling. It's just that sometimes the situation makes me tired. And, right now, I've slept with neither woman I love and so would probably sleep with any woman who looked my way." Yet, many women had looked his way today, as they did everyday. Jud continued, "I have something to tell you that I'm not supposed to tell any-one. For better or worse, I've told Mara. I keep no more secrets from her. Do you remember Georgina Binakas?"

"I remember her."

"On the day you and Linda came to my parents' home for dinner, she had come to see me."

Bill was stunned. "What about? Wait, don't tell me." He looked at Jud's face by the firelight and was reminded of the firelight that had gilded him twelve years ago in front of Georgina's fireplace. Bill said, "She has a child and is saying you're the father."

"You knew what happened that night?"

"I would have had to have been dead to miss noticing what Georgina was up to. If I had been the object of her attention, as I had hoped for, I would have been as lost in the sea of desire and in the fog of oblivion as you were. So, I don't blame you." He paused and said, "Go on."

"The child is a girl, Diana."

"And so you are going to Crete to see her."

"Yes." Jud pulled out the small photo of Diana and showed it to Bill.

Bill turned on a reading light over his shoulder and looked at Diana's face. He said, "Wow."

Jud took the photo back.

Bill asked, "Why has Georgina waited for all of these years to pass before telling you? And why would she tell you at all?"

"Those are the right questions. I don't know. She says that her husband has discovered her indiscretion and, since he has, he accepts it and feels that it would be good for their daughter to meet her biological father. Mara thinks that David and Georgina Binakas have an ulterior motive. But I don't know what that would be. Or why they would even have one."

"I asked you to stay in Massachusetts rather than go to Indiana last March. Now, I am asking you to stay here rather than go to Crete. You've barely recovered from this last event. Find out more about the Binakases before you put yourself on their doorstep."

Jud felt the wisdom in what Bill said but he had waited too long as it was to see Diana. He had re-read her e-mail letters many times. Each one had impressioned his heart. Nothing could change his mind about going to see her.

§

In Washburn, Mara lay in bed. She was restless and had thrown away her sleeping pills. Bos had been unable to send another reporter to take her place at the Farnham trial, which could have ended today—the first day of jury deliberation, predicted by news pundits to end with a quick decision—but it had not. Thus, Mara would be unable to use the flight reservation she had made for tomorrow morning to return to Massachusetts—she couldn't walk out on a story; Bos was relying on her. Even if the jury came to a fair decision by tomorrow afternoon, she would be too late to see Jud before he left for Crete tomorrow night. She had a bad feeling about his venture.

She sat up, picked up the telephone, and called Jud. There was no answer. She left a message for him to call her at any time. She knew he might still be at the Harcourts and called there. Bill answered the telephone and told her that Jud had left and should be at home. Mara didn't tell him she had already called Jud there.

§

Jud let himself into his parents' household and punched in a security code within the allotted seconds before the alarm would go off. The house was dark. He took off his coat and left it in the foyer. He found his way upstairs; he knocked on his parents' bedroom door and said, "It's Jud." He stood and waited. He knocked again. As he turned to leave, the door opened.

Ogden stared at his youngest son. At last, he said, "What do you want?"

Jud was glad that it was his father, a light sleeper, who had awoken. He said, "I want to speak with you."

"Your mother has already told me that you are leaving the country tomorrow."

Jud stood there and waited.

Ogden recognised his own stubbornness in Jud. As he heard his wife stir, he said to Jud, "Let's go downstairs."

"We can stay up here and go to my room."

Ogden agreed. In the hall, he put on a light. Father and son walked along the wide hallway. Once inside Jud's room, Ogden closed the door. He looked at his son's hair—dark for the Thorensen family—his striking features, and his lean strong tall physique, different from his or Jared's which, although also tall, was stately. And whereas his and Jared's faces were pale and poetic, Jud looked as Ogden's own father had, as a mythological god and different from other Thorensens. Yet, Ogden's father had behaved as a Thorensen, dignified and traditional. Jud did not.

He said, "Jud, I want to disown you and, legally, disinherit you. I haven't told your mother, yet."

Jud swallowed hard. He looked into his father's face and asked, "What have I done that makes you want to do those things?"

Ogden sat down on a chair in Jud's room. It had seemed that his children would remain as children forever until, one day, they had grown up, except for Lisbeth—she hadn't quite, yet. He was unsure if he could talk in here, after all. It was permeated by his memories of Jud as a child, although there were no physical reminders in a room that had become very different as Jud had grown more mature. Yet, Ogden recalled the papers filled with scribbled stories stacked in piles around the room and the nights he had tucked his boy into bed, told him tales, and kissed him. Ogden said, "You have done too many things. There have been too many years of things. But the Washburn event was the proverbial straw; it was too much for me.

Do you know what it's like for me to have watched Jared suffer, because of you, while he waited to hear if he could keep his ministry. His fiancée nearly left him. And during these years that Jared has had his ministry and has abstained from sex—and still is abstaining until he marries—you disregarded his feelings whenever he visited here. Between the girlfriends you brought home to sleep with and the escapades you had with your rock band members, including Bill, you were less than an ideal university student. And a bad example for your little sister. Your influence on Jared is poor—when he's around you, he struggles to stay on the path he's chosen.

Then, there's the fact that my friends are still laughing at me because I had no clue that you were a published author, especially of The Crucifixion. I look like a fool. Have you no respect for my feelings?"

"I thought I was saving the literary reputation of the Thorensen name by using a pen name."

"But you didn't tell me or your mother. And I am not going to begin to touch on the matter of religion."

It seemed to Jud that, lately, sometimes, when he had something to tell someone, he had to hear what the other had to tell him first. He felt as he had with Mara when she had told him about her parents and he had no longer wanted to say what he had come to say. He said, "Maybe I didn't make choices that you like. And maybe I've made bad ones. But they were mine to make." And he thought, *even though we disagree, I love you. But do you still love me?*

Ogden stood up. He took a deep breath. He asked, "Just why did you come here tonight?"

Jud felt a rising anger, a rare emotion for him. He said, "My reason will make no difference to you if you disown me. And if you don't disown me yet, you will after this." He turned to go.

Ogden grabbed his arm and asked, "What do you mean?"

"Nothing." Although Jud felt tense inside, he stood relaxed as he waited for his father to release his arm.

"Disown you after what? What more could there be?"

Jud pulled his arm away from his father's grasp and went to the door. He opened it and saw his mother. She had raised her arm, ready to knock.

Helen saw the tears in Jud's eyes—and the blaze in them. She looked at her husband. When Helen had been disturbed in her sleep, she had, at last, risen from her bed, walked down the lit hallway and heard voices in Jud's bedroom. She asked, "What is going on?"

Jud could barely speak but he said, "I was just leaving." Though he had wanted to talk about Diana with his father, he had not wanted to tell his mother about her because, if things didn't work out, she would be disappointed. He looked at her troubled face. He didn't know how to hide his own hurt. He just wanted to live through the moment. But the moment was lasting too long. He said, "You have a granddaughter." Then, he left.

At home, Jud listened to Mara's message and returned her call. While it was just after one a.m. for him, it was just after eleven p.m. for her in the Midwest. He assured Mara that everything would be fine and he would see her in a couple of weeks. She told him that she hoped the Farnham trial would end tomorrow, Thursday, with a jury verdict. Because, then, she could come home. That night, Jud was aware of being awake all night while thinking he'd been asleep.

§

Jud left his bed before Thursday's dawn and lifted weights. It was the twenty-fourth of October. He put on a heavy jacket over a sweater and jeans; he went for a walk in the cold morning and smoked a cigar. Once at home again, he called his mother to see how she was after last night. Lisbeth told him that Helen was on her way to see him. Jud showered and shaved, dressed in a wool sweater and trousers, and ate breakfast while he waited for his mother to arrive from Clinton. He had packed his luggage yesterday morning. His flight to Greece was in the early evening, which would put him there the next day on the twenty-fifth, a Friday, and, then, he had a connecting flight to Crete.

When Helen buzzed his intercom, he let her in and took her coat. Light-haired and darker-skinned than he, she was average in height but exceptional in looks. Underneath an umber wool coat, she wore a classic suit, burnt brown, because after visiting Jud she was staying in town to lunch with friends and attend a concert at the Stella Gartner Museum. Before she even took off her coat, she said, "You know your father loves you."

"Let's talk about something else, Mom." He went to the stove and poured hot water over a tea-bag in a cup.

Helen looked at his tired face. She said, "All right. But I hope you believe me." She paused and asked, "What is this about a granddaughter?"

"I would prefer to not talk about her until I return."

"You cannot expect me to ignore this situation. I need to know about her."

Jud brought a hot cup of tea to his mother. He said, "Hold on a moment." He left the room.

When he returned, he handed her an oil painting. Helen put her cup down and took the portrait in both hands. Having expected a baby or a toddler, she looked up at Jud's face and said, "You are hardly old enough to be her father. Just how old is she?"

"She recently turned twelve. Her name is Diana."

"She may look like you but she's not necessarily yours."

"A DNA test was done. She is mine. She's the reason I'm going to Crete."

Helen leaned Diana's portrait on a small table against a wall. "You've traveled to Crete a few times but I have to assume that she was conceived during your first visit when you and Bill went during high school at Christmas-tide." She was about to ask who the mother was when she suddenly knew. "Georgina Binakas. The mother is the woman who came to see you last spring. Oh, Jud—how could you not have told me then?"

"I was asked to not tell anyone. But, in the course of time, I've told Mara, Bill, and, now, you and—Dad. This first time that I see Diana might be my last so there's no point in going into any details about how all of this came about."

She looked at him. She could see he was upset and asked, "What is it?"

Jud turned his back to her and stared, without seeing, at one of the many oil paintings he owned of today's artists. He said, "I don't know if I can live with meeting her and then never seeing her again. I don't trust her parents. I don't think they have her best interests at heart because, if they did, they would surely have left well enough alone and not told me about her. I don't know if they've told her about me, yet. I probably shouldn't go—maybe I don't have Diana's best interests at heart either."

"As much as I would love to have a granddaughter—although I'm sure that I would be disallowed by her parents to treat her as one—I have to say that blood ties are not everything." Yet, Helen wanted to meet the happy child in the painting. Very much.

Jud turned to face her and said, "It isn't all to do with blood. She and I have shared brief communications as friends. Somehow, from them, I feel an affinity with her. You know how you can meet someone and feel indifference, even aversion, or you meet someone and, right away, you feel good with them. Those feelings of compatibility and incompatibility exist within families—between siblings, between parents and children, and so on. I feel tied to Diana, not only because we are of the same blood but because we are of like minds and hearts. I know I will want to continue a relationship of some kind with her—but that might be unlikely."

Helen put a hand on her son's chest, over his heart. "Just go and see what happens. As you often tell me, worrying is a waste of time."

"I know. I hope for the best."

§

On Thursday night, October twenty-fourth, on Greece's mainland, Diana lay on her dormitory bed. She anticipated leaving St. Mary's High School tomorrow for another of her occasional weekends at home, this time for Ochi Day on October twenty-sixth, a Saturday, when she would be able to partake of a feast and stay up all night playing games.

Diana looked forward to flying with Constantine and Stephen in Stephen's private plane. Once they had landed in Irakleío on late Friday afternoon, they would take a taxi to Ágios Nikólaos where Diana would spend the night with Ariadne, Georgina's friend, whose children were now young adults, while the Sgouroses would go to her parents' villa. On

Saturday morning, the Sgouroses were to pick up Diana from Ariadne's and stay in Ágios Nikólaos to see the parades there, while her parents continued to entertain their guest. Diana had asked David why she couldn't come home until Saturday night and he had told her he would be entertaining a business guest, who would be gone by then.

That Stephen would be her husband four years from now had no reality for Diana. Through her young eyes, he looked old, although that did not bother her—that he acted older than his years did. Diana rarely saw him and not usually during a holiday. Because reaching sixteen years of age seemed light years away, she was sure that she could figure out an escape from marriage to Stephen by then.

Under her covers, Diana held the small white prayer book Jud had sent to her and inscribed: *To Diana with love, Jud.* She often wondered about him. Since the day she had seen his name in her mother's handwriting, she had watched her parents' relationship become like ice that had grown colder, until cold enough to evaporate and motivate her mother to move into her painting studio, across the courtyard, diagonally opposite to the master bedroom of their villa—whose top third floor was one room of glass walls overlooking the villa's back, where hills lay strewn with rocks and, during fall and winter, with poppies, euphorbia, and violets, before sweeping to face the Aegean Sea, which her mother now faced every night as she lay upon the bed she had put into her studio, along with her clothes. Diana still associated Jud with her parents' mutual estrangement and her father's coolness toward herself; she still believed that Jud was her father. While she had obeyed her mother by not communicating with him in tangible ways, Diana imagined that her thoughts of him must be bouncing off the stars and reaching him. She doubted that she would continue her obedience and be silent toward him for much longer. She wished she would dare to discuss their blood relationship with him. Then, she thought, perhaps it was up to her to be the first to bring it up.

CHAPTER TEN

Late on Friday morning, October twenty-fifth, David Binakas sat working at home in his office, on the same side as his now solitary bedroom. He was having a conference call with his Pharmakon managers. He had much to do for Monday and would not have time this weekend to work since he would be entertaining Jud Thorensen with the Sgouroses tonight, celebrating Ochi Day with his family on Saturday night after perpetrating a lethal incident, and adjusting his life on Sunday to the resulting circumstances. He looked at hills with the hundreds of white stones interspersed by thousands of colorful wildflowers. Two days of rain had passed. Today, the sky was darkening, the wind was blowing. But with a recent pattern of three days of rain and one day of sun, David assumed that tomorrow would be bright and clear for the parades and other festivities.

With the sea at his back, Georgina's chauffeur drove through the villa gates and up the winding drive. Inside the black car, Jud felt anticipation in his heart and fear in his stomach. Almost thirteen years had passed since he had been in this area of Crete. And since he had been in front of this door. Jud thanked the driver and stepped out of the car with one suitcase; he walked up to the door, which opened before he rang the bell. Rain began to splatter down. The sky deepened into heavy blue with green tinges. Clouds crowded together, ready to watch the humans below as they created their own storms.

Georgina opened the door and faced Jud. She and he had each thought that he would feel distress upon seeing the other. Instead, each felt relief and unexpected joy as they gazed at each other's faces. And so, as storm clouds that break apart for sunny skies, they smiled at each other. Despite being strangers who had been intimate and then been apart for years, each with his own life and secrets, Jud and Georgina, with all of that washed away, liked each other. Jud put down his suitcase and without thought pulled Georgina into his arms. Then, he released her and touched the deep line that lay between her eyebrows and had not been there when he had seen her last. Jud picked up his suitcase and walked inside the villa. Georgina took Jud to a bedroom, to the right of the top of the stairs. Jud set down his suitcase again and took off his coat, laying it over the case. He knew what was going to happen—what was in his mind was in Georgina's eyes.

Georgina locked the door. Because she might be making love to Jud, she was using her birth control device and told him so. She had nothing left to lose with David and, although Jud didn't know it yet, neither did he. No matter how different each one's thoughts were from the other's, neither cared about anything else other than making love. Jud kissed her lips as if he couldn't get enough of them, she kissed his in like manner. She pulled off his sweater. He unzipped the back of her slim dress. He leaned down and put his hands underneath her dress on the sides of her thighs, moved them over her hips and torso, raising the dress and then letting it fall again as he put his hands on her shoulders and slid the straps off her shoulders and slid the dress down. She undid his trousers and they went to the bed to continued their foreplay.

Jud couldn't rationalise his behavior. He thought about Mara and her wish for his faithfulness, his loyalty. Yet, he was seduced by Georgina's short dark hair that took away her elegance and gave her a rakish beauty, by her thinner curves, and by her irrevocable status of being Diana's mother, who deserved to be loved and cherished, no matter what. And while her status of being Diana's mother was not his excuse, he felt as if he had a right to Georgina and she to him. He felt that the world could not deny them the pleasure of each other. Or condemn them. And if the world would do those things, it still wouldn't matter. Having shared carnal knowledge that had led to a child, he could not feel that they were doing wrong.

But Georgina was sure she would go to Hell, even if she confessed her sin. Yet, she didn't care. This was heaven now. And Hell couldn't be any worse than the hell-on-earth that would be here tomorrow.

§

Jud stood on the woven rug near the fireplace. It was early evening. He was feeling the effects of jet lag—when his flight had landed in Athens at about nine this morning, it had been two a.m. in Massachusetts. So, by now, having had scant sleep during the night flight and having been up a few hours earlier than usual, he wanted to go to bed. But he was waiting for Georgina, who had left him a short while ago. Although Georgina had not said so, he knew that Diana had been in school today and that he would not be seeing her tonight because, while the storm persevered with strong wind and rain, she would be unable to travel, by ferry or plane; he assumed that David was on the mainland waiting for clear weather before bringing Diana home.

Yet, David was still in his office. He called Ariadne to confirm what she already knew, that the storm was preventing Diana's departure from Athens and, thus, her arrival to Ariadne's home this evening. David thanked her for her availability and wished her a good evening. He told her that Georgina was making dinner, since Leesa had been given today off—otherwise, Georgina would have called Ariadne.

David emerged from his office and approached the living room. He walked up to Jud, held out his hand, and said with a smile that he didn't feel, "Welcome Mr. Thorensen. I'm David Binakas." He saw surprise on Jud's face and realised that Georgina had not bothered to tell their guest that his host was at home nor had she brought him to his office upon his arrival as he had expected her to, which, because of his work overload, had not troubled him.

Jud shook his hand and asked, "Would you mind if we are informal?"

"Not at all, Jud. Shall we go into the dining room? Georgina will be there shortly."

As they entered the dining room, Jud observed five place settings on the white tablecloth and assumed that one of them had been for Diana and the other for her chaperone from the mainland. Covered silver serving dishes sat on the table. David removed the two place settings that had been intended for Constantine and Stephen. He excused himself and left the room with them. Jud looked at the storm outside. David returned.

Just as Jud turned to face David, Georgina entered the room. She wore red. She kissed her husband's cheek and offered her hand to Jud, whom she admired in a gray blazer, white shirt, and dark gray trousers. David had not seen Georgina wear color for a long time. Her eyes looked bright. He saw the way Jud looked at her, the way any man remotely attracted to the female sex would look at a woman who was beautiful and sexy. David looked at her that way himself. He couldn't help it. But, whereas he had used to see the light of love in Georgina's eyes directed toward himself, he saw, instead, a look of pleasure directed toward Jud.

As the three sat down to make thin conversation and sate their appetites, the storm experienced its own satisfaction—then, once no longer voracious, it released its severity and allowed the winds to taper down to a slow death. After dinner, Jud offered to help Georgina clear the table but she refused. David said good night to his wife and asked Jud to follow him upstairs.

On the third floor of glass walls, a circular fireplace stood in the middle. Stationed at intervals around the room were low-backed couches and chairs. Soft, yellow spotlights—ceiling insets—cast yellow columns of light. Because of the interior dimness, the exterior dark landscape could be witnessed. Jud stood with David by a window. David looked at the man before him and thought that he seemed too young to have a daughter of

Diana's age. And too young to have slept with his wife thirteen years ago. David didn't know what Jud and Georgina had done this afternoon but he would imagine that they had not made love. Not again, in his house. Not with him there. And he wondered why he was even thinking of such a thing.

As he looked Jud up and down, his jealousy of Jud's youth and beauty surged. David's bitterness regarding the father of Diana had grown during these last few months. That Georgina refused to sleep in his bed was almost intolerable; he had become sexually frustrated because of that—and because he had not sought satisfaction outside of his marriage. He had to overcome his anger. In an even tone, he said, "I'm sorry that Diana isn't here tonight." Even though the storm was abating, he used it as an excuse for her absence, and, with ease, still pretended that he wanted Jud to meet her—even though, according to plan, Jud never would.

Jud said, "I'm sorry, too. I've been looking forward to meeting her—I hope that the weather will let up and she will be here tomorrow."

"Let's hope so."

Jud felt that insincerity shrouded David, unconvincing as a man who would be willing to share his daughter, so Jud asked, "Have you changed your mind about introducing me to Diana?"

David said, "I feel as I did before," and left his comment up to Jud's interpretation. He added, "I want you to know that I forgive you and Georgina for what you did. How old were you?" David barely breathed while he waited for an answer—Georgina had not told him everything on that afternoon in Pherma.

Jud said, "Almost seventeen."

David thought, *Jesus Christ. What had Georgina been thinking?* It was acceptable to him to see an older man with a younger woman—but not the other way around. He waited for Jud to thank him for his forgiveness but Jud said nothing more. Nor did Jud offer the apology that David had expected he would hear once he and Jud had met. At last, David said, "I love Diana and am glad to have her. But, I am in an awkward situation. I have arranged a marriage for her—to take place when she is a few years older. That is why I asked Georgina to contact you—because I thought that Diana should know her true lineage and that I should be honest with her prospective parents-in-law. What do you think?"

"I don't know." Jud was surprised that Diana's future was being planned for her. "I suppose if you feel that her future husband and his family need to know, then you should tell them. I don't know your modern-day customs. Would the circumstances of Diana's birth matter to the family?"

"I think it's going to matter a great deal."

"Then, why did you want me here? Why expose your secret?"

"First, tell me why you came here. I wonder, if I had been in your shoes, if I would have trekked to another country to meet a stranger, which is what Diana is to you."

Jud thought about not explaining anything but, on a whim, opened up his heart, even though Constantine's last words had struck him there. He said, "Although Georgina was persuasive, I came because I want to know what Diana is like. Knowing that she is mine in the natural sense, I want to meet her. And I saw her photograph. The reasons may sound weak but they are backed by a strong desire. I think you are lucky that you have a daughter. And that she is yours is unquestionable. I've never wanted children for myself but I think you are lucky that you have Diana to take care of, to spend time with." Jud's throat tightened—yet, he was able to say, "From my perspective, I have missed twelve years of watching Diana grow up and of being a parent. Regardless of how I feel, I stand aside and accept whatever you might allow for me. Yet, although I missed all of those experiences with Diana, you are giving me a chance to see her now—I am happy about that. I think you are generous. I don't mind telling you my feelings, even if you think I'm crazy or laugh at me, but I wonder what yours are. I sense that you are unhappy about this. If you are—just let me know—I'll leave tonight. Even though I would rather stay. I have no rights in this matter—you have them all."

David almost began to think of letting Jud go. But he couldn't. He asked, "Do you love my wife?"

Jud said, "No."

David heard the doubt in Jud's voice and felt his own jealousy rise afresh.

Jud felt his own doubt. Today, he and Georgina had been lost in a sea of sensuality and then drawn into a net of love that had bound them together into unheard of ecstasy. He still felt the remnants of their afternoon experiences swill around him as soft streams of water. He hoped that David could not read his eyes. Not because he felt guilt, which he did not, but because David seemed to be a jealous man. Jud wondered what sex had to do with loyalty, a subversive concept, perhaps.

David was saying, "Of course, I haven't told Diana's prospective groom about you, yet, because—and I've had many months to think about this—I think that he just might become upset. Actually, Diana doesn't know about you either, yet. Perhaps I should change my mind about telling her about you. You must have an opinion about that. Now that you've come all this way and might not see her." David laid a hand on Jud's shoulder.

Jud was thinking that he should leave David's home, tonight, and was about to say so when he heard a doorbell chime, faint but distinct.

David said, "Ah, Diana is here tonight, after all. You shall meet her tomorrow. Please, don't mind what I said before."

On the ground floor, Georgina had pulled on a robe. Although she had wanted Diana to remain in Athens this weekend, the choice had not been hers to make. It had belonged to David, whose wish was to have Diana join them on Crete because she was David's hold over Georgina's co-operation. Yet, Constantine had seemed particularly interested in Diana's presence. When she had commented on this to David, he had said that Constantine was just interested in protecting David's plan for Jud.

As Georgina let her daughter and the Sgouroses inside, David led Jud downstairs to the second floor. He opened Jud's bedroom door and bade him good night. Before entering his room, Jud looked over the railing; he glimpsed two men and Diana. David stayed where he was until Jud closed his door. Then, David walked away.

Jud went into the bathroom and stared at his face in the mirror. He felt as if he were looking at someone not himself. He was changing more. He had been nothing like his older brother and was even less so—Jared was reliable, conforming, and would likely know only one woman in his life. But Jud couldn't change to become as Jared was any more than Jared could become as he was. And that had to be okay—for both of them.

The world was full of rules, formulated by people, about what was good and bad or right and wrong, often conflicting with each other. The only things Jud knew to be wrong was when a person set out to psychologically or physically harm another human being—or kill him. Then, he had the thought that David was interested in killing him. And he wondered where the idea had come from.

Yet, Jud had seen Diana. So, rather than leave the house in the dark of night, he was going to stay.

§

Diana's bedroom was on the opposite side of the staircase to Jud's room. As Diana reached the top of the stairs, she noticed a light, to her right, coming from underneath the first bedroom door. She went into her room. She was unaware that Constantine had thought that it was late enough that there would be no risk of her running into Jud Thorensen, unimportant to himself if she did but, to David and Georgina, critical that she did not.

In his room, Jud changed from his dinner clothes into a sleeveless tee-shirt, jeans, and sneakers. He turned down the temperature control and paced the warm room, wondering what was next. He had no idea who those two men were or why they hadn't waited until morning to bring Diana here. He opened his door and sat in the dark hallway outside his room. He kept an eye on his limited view of the downstairs and caught the cool air from the passage. As he relaxed, he sat with his feet together and his knees apart, with his arms leaning on his knees. He let his head drop forward. Then, something made him look to his right. He saw Diana. She was standing, in her nightgown, near the stairs peering at him through the dimness. Despite having been told to stay in her room, she had been on her way to the kitchen for a sandwich, since she had not eaten all evening while at the airport with the Sgouroses, hoping the storm would subside and enable them to fly to Crete before morning.

Maintaining the quiet, Jud opened his door so that the light came out and Diana could see who was there. Then, he stood up. He held his finger to his lips but Diana, realising that she had been deliberately kept ignorant about his visit, needed no warning to be silent. She walked across to him. She was astounded to see him here—she felt a thrill in wondering how he came to be here. After all this time of wishing to see him, he had shown up—just like that. She walked with him into the guest bedroom; Jud closed the door. They stared at each other in the lamplight. Jud breathed her name, "Diana."

Outside Jud's door, a figure passed by and entered a bedroom—Stephen was two doors down from Jud; his father's room was next door. Diana and Jud thought they had heard something. While she knew, he presumed that the two men were staying overnight. And one of them had come upstairs.

Jud held his breath. It was as if he were in the Vermont woods and facing a fawn. If he moved, it might leave. Then, Diana sneezed as Stephen's cologne seeped under the door and drifted up to tickle her nose.

Jud said, "Bless you."

They moved closer to each other. Diana saw her face when she looked at his. She felt his gentleness and love. She felt comfort in his presence. She walked closer to him. She said, "Thank you for the English prayer book."

"You're welcome."

Diana put her arms around him and felt as she did when she hugged her mother, she was at home. Then she felt his arms around her. They stood that way for long moments. Then, her body shook as her tears came. She not only knew but she felt he was her father. And she knew that he had already known this was so. As she asked, "Did you come here to see me," she wondered why secrecy veiled his visit.

"Yes."

She had to say it because he had not, "You are my father."

"Yes."

"Why did you wait all these years, I wonder."

"I didn't know about you, Diana. But shall we try get to know each other—now that we have met?"

"Yes."

Neither could take his eyes off the other's face. At last, Jud said, "I imagine that your mother would like you to be in bed. May I walk you back to your room?"

Diana nodded her head. "In fact, I want you to." When they came to her door, she opened it and said, "I want to show you something I didn't understand until now."

He walked inside. Her room was full of books in bookcases. Georgina's paintings hung on the walls and seashells lined the window ledges. A signed photograph of Romeo was on the wall above Diana's bed, next to which was a computer notebook that Georgina had given Diana for her birthday so that she would have a computer to use at home during the school year while her main computer was left in her dormitory. Diana turned on her computer notebook and logged onto her e-mail account. She brought up an e-mail from Mara Sylvan that asked her to let Jud Thorensen know that she would arrive on Crete on Saturday morning and to ask him to stay at the Binakas house until she got there, before he might leave for any of the Ochi Day celebrations. Diana said, "I saw this message before I left my room and then saw you."

Diana noticed Jud's surprise and said, "When Mara sent the Romeo photograph, she sent her business card, which had her e-mail address. I sent her an e-mail to thank her—and that's why she has my e-mail address." Jud looked at the time on the computer notebook and realised that Mara had already been on an airplane for a few hours. Jud said, "Thanks, Diana, for the message."

Diana shut down her computer, climbed into bed and sat up. She held out her arms. Jud sat on the edge of her bed and hugged her. He said, "Good night, Diana." He scarcely believed he was holding his own child in his arms. She felt thin and light, sweet and innocent. He kissed her soft forehead, her skin softer than eiderdown. *I love you Diana*—he thought what he dared not say.

Diana said, "Good night, Jud." She kissed his cheek.

As Jud rose and turned, he faced Georgina who had come to say good night to Diana. Georgina thought she was dreaming when she saw father and daughter together. She became breathless. She said, "Jud, would you please wait for me?" Jud nodded.

Diana watched Jud walk out and then looked at her mother, who made no comment, turned off the lamp, and left her room.

§

Jud stood outside Diana's door, which Georgina closed after exiting from it. She brushed by him. He followed her down the hallway on Diana's side of it and into a room that was pitch-black and seemed to be empty. She shut the door. If there was a window, no light came through it.

Georgina asked, "What were you doing in Diana's room?"

Jud could feel her fury. Although he couldn't see her, he felt her whisper against his face. He said, "We ran into each other in the hallway. She showed me her room."

"How is it that you two know each other well enough to kiss good night?"

"I don't know, Georgina. We wrote back and forth for a while and when we met, we—had a bond. It just happened that way."

"You are to stay away from her."

"I thought I came here to meet her."

Georgina shivered. She said, "When I say so."

Jud said, "I think you're overreacting but you are her mother. I'm sorry."

Georgina reached around his neck with her arm. She hadn't realised how much she cared about him. *If only tomorrow wouldn't come,* she thought. She put her other arm around him, pulled him toward her, and kissed him hard. She almost hurt them both. Then she ran her hands through his hair and clenched strands of it in her hands; then, she caressed him.

Jud couldn't understand her passion. Anger and desire lay in it. And something else. He wanted to pull away but didn't.

Georgina held him tighter. Then, she lifted up his shirt and undid his jeans. She parted her robe and pushed her body against his. Then, she kissed him hard again.

Jud felt her arms move from around his neck to his waist. He took a deep breath. He didn't understand Georgina's intensity or roughness. She held him tight and pulled on him until he responded with the same ardor. It was unlike any experience with her before and, although it held none of the slow, sensual passion, it was erotic. He fondled her breasts; then, he moved his hands downward and lay them on the inside of her thighs and then on their outsides and back up to her hips. When he picked her up, she wrapped her legs around his hips. As they made love, the room remained black—with no light for their eyes to adjust to.

Then, Georgina's kisses turned into the sweetness of light rain and Jud felt her tenderness. He kissed her gently. He let her down.

Jud adjusted his clothes while she fastened her robe. He was about to ask her a question when she opened the door and walked out. He followed after her down the hallway. He reached out a hand and touched her arm.

He whispered, "Are you never going to speak with me? Tell me what's going on."

She breathed, "Tomorrow." Near the top of the stairs, with a view of the empty living room below, she turned toward him. They kissed. Then, Georgina ran downstairs.

Jud watched her turn left at the bottom of the stairs and turn toward her studio. He walked along the landing to the first door in the hallway, its silence in unison with nature's silence outside.

Inside his room, he lay on top of the bed with his clothes on. He was asleep when he felt a mosquito bite his arm. Greece had no mosquitoes, so he thought he was dreaming but when the sting persisted, he moved his palm over it and felt a hand holding a hypodermic needle. As he fell into an oblivion that could capture a mind more fully than natural sleep could, he barely heard a voice say, "Sweet dreams."

§

In the kitchen, David, still in his three-piece suit, joined Constantine and Stephen Sgouros, who wore casual clothes. The Sgouroses had eaten the sandwiches that Georgina had given them earlier and were leaning against a counter, drinking wine, warming up for tomorrow's festivities. David had given verbal and written clearance to Diana's school to release Diana to Constantine Sgouros, since he was coming to Crete to meet Jud. When Georgina had begged David to keep Diana away from Crete on Saturday and promised her full co-operation without Diana's presence, he had nearly given in to her. Yet, after their dinner threesome tonight, he was glad he had not because he was sure that Georgina would have backed out tomorrow. He had seen her eyes. She would no more want to see Jud harmed than she would Diana. True, he, David, could have reached Diana before Georgina could have, if Diana had been left on the mainland, but there would have been a risk that he might not. He was relieved that Diana was here at home, tonight, despite the inconvenience of her presence to his plan. David refreshed Stephen's glass of wine and poured a glass for himself.

Stephen thanked him. He had hair like his father's, thick and wavy, but with a few gray strands among the black rather than bands of gray. Like his father, he was a notch taller than David and had more bulk and strength. As his father was, Stephen was tired and was glad to have reached the Binakas home tonight. Now, all he had to do was sleep. It was by Constantine's request that Stephen had brought Diana and his father to Crete tonight. He planned to fly back to the mainland the next morning.

Constantine said to Stephen, "I want you to stay on Crete tomorrow."

Stephen stared at his father as if he were crazy and said, "I have plans for tomorrow in Athens. All my friends are there—and the celebrations are bigger."

"This is important, Stephen. There's a situation that involves you. And, since we cannot change the past, David and I have worked out a solution."

"What are you talking about?"

"Take it easy. Just remember that, after you hear what David tells you, we have ensured that everything will work out well for you." Constantine was afraid that Stephen would become self-destructive after hearing what David would say. As a child, when Stephen couldn't get his own way, he had clawed his face and arms or screamed bloody murder, causing his face to redden and his veins to swell. Now, Constantine did not want Stephen to jump into a plane tonight and leave in a state of anger. He loved his only son more than his three daughters put together.

"I'm fine, Pater. You are the one who is melodramatic and needs to relax." With his arms folded, Stephen looked at David and said to him, "I am listening."

David said, "I am sorry, Stephen, to have offered my daughter's hand in marriage to you. It's based on a lie—recently found out. I am not Diana's father."

"What do you mean," Stephen asked.

"Diana is not of my blood."

"Where are you going with this, David?"

"Your father wants me to withdraw the marriage arrangement between you and her."

Stephen unfolded his arms and stood up straight. He said, "We can keep secret whatever the details of Diana's birth are. I didn't give up the woman I love and watch her marry someone else so that you two can play this cruel joke on me."

Constantine stepped in and said, "You cannot marry Diana." He could see there was no gentle way to let Stephen know what was going on. She has bad blood. And if anyone should ever discover her true father, our family's humiliation would last for generations." He said, "I will not allow your marriage to her."

Stephen was bewildered—at the revelation and at the idea that he would have to give up the powerful connection to the Binakas family. He wasn't sure he could do that. "Would I know the man who is her father?"

"Yes," David said. "Jud Thorensen."

Stephen said, "So?" The name was familiar but he hadn't heard it in a while. And, even so, he did not understand its significance to breaking the marriage arrangement.

Constantine said, "You must recall the news about the author of The Crucifixion."

Stephen said, "Yes, the man you call the Antichrist. You are a superstitious man, Pater. Do you think I care about Diana's bloodline—it's a technicality. She has the Binakas name—and that's good enough for me. I will marry Diana." Stephen had shaken off his latest depression and looked forward to drinking all of the next day and night with his friends. In four years, he anticipated Diana's generous dowry and eventual exorbitant inheritance, alternatives to losing the love of his life, although modest ones. He had to marry Diana to make his anguish worthwhile. Although she was a cute girl and was unlikely grow up to become his type of woman, he thought he would get along with her.

David felt relief—he would be a happy man if the marriage plan stayed intact. Then, all he would have to do was take his revenge on Jud—he couldn't imagine how his relationship with Georgina would be after Jud's death but that didn't matter, for now.

Although Constantine was glad that Stephen was calm, he was disturbed at his insistence on marrying Diana. Thus, Constantine would not let Stephen be and said, "You will not marry Diana. The risk of dishonor to our family is too great. His face is well known and she looks like him."

Stephen felt a seed of anger. He said, "I don't care who her father is or if she looks like him. You both have meddled with my life before—I had not wanted this future wedding but, since I agreed to it, I will have it stay as it is."

Constantine was furious but realised that pushing against Stephen was useless. Yet, he didn't know how he would get Stephen to co-operate in David's plan tomorrow morning. Constantine had not counted on this. When he had complained about Jud Thorensen months ago, Stephen had commiserated with him. That his son thought differently now was a shock to him. Constantine doubted the wisdom in telling Stephen about David's plan. Perhaps, he should let Stephen return to the mainland tomorrow. He said, "Stephen, why don't we talk about this in the morning. Let's all get some rest before the festivities."

Stephen said, "There is nothing more to discuss." Then, he asked, "By the way, who is your guest?" He added, "I took my overnight bag upstairs earlier. I heard Diana sneeze—she was in the first guest bedroom, talking with someone."

David felt surprise but, in an even tone, said to Stephen, "Jud Thorensen."

Stephen whistled. He asked, "How did he come to be here?" As he looked into David's face, he saw an angry man. As David had said that he had invited Jud here to meet Diana, Stephen decided that he would stay on Crete, after all, and meet the American writer, younger than himself, whom he might expect to have an association with, after marrying his daughter.

David knew that, after hearing Stephen's responses about Jud, he would not tell Stephen about his plan for Jud. In private, David would have asked Constantine for his silence about it but Constantine seemed to already have the same thought.

§

After David said good night to Constantine and Stephen, he thought he would go to Diana's room and interrogate her about her meeting with Jud but decided not to. Instead, he entered Georgina's bedroom studio. He hoped she would be asleep and then he would just leave but Georgina was rinsing brushes in turpentine by the sink. Because she had felt wide awake, she had been painting but, then, unable to focus on what she was doing, she had stopped. David had not been in this room for weeks. He sat on her bed. He noticed an open copy of The Crucifixion face down on the floor at his feet. Then, he saw that the drawer of the small table next to her bed was ajar. He glimpsed inside and saw the case for a diaphragm. He recognised what it was because, when he had first married Georgina, they had not wanted children right away and, unaware of his infertility, Georgina had used birth control, the diaphragm, during the first year of their marriage. This case had a drop of water on it. And he knew that its content had been used and then washed tonight. David closed the drawer.

When Georgina came to stand next to him, he gave her two sleeping pills; he watched her as she took each one. He did not want her to run away with Diana tonight, as he thought she might. Yet, if she could run away with her and wanted to take Jud with them, she would be unable to.

David told Georgina to get a good night's rest so that she would be fresh for tomorrow. He moved to kiss her. She turned her head—not because she didn't want him to kiss her as a loving husband—but because she did not know who he was anymore with his mind bent on revenge.

§

Diana was almost asleep. She was feeling happier than she had in a long while—she had met her real father. She still loved David who, while he had loved her mother during all these years, had been a happy man. His happiness had showered her and her mother with feelings of security and, if not compatibility for Diana, companionship—that, sometimes, had been very pleasurable. But during these last few months, David had shown other aspects—he had become more restrictive with herself; he had become harsh and restrictive with her mother. Wherever her mother was, David was there with a watchful look, especially if Diana was with her. Diana had observed David's treatment of her mother change from loving and pampering to loathing and criticising. She thought that if her grand-mother, Athína Binakas, had still been around, that David would have tempered his behavior.

Yet, Diana understood that David must feel devastated that she was not his own child. Although neither parent had mentioned Jud and his rela-tionship to her, she had never wavered from her belief, since it had formed, that Jud was the reason for the discord between her parents. His presence, whether by name only or by physical form, was the only new element in their family environment. It bothered Diana to see her parents wrapped in misery, enough to disregard her, Diana's, feelings. Yet, she was extra kind to them.

Georgina continued to show Diana love—without having to make an effort, usually. But David paid scant attention to Diana and rarely kissed her good night—now, it was past the hour that he would do so. Tonight, in her distraction, even Georgina had just tucked her in without kissing her. Thus, Diana had lain awake thinking. When she had heard quiet voices and peeked out of her door, she had seen Georgina and Jud kiss.

It was then that Diana had begun to realise the physical nature of life— she had not thought that Jud and her mother had actually made love to conceive her, even though, when Diana had started her new school year, Julia, her best friend and roommate, whose parents had informed her dur-ing summer vacation about sexual intercourse between men and women, had been anxious to tell Diana about sex and had taken one step more— after finding a stack of pornographic magazines for men and some for women in a storage room at home, she had smuggled a porn magazine of each genre into her dormitory room at St. Mary's and shown Diana.

Thus, after Diana had seen her mother and Jud kiss, she had begun to understand how badly David must feel and why. Yet, she saw him as a blind man because her mother still loved him and he couldn't or wouldn't see that. If he had been different, Georgina would not have left his bed. Often, her mother talked about David and told Diana stories of their life together before Diana had been born and since her birth, including stories Diana had been too young to remember into her future years.

For a brief while that night, Diana had felt animosity toward Georgina and Jud, especially Jud—she wondered how he could have dared to kiss her mother in her father's house. If Jud had not been her father, also, she might have stayed angry with him, angry that he would kiss a married woman, even if she wanted him to. But Diana supposed she would prefer that Georgina and Jud like each other than not. And there was something about Jud that held no pride. He was just himself—not perfect—she didn't know anyone who was and she was unsure just exactly what being perfect meant, anyway. When Jud had held her tonight, Diana had felt his warm strength and perceived that he adored her. And that was her dominant thought.

CHAPTER ELEVEN

David and Constantine rose at dawn on Ochi Day and met in David's office. They had excluded Stephen from their mission because he was not aligned with their thinking: he had none of David's malice toward Jud or a shred of Constantine's belief that Jud was a valid reason for breaking the Binakas-Sgouros marriage arrangement. Therefore, just the two of them went to Jud's room. David turned on a light. Since he and Constantine had to remove Jud from the villa sooner than planned because of Diana's presence and her habit of rising early, David again injected Jud, this time with just a micro-dose of aconite, to ensure he was well under. Constantine watched David withdraw the needle and asked what had been in the shot. David told him it was a sedative made from monkshood roots. Then, between the two of them, in the dark house, they carried and dragged Jud, heavier in his unconscious state, down the living room stairs.

From inside Diana's room, Georgina heard sounds at the top of the stairs and knew what was happening. After David had left her room last night, she had taken the dissolving sleeping pills from underneath her tongue. Then, she had gone upstairs to Diana's room; she had climbed into bed with Diana and put an arm around her. She felt worried because Constantine and Stephen would be taking Diana for the day. That David had already told her that Constantine would harm Diana if he learned that Georgina let David down today did not worry her because she knew she would carry out David's plan but she was afraid that because Constantine hated Jud, he must also hate Diana, who had Jud's blood running through her veins. And she mulled over why Constantine had left the marriage plan intact between Diana and Stephen. And why Constantine knew of Diana's real father while Stephen, it seemed, did not.

After all of this was over and David was no longer monitoring her, she was going to run away with Diana, because each day brought a greater realisation that she could not live with David once he had murdered another man, even if not with his own hands. Nor could she live with herself, because she would be as guilty as David, although his unwilling accomplice. And yet, she would have to live with herself for Diana's sake.

As footfalls faded down the stairs, Georgina closed her eyes and fell asleep again. David and Constantine continued lugging Jud from the living room and down the passageway stairs that led to the underground garage. They put him into a car and drove a short distance to the designated locale. They removed Jud from the car and lay him on the ground. They returned to the villa.

After dawn had brightened into morning, Georgina awoke. Diana was lying awake and enjoying the comfort of snuggling next to her mother, who had not climbed into bed with her for years. Georgina hid her anxiousness and smiled at her. Then she rose from the bed and went downstairs to make breakfast for Diana, David, and the Sgouroses.

David heard Georgina's steps as she approached the kitchen. He had started the coffee. Stephen had joined him and Constantine. Then, Diana entered the kitchen. She asked where Jud was. David said that Jud was sleeping in—he had jet lag. Although Stephen accepted David's lie as the truth—which it was in a way, David thought—Diana was doubtful. It was common gossip that, after escaping a dawn crucifixion, Jud Thorensen couldn't sleep past dawn. Yet, Diana accepted what David said because: there was no reason for him to fib, jet lag could alter a person's sleeping habits, and Mara had said in her e-mail that she would arrive here late in the morning.

After her meal, Diana asked her parents why they weren't coming with her and the Sgouroses. David said that he and Georgina had seen enough parades this year and so he would catch up on his office work while Georgina worked in her studio. He added that Jud would join them during the evening celebrations for Ochi Day, unless he had to leave here early tomorrow to see one of his colleagues, who was expected to be in Athens then.

Then, David told Constantine that there was a set of car keys on the seat of the blue convertible and gave him a garage door opener. Georgina watched Diana walk between the Sgouroses toward the passageway door leading to the garage. Diana turned and blew her a kiss.

After Georgina had showered and put on a dress and sweater, both white, she tidied up her studio while waiting for David. She heard the intercom. Leesa did not work on Saturdays and so was not there to answer it. As David did, Georgina also left the buzz unanswered and the ensuing ones. A short interval after the last one, David knocked on Georgina's open door and told her that it was time. Istron, the small village nearby, was alive with festivities. People were everywhere; David was pleased.

David and Georgina walked down the driveway and through the villa's outer gates. As David turned right outside them and walked down the road, Georgina leaned against the stucco wall, lined by cypress trees. It was a beautiful day. Then, too soon, she watched David return. He had just given Jud another injection. As he walked toward her, she moved toward him. In the distance, he saw a rare sight in this area, a taxi.

§

Mara arrived on Crete in the late morning. She hired a taxi to take her from the airport to the Binakas villa. But when she got there, the gates were locked and no one answered her repeated buzzes of the intercom. She returned to the taxi. The driver, who spoke English, told her that the largest town where she could find a good hotel room was Ágios Nikólaos.

But Mara wanted to stay in this area and asked him to drive her the short distance back to Istron's square, that they had passed, usually sparsely-inhabited and quiet but now lively with families celebrating the holiday. There were a few scattered houses, one taverna, and one main road with veins of paths on either side.

Tables had been brought outdoors and laden with food dishes. The sea air was full with the smell of cooked lamb, fragrance of fresh-baked bread and desserts, and drifts of coffee aroma. Wildflowers bloomed and, although the air was cool and the ground was damp, the sun was bright and the clear sky was blue. Mara heard mandolins and guitars.

Adults and children were dressed in their best; the children were already getting dirty. Dog and cats mingled with people as they hoped to become recipients of scraps from the feast. Laughter tickled the air. Mara used gestures to ask some of the revelers about acquiring a room for the night and a man told her she could have one for twenty dollars. A few nearby villagers laughed—they knew that twenty dollars, translated into drachma or not, was too much money for Alek's stucco square room with a hard cot and no bathroom, less than tourists were used to. The villagers were unsure that Mara was American because she looked European. Mara told Alek that she would take the room. She paid him with drachmas from her belt bag, which also held her passport.

As she was passing a line of dancers, she was pulled into it; she laughed with exhilaration as she danced. She and Jud had done Greek and other international folk dances in Ocean City on many Friday nights. If Jud had been waiting for her at the Binakas villa, she would have celebrated with him here in Istron. Although she gracefully withdrew from the line before the next dance started, she stubbed her toe on one of the ancient rough stones that inundated Crete. She returned to the taxi driver. He had waited for Mara, per her request, in case she did not get a room in Istron. He took her two suitcases to Alek's house. He was happy to oblige her— she had already paid him well. Mara debated where to go next. She asked the driver to take her to Ágios Nikólaos, after all, to see what she could find. As she climbed into the taxicab, a police car drove past.

§

Jud started to come to consciousness. He felt a fresh sting from where he had felt a mosquito bite last night. But things were different. He was out-side. The sun was warm on his face. He felt pain in his body. A drug had put him to sleep and another drug, injected a few minutes earlier, was striking at his nerves, forcing him awake. He opened his eyes. A dark shape moved and blocked the sun. Jud leaned up on his elbows. He felt earth and rocks underneath his body. He began to see that a stranger stood over him. Jud sat up and felt dizzy. He could see that the stranger kept looking back, down the road, beckoning to someone who was calling out to him. Jud tried to get up but blackness covered his eyes. As he sat on the grass, he bowed his head between his legs. But the sickness stayed; he got onto his hands and knees and retched. He heard running footsteps and a voice speak in English.

"This is the man."

Jud looked up to see who had just arrived and then spoken. It was David Binakas. Jud looked at the stranger again who was still looking at him.

The policeman said, "Stand up."

Realising that he was the object of the command, Jud got up. The earth swayed. The policeman held Jud by the arm to steady him and then to pull him onto the road.

David said, "I'm very lucky you have found my house guest. He's drunk. I can take care of him from hereon. Thank you."

David had wanted Jud to be found. But by revelers and not by a police officer. Twenty minutes earlier, alone, David had come a few yards west of his villa to this quiet dirt road—where he and Constantine had laid Jud down into a grassy roadside hollow at dawn—and injected another drug, an amphetamine, into Jud's system to wake him up, since Jud had not even been stirring. Then, David had picked up Georgina, waiting outside their villa. They had been ready to walk northeast to Istron when David had seen the squad car pass the taxi and head west toward where Jud lay. Thus, rather than take Georgina with him into Istron to entice, with a story of Jud's wrongdoing, a group of villagers into helping him find Jud, David had taken Georgina in the direction of the squad car, which had then stopped near Jud. The policeman had left his car and, as he had approached Jud, David had called out to him, saying that he was looking for a house guest who had begun celebrating too early. The policeman had beckoned to David, already on his way, to identify the prone man. Georgina had separated herself from the scene—she acquired anonymity by standing nearby underneath the dark shade of a large olive tree.

The policeman said, "Perhaps he should be in a jail cell. It would teach him a lesson."

David looked at the police officer, who wanted to take Jud out of his grasp and so turn his plan into an unrealised one. The officer winked at David and, continuing to speak in English, asked the foreigner, "What is your name?" The man was obviously too drunk to answer—he was starting to fall again. The officer and David reached for Jud.

But Jud was blacking out from the pain that, stronger than the stimulant drug that was to have awakened him and then kept him awake, stemmed from the battle between two drugs over control of his body. Yet, his descent into oblivion was slow this time. And, ignorant of the Greek language, he did not understand what the police officer spoke in his native tongue as the officer said, "I recognise him. Any self-respecting Christian would stay away from him—no offense to you, Mr. Binakas. He's—" Jud was unaware that the officer and David were putting him into the police car.

§

With its multitude of white groups of stucco buildings, Ágios Nikólaos looked white under the sun. In the harbor, small boats bobbed and large sleek craft sat in imperceptible motion. Mara sat at a table on the perimeter of a taverna's outdoor seating. Surrounded by men with black hair and sun-dark skin, Mara drank steaming coffee with milk. The men seemed to be staring into thin air when they looked at her. They were subtle compared with the Latin men who, when she had been in Central America had not only looked at her but made comments that, from her knowledge of Spanish, meant very beautiful. She looked up at the blue sky and white clouds. She couldn't believe that she had gotten herself all the way to Crete and not thought about what she might do if she didn't see Jud at the Binakas villa. She was at a loss regarding what to do next, other than to return to the villa and camp outside the villa gates.

A parade went by. And as it went by, she thought she was dreaming when she saw Diana Binakas. There was an unreal quality to seeing someone in the flesh that, up till now, she had only seen in a photograph. And there was a more unreal quality to see Diana's likeness to Jud. Even her mannerisms were similar—the way she waved, the way she stared into a person's eyes. Mara smiled at her as Diana reached her.

Diana caught her breath and said, "Miss Sylvan. When I saw you, I had to look twice but then I thought—no one else could have your hair color and look that much like you."

"Diana, it's wonderful to meet you. Please, call me Mara." Mara stood up and was surprised to find that, from her standing position, she had to look down only ever so slightly into Diana's face.

Constantine and Stephen had recognised Mara from the newspaper and TV coverage of the American crucifixion. One thing that Constantine knew about Mara, other than her erogenous property of energy which he felt from where he stood, was that she was detailed in her investigations, as he had learned from his American friends and David Binakas. Although Constantine knew that Diana did not know that Jud was being killed or was already dead, he did not want to leave Diana and Mara alone together because Mara must be here looking for Jud. And Diana might tell her that she had seen him at the Binakas villa last night but had not seen him this morning. Yet, Constantine had stayed back with the hope that Diana, who had left his side without permission, would say a brief hello and return quickly, alone; he had put a hand on Stephen's shoulder to indicate his wish to stay back. But, now, Diana was pointing to them.

Mara saw the two men come up from behind Diana. Clouds passed in front of the sun, causing the air to feel cool and the light to seem gloomy. Yet, as quickly as the clouds had moved to hide the sun, they moved onward to allow the sun's warm favor to shine anew on the city.

Diana was about to tell Mara that she had received her e-mail and to ask her if Jud was with her when Constantine and Stephen reached her.

Constantine interrupted Diana as she began to introduce him. He smiled and said, "Mara Sylvan. This is an honor. I am Constantine Sgouros and this is my son Stephen." Although Mara couldn't jeopardise his plan for Diana, he was displeased about her presence. He thought, *Damn Diana for this.*

Mara stood up and said, "I'm happy to meet you both."

Stephen took her hand and kissed it. He said, "I am pleased to meet you."

She looked at the two men, whose names she recognised, and assessed that they knew Jud was on Crete. They were friends of David Binakas's. When she had investigated the American drug company, she had learned about David's pharmaceutical company and of David's marriage scheme for Diana Binakas and Stephen Sgouros, son of the Greek City Planner. Yet, Mara had not told Jud that his daughter was slated for an arranged marriage because, until Jud had a connection with Diana, it was unnecessary information. Right now, she wanted to know if Diana had read her e-mail about her own arrival on Crete this morning—and if Diana had met Jud and relayed her message to him. Although Mara had no reason to suspect the Sgouros men of wanting to harm Jud, just as she had no solid reason to suspect David of the same thing, she wondered if she should question Diana in front of them. Mara asked, "Would you like to join me?"

Wanting to know why Mara was here and how she knew who Diana was, Constantine said, "Yes, we'd be delighted." Mara was not supposed to know of Diana or know of Jud's visit here, according to David. Much less be here herself.

They all sat down. Constantine ordered an Italian soda for Diana and coffee for Stephen and himself.

Constantine asked, "Are you here on vacation, Miss Sylvan?"

"Yes, I am."

"Alone?"

Mara answered Constantine by saying, "I'm here with someone."

Once he and Stephen were served coffee, Constantine asked, "May I ask whom you are with?"

"I'm with Jud Thorensen."

Constantine knew that he and Stephen would have to be careful about what they said to Mara, without telling lies, if possible. Constantine said, "I had heard that Mr. Thorensen was here—he's unpopular among the Greek Orthodox Church members—of course, we are all Greek Orthodox." Constantine laughed at his own joke. He added, "I hadn't heard that you were here."

"I arrived today."

Unaware of Jud's dire straits but sensing his father's reserve with Mara, Stephen was cautious as he asked, "Has Jud not come to Ágios Nikólaos with you—or is he somewhere around here?"

Mara was unsure if Stephen was playing a game with her but she sensed that his question was genuine. She said, "I was to meet him at Diana's home this morning."

Constantine was surprised at this information. There was an undercurrent of activity that he and David were unaware of.

Diana had expected Mara to say that Jud was nearby. It was the afternoon, past the loosely-timed morning rendezvous. Diana then realised that Mara had been to the Binakas villa and not found Jud there. She was about to ask Mara if she had met her parents, who were home for the day and would know where Jud had gone.

Instead, Mara spoke. She asked the Sgouroses, "Have either of you met Jud?"

Constantine said to Mara, "No. But we'd like to meet him, of course." Constantine did not count helping David with Jud this morning as an actual meeting. He continued, "We're very civilised these days and don't torture the dishonorable—not that your friend is dishonorable but he has come to an island with beliefs very different from those of our inhabitants." Constantine was trying to get a rise out of Mara so that she would be forthcoming with information about her visit here but his needling comments fell as dried pine needles, slipping down with barely an impact.

Diana was trying to piece information together. She thought that the Sgouros men, while they had not been introduced to Jud last night, must know that Jud was in the Binakas house. She had no inkling that danger existed for Jud, certainly not in her home. But she had a sudden urge to go there. She turned to Constantine and asked, "Mr. Sgouros, would you please take me home?"

Constantine glanced at his watch. Jud should be long dead and whatever mess that had been made should have been cleaned up. Constantine's concern was for Stephen, not Diana. He wanted Stephen to be ignorant of Jud's death and of David's hand in it, for now. He determined that it would be safe to return to the Binakas villa. And a good time to get away from Mara Sylvan. Constantine knew that David would not want Mara to investigate Jud's death soon after it had occurred because, although it would not be traceable back to David after a time elapse, it could be now, despite David's unsoiled hands. Thus, to avoid cause confusion to Mara regarding his next destination, the Binakas villa, Constantine said, "It's too early to leave the festival, Diana, but we should take no more of Miss Sylvan's time." He turned to Mara and said, "Please excuse us."

Mara realised she needed to hasten her questions. She said, "Of course, Mr. Sgouros. Diana, have you seen Jud in your home?"

Midway through Mara's question, Constantine stood up and took Diana's hand.

Stephen stood up and said, "It's been a pleasure, Mara." He nodded his head. If his father would not allow Diana to answer Mara's question then neither would he.

Mara was looking at Diana. But as Constantine was saying, "Thank you for your company, Miss Sylvan," he pulled Diana away.

As Diana reached the crowd with Constantine and, now, with Stephen at her side holding her other hand, she turned her head and called out, "Yes."

Mara stood up. The three of them had disappeared. She paid the bill and ran to find a taxi. She found a road that had not been blocked for parades. As she hailed a cab, she realised that Diana had told Jud that she was coming to Crete and that Jud must have a reason for not waiting at the Binakas villa for her, just as the Binakases must have one for not spending Ochi Day with their daughter and, instead, letting her spend it with two men who seemed as if they would more likely celebrate the holiday with their own family or with carousing friends. Mara mused on why Constantine was hiding Jud's whereabout from her and why he was possessive with Diana—he had watched her every move.

Mara climbed into the taxicab that had stopped for her. She gave the address of the Binakas villa and hoped that the Sgouros men were taking Diana there now.

§

Jud awoke in the late afternoon. His pain had lessened. He was lying on the floor of the living room in the Binakas villa. David sat nearby. Georgina watched Jud, who seemed to be unaware of her or David as he opened his eyes.

David had persuaded the policeman to bring Jud here and hoped the man would continue his duty in another town. The morning had gone awry because of Jud's second blackout, which had occurred despite the amphetamine. Yet, David had been glad, after all, about the officer's appearance because, then, he had paused for thought: it would be useless to gather together a group of people and rile them up while Jud was unconscious and already down. And Jud would be in no condition to appreciate David's revenge.

Thus, David was waiting for the drug effects to wear off Jud, who should not have been this affected—even considering his jet lag. The timing was bad—Jud was supposed to be dead by now; the Sgouroses could be back at any moment with Diana. He felt tense about that, as did Georgina. And she also felt tense because she had already lived David's plan many times in her mind and felt unsure she could handle it one more time, for real.

Jud leaned up onto an elbow. His vision was blurred but he could see Georgina and David. He got onto his knees and sat on his heels in readiness to stand up but then felt a need to vomit. He leaned forward onto one hand and covered his mouth with the other. He gagged but nothing came up. David asked Jud if he could walk. Jud said nothing. Then, David took Jud's arm and tried to help him to his feet. He told Georgina to help him with Jud and then get some water for him. Georgina helped him and then left. She returned with a glass, which she held to Jud's lips. David took the glass from her and splashed the water into Jud's face. Then, he told Georgina to make coffee, extra strong. She left to start the process and then came back to help David to bring Jud into the kitchen. Georgina put an arm around Jud's waist as she helped him to walk. On the other side of Jud, David put an arm around his back and led the way.

Jud became aware of the smell of coffee. David and Georgina stayed near him as he slowly sat down at the kitchen table, onto which leaned his arms. His legs were like rubber. All he wanted to do was lie down to sleep because he could scarcely keep his eyes open, despite his pain and nausea.

When David commanded him to drink the coffee, Jud spilled the coffee as he picked up the cup and brought it to his lips. He had scant control over his body and so, instead of sipping the coffee as he had intended, he took more into his mouth than he had thought he would. He scalded his tongue and throat, he felt the burn travel down his esophagus. He clenched his jaw as he waited for the new pain to subside. When he looked up again, he saw David looking into his face.

David thought that Jud looked awake enough now. He said, "Come with me."

Georgina held Jud again. He leaned on her as they followed David, who helped them down the passageway steps leading to the garage. He told the two of them to get into the Mercedes. David sat in the driver's seat. He ordered Jud to lie down in the back seat but, when he looked back, he saw that Jud was already lying down, with his head on Georgina's lap; David was shaking with anger as he drove the short distance to the road where Jud had been found by the officer. David parked. He told Jud to get out of the car.

Jud got out and felt the warm sun of the fall day and the whisks of wind. His vision was sharpening, although not by much, and he was becoming more aware of his surroundings. Yet, he did what David told him to do because David seemed to be the center of his world. Without David, the fog might begin to close in again. Jud stood in the road. Georgina stood behind him. As David got into the car, Georgina left Jud standing all alone. She walked toward Istron.

Jud felt as if he were standing in endless silence—he was unable to speak or move. He would have sat down if he could have controlled his motion and not crashed to the ground. Then, Jud decided that he needed to learn to walk again. He put one foot in front of the other, slowly. He thought that Georgina was somewhere ahead of him.

David drove his car just inside of the villa gates, which he closed after he walked out onto the road again; he headed to Istron. Once in its square, he spoke Greek in a loud clear voice to the revelers in various acts of sitting, standing, eating, and dancing to the music. Children laughed and played. As David spoke, many revelers came to stand around him. A few tourists, who knew no Greek, joined the crowd that had gathered near David because they understood by David's tone that something serious was happening.

David led the rumbling crowd to the road. Coming from the other way, Georgina now ran toward David, who put his arm around her— together, they led the crowd to Jud.

Jud heard a roar in his ears. He looked around him and watched the large crowd that had been behind David form a circle around him. Feeling conspicuous, he moved away from its midst and from David and Georgina who had just joined him. Jud stopped moving as David spoke in English to the crowd, whose hostile looks were tangible in the form of an invisible barrier of misunderstanding, anger, and hate, inexplicably touchable to Jud's senses although unfelt by his skin.

Jud gazed at Georgina as she stood with David's arm around her. She looked frightened. Then, she spoke to the crowd in Greek and glanced at Jud. He saw her eyes, welled with tears. He kept looking into them and wondered what they were trying to say to him as their shining tears spilled down her cheeks, even after she stopped speaking.

Georgina was crying over what she had said but the crowd thought that she was crying over what had been done to her. The crowd remained quiet as it waited for David's lead.

"Georgina, repeat what you have said in English so that this man," David said as he held out an arm to Jud, "realises that these people know exactly what he has done."

She looked around at the crowd to see if Diana and the Sgouroses were there. She didn't see them. If she could have grabbed Diana and run away with her now, she would have—rather than reveal to Jud what she had spoken in Greek. But Diana was not there so Georgina gave the full story that David had told her to give, in English.

She said, "This man was a guest in our home last night. While my husband worked late in his office, this man raped me. I cried and tried to get away but he covered my mouth and overpowered me. He left just before my husband came into our room. Then, I told my husband what had happened and we ran upstairs to our daughter's room. It was horrible. He had just entered her room and pulled back her bedclothes. He had put his hand over her mouth so that she couldn't scream. When he saw us, he ran. My husband chased him but couldn't catch him. We called the police. But this man is sly—he convinced the officer that he was not the one who had violated me or tried to violate my daughter." Georgina felt as if she were killing herself with each unwanted word. She was aware that Jud's eyes were on her. She had dared not look at him as she had spoken but now, from the corner of her eyes, she saw his disbelief and shock. She looked away and clung to David. Her body shook.

David said, "I want to take this man to the police but I'm afraid that he will persuade them again that he is innocent."

Someone said, "The crucifixion writer holds nothing sacred."

As David moved away from Jud, Georgina backed away with David while he still held her shoulders. Their withdrawal left Jud isolated in the middle of the crowd's anger, judgment, and urge to punish him by death. Jud saw that one of the men had a shepherd's staff and other men held large jagged stones. He looked at Georgina's face as she looked back before she turned around again and then disappeared through the crowd with David. An apology had sat somewhere in her eyes, frightened and desperate, but Jud hadn't seen it. He stood alone as epithets were spit out at him in English, German, and mostly, Greek. People came closer to him. Someone said, "Leave him alone." But the words that soundest the loudest to Jud were the few English ones—rapist, heathen, Antichrist. They were deafening.

The first stone that hit Jud hit his thigh in the same place Georgina's car had twelve years ago. The roar in his ears was unbearable and, as the second stone smashed into his right side, cracking a lower rib, he fell onto his knees and covered his head with his arms. He felt a stick hit him. He heard more words. A third stone cut into his arm. He fell forward onto his elbows. If he could have blocked the ocean roar from his ears, if he could have cleared the fog from his eyes, and if he could have breathed without pain, he would have stood up, pushed through the crowd, and walked away.

§

Diana sat in back of the open convertible on the drive home. Because Constantine drove too fast, she held onto a door arm. Stephen didn't know what was going through his father's mind but knew that Mara's presence had disturbed him.

Constantine was beginning to worry about carrying out his murder of Diana with Mara here. Once Mara discovered that Jud had been murdered by an angry mob, although she would be as unable as the law to do anything about it—whatever the deed that David and Georgina had accused Jud of would be sufficient reason to let the incident go unheeded and its many participants go unpunished by the law—Constantine was yet afraid that Mara might investigate Diana's death, particularly because it would occur soon after Jud's and because she knew that Diana was Jud's child, evident in her manner toward Diana, which had been more intimate than friendly. Thus, because Diana was to die by his own hands, Constantine would have to ensure that he would be above and beyond suspicion.

He drove the convertible up to the villa gates and saw a thick circle of people down the road. Constantine used a remote to open the gates. As he waited for the gates to open, Diana saw David and Georgina emerge through an opening in the circle. Before Constantine could move the car onto the villa grounds, Diana opened her door, jumped out, and ran toward her parents as fast as she could. Constantine let her go. He knew what was happening and he didn't care if Diana witnessed it. If what she saw distressed her, she would become an easier prey for him. Stephen was bewildered. He would have gotten out of the car but his father drove it, with Diana's door still open, around David's car, up the driveway, and into the underground garage of the villa.

Georgina and David had barely emerged from the crowd, that had let them pass through, when Diana reached them. Diana saw the stern face of David; she saw the stream of tears from her mother's eyes. She heard foul epithets from the crowd. Then, she realised that her parents did not have their arms out to hold her but to block her from joining the throng, tight and strong. She would have walked away from the crowd with her parents if she had not just heard the word Antichrist. Thus, she dodged her parents. Georgina almost caught her but stumbled over a stone and fell on the dusty road. David was fast but Diana was fast, agile, and driven by a rush of strength she hadn't known she could call upon. She dove onto her hands and knees and pushed through the first row of legs. Some people staggered from her onslaught. Diana kept shoving through. She raised herself to her feet and thrust through the innermost row of the tight mass of figures. She almost fell once she broke through.

She saw Jud bowed over in the center. Three heavy stones lay near him. Someone with a staff was backing away from him while almost all of the others had raised their arms in readiness to hurl the stones they each held with two hands. Diana didn't know what to do. As she dashed toward Jud, she pulled a white handkerchief from the inside of her cardigan sleeve and waved it; she hoped that the crowd would know from Greek history that a handkerchief being waved meant that the life of a favorite gladiator now fallen should be spared. When it seemed that no stones would be heaved, Diana turned from the crowd to face Jud and held the handkerchief against Jud's bruised and bleeding arm. She put an arm behind his back and held him.

Jud raised himself up to a kneeling position and leaned back on his heels. He knew Diana was beside him. The ocean roar had died down to soft lapping waves and then to silence. His vision, still indistinct, saw

Diana's face with light in and around it as she looked into his face. She was kneeling beside him.

She asked, "Jud, can you get up?"

He nodded. He put an arm around her shoulders and, without leaning on her, balanced himself as he slowly raised himself up.

As Diana kept her pace with his, as she rose from her knees to her feet, she slid her arm from his back to his waist. She saw that the ones in the crowd who had held stones had returned them to the ground. She looked into the eyes of people surrounding her. Although their eyes showed different emotions, all shared the same one of surprise.

A few of the crowd members knew Diana Binakas but most didn't. Most knew of Jud Thorensen. They had stopped their attack on him, even though many had not wanted to, because they had no wish to hurt the young girl in their midst. But when they observed the young man and girl together, they saw the resemblance, regardless of what the kinship might be: cousins, siblings, or father and daughter. And they were beginning to consider what had just happened and to wonder where the man and woman, known as David and Georgina Binakas to some of them, had gone to. It was too much to suspect, at the moment, that Diana Binakas was not the daughter of David Binakas but was the daughter of Jud Thorensen, a pagan American author. But in the next moment, some of them began to doubt Georgina's tale of rape—unless the American had raped her twelve years ago, also, and had sired her daughter.

Someone—Jud couldn't see who—came up to him and squeezed his shoulder. Jud felt relief in the kind human contact. He nodded slightly. A few others came around and said they were sorry. And others wanted to touched him, his back and bare arms.

Jud and Diana walked away through the crowd as it parted. That Diana had saved him was still coursing in waves of gratefulness through Jud's mind.

Georgina had watched Diana disappear through the throng and prayed she would be unharmed. And she hoped that her own failure to bring Jud to his death would not cause David to bring Diana to hers. Then, she saw Diana—with Jud. That he was alive was a blessing. David gripped Georgina's arm but she pulled away from him. She waited for Diana and Jud.

David walked to the Mercedes, climbed in, and drove it up his long driveway. He put it into the garage and walked into the house, minutes behind the Sgouros men. He didn't know what to do. If a crowd hadn't killed Jud, then, other than hiring an assassin, something David had never done and would not do now, he would have to allow Jud to live, because he would not soil his own hands. But, then again, another thought occurred to him.

§

Mara's taxi driver found an open route out of Ágios Nikólaos. He made good time. Thus, although Mara did not see the Sgouros men enter the villa gates, she arrived at the villa soon enough to see the black Mercedes go up the driveway. And she saw Jud and Diana, each with an arm around the other. Jud's walk looked different. Mara saw a large crowd walking behind them.

Mara thanked her driver and paid him too much. She jumped out of the taxi and ran toward Jud.

He said his first words since last night, "Hi Mara." He put an arm around her. It had been seven weeks since he had seen her.

Mara heard his slurred speech and saw the glassy look in his eyes. If he had not said her name, she would have thought he had not recognised her. She touched Diana's cheek and saw that her dress was covered with dirt. Jud looked bad. His breathing was shallow. Against his white face, his hair looked darker. Mara looked at Georgina, a few feet away, and recognised the likeness between her and Diana. She tried to read Georgina's face and stance.

As Georgina saw Mara put her arm around Jud and walk on the opposite side to Diana, she turned away and walked up to her home, alone.

It escaped Mara's and Diana's awareness that Jud's walk toward the Binakas villa was unbelievable because each was unaware that David and Georgina Binakas had set him up for murder—almost successful. But Jud was aware of how astounding it was. Nothing would have induced him to set foot in the Binakas home again if it were not for Diana. And he began to wonder just how safe she was.

CHAPTER TWELVE

Once in the house, whose dominant occupant was cold silence, Diana closed the front door and took her arm away from Jud as her mother called her from the direction of the kitchen. She watched Jud lean on Mara as they went upstairs to his room. As Georgina came out to see Diana and take her upstairs, Diana glimpsed David heading toward his office. Diana had a bath while her mother turned down the covers of her bed and plumped up her pillows. Diana assumed that Constantine and Stephen, whom she had not seen since getting out of the car, were in their rooms. She wanted to ask her mother why Jud had been called a rapist but dared not—as she had time to think, she began to suspect her parents of inciting the crowd today.

Once downstairs again, Diana ate an early dinner as she watched Georgina preparing the planned Ochi Day dinner—for more people than Georgina had planned on. Diana would usually have joined the celebration dinner but she accepted her exclusion from it without protest. The atmosphere in the house was funereal.

Stephen came into the kitchen. He had just asked Constantine, who was lying down in his room, if he wanted to have a cigar outside but Constantine had said that he did not. Stephen wanted company. Here, though, he saw that Georgina's eyes were rimmed with red and her hands were shaking as she cut vegetables. When Stephen asked her what was wrong, she made no reply. So, he returned to his room. He was tired. Last night had been a late one and his morning had been an early one. So, once he lay down, he fell asleep.

Still downstairs, Diana finished her meal. Then, Georgina took her upstairs. As they entered Diana's room, Diana glanced at the first bedroom door across from the top of the stairs. She knew Jud and Mara were still in there. She wondered how Mara would feel if she knew that Jud had kissed her mother. And she wondered how Mara felt about Jud having had a child with another woman—Diana knew that Mara knew that she was Jud's child. Georgina tucked Diana into bed. She stroked Diana's hair and kissed her lips. Diana lay back. She felt short-circuited from her thoughts, too many, too confusing. She closed her eyes. Sleep came before her mother had closed her door.

§

Mara wished she knew what had happened today. Jud had spoken no words other than when he had first seen her. He was not alert and she was worried. He had a drug in his body. Jud smoked an occasional cigar, drank an occasional glass of wine, and ate fruits and vegetables—he sometimes ate fish but rarely ate meat, simply because he had never liked it and still didn't—she knew he was unused to her father's English meals. Nor was his system used to medicine or any other foreign substances.

Mara turned on the shower water and undressed. She had seen the dirt on Georgina's dress. She had seen the tragic look on her face. She had not yet seen David, who must have known what was happening outside of his own home, especially since his wife and daughter had been involved. She hadn't seen the vehicle in which the Sgouros men and Diana had left Ágios Nikólaos but she guessed by Diana's involvement with Jud and the crowd that they had not been in the black Mercedes she had seen going up the drive. She now thought that David had been in that car and she wondered why he had left a bad scene, his wife, and his daughter. And Jud.

Mara came to the doorway and told Jud the shower was ready. He entered the room and stripped off his clothes. He came into the large shower stall with her. It was not romantic—she was afraid he would fall. He had bruises that looked painful. They lathered each other with soap. She was gentle near his ribcage. They began to kiss. Lather from shampoo and soap slid down their bodies. Their kisses were wet and slippery as the shower-head doused them with hot water. The shower room was hot and steamy. Jud kissed her breasts and slid his hands down her body. He put his arms around her and massaged her back as he kissed her neck and then slid his hands down low. She felt sensations in her body pulse upward as water pulsed down. He held her face in his hands and gave her French kisses. She wanted to resist him. She knew he had slept with Georgina, again, and she swore that if there was someone else she wanted to sleep with, she would do so—but, there again, her sexual loyalty did not depend upon his. And in this moment, as in countless moments, she wanted him and he wanted her. Everything felt good and so she responded. Their wet, hot bodies molded together in rhapsody.

At some point, Jud turned off the water. They left the shower. Jud wrapped a towel around his waist and lay on the bed. His rib hurt with every breath. But his mind was on Georgina. And what she had done.

When he realised that Mara was dressed, he sat up on the edge of the bed and put his feet on the floor.

She had on the same clothes she had worn earlier, tight black pants and a white sleeveless top. She had left off the black sweater. The rest of her clothes, mostly suits worn for the trials in Washburn from where she had come to Crete, remained in the room she had rented. On a last-minute impulse, she had bought a ticket to Greece once the trial had ended yesterday. Mara walked to the bed and put her hand on his shoulder.

Jud stood up and understated his feeling when he said, "I'm glad to see you." He took her hand and kissed it. Then, he dressed for dinner.

Mara discerned that Jud's silence was not due to the drug in his body but because of a secret he kept, deep and seething. He knew what had happened and, yet, he refused to bring it to the surface and tell her.

Once Jud was dressed but before he went downstairs with her, Mara said to him, "There's something you should know. David has arranged a marriage for Diana once she turns sixteen—"

"I'm aware of that, Mara."

Mara ignored his edginess and continued, "And are you aware that Stephen Sgouros is Diana's betrothed—and that he is probably in this house now?".

"I didn't know his name. I saw two men in this house last night—they looked like father and son. But it was only a glimpse."

When Mara described Constantine and Stephen, Jud said that the two men fit her description. Jud thought that his being here at the same time they were here was odd because David had said that Diana's future groom and in-laws would be very upset to find out that he, Jud, was Diana's biological father. If that were case, the last thing that David should want is to have himself, Jud, under the same roof with the father and son.

§

David had knocked on everyone's doors earlier and informed them that dinner was at nine. Thus, his guests were gathering in the living room around that hour. Jud and Mara were the last to descend the staircase. While the other men wore suits and ties, Jud wore jeans and a white shirt, open at the collar. His only evident injury was an old one, a scar line at the base of his neck. This was the first time that Constantine and Stephen had seen Jud in person. What Constantine saw confirmed his feelings about the arranged marriage. It had to be stopped. Stephen felt as if he'd had a physical blow—until now, Jud Thorensen being Diana's father had seemed unreal.

Mara greeted everyone. Jud, his eyes dark and veiled, remained silent. He shook hands with the Sgouros men. He didn't look at David or Georgina, yet. David and Mara, having spoken once on the telephone, needed no introduction to each other but David introduced Mara to Georgina, who wore a sleeveless silk dress, the color of moonlight-pink, and spike heels of the same hue. She wore the ensemble in honor of her private celebration: that Jud had lived through today.

That dinner was awkward surprised no one. A sumptuous feast with a main course of rack of lamb sat before them all. Jud was starving. Having been under the influence of drugs since the night before, he had not eaten since before then. He seemed to be the only one with an appetite. Despite the pain from his rib, he began to feel better because his vision had cleared and, as he ate, he was becoming more clear-headed. He drank several glasses of water but left his wine untouched.

As Jud observed Constantine and Stephen as the respective future father-in-law and husband of Diana, he wondered what, exactly, their interest might be in himself. Although David wanted him dead, the Sgouroses seemed to not care whether he lived or died. Thus, Constantine's underlying anger, shown by the tense muscles of his face and each tight grasp of his wine glass, might be directed toward Diana, whose birth, legitimate by its occurrence during lawful wedlock, had come from an unlawful conception. If Constantine and Stephen were upset that Diana was not David Binakas's daughter and were not taking out their anger on himself, then they were here because of Diana. But what was their intention toward her. Or, rather, Constantine's.

Mara hoped to find out what had happened with the crowd today. She could ask Diana tomorrow but Diana was unlikely to know much more than she herself did. Since this afternoon, Mara had become sure that the incident had been David's orchestrated attempt on Jud's life, whatever that had entailed. That David had ignited a crowd's emotions, then fueled and sustained by Georgina's lies, was unknown to Mara—she had not seen David or Georgina with the crowd, although either or both could have taken part with it earlier. Mara was also sure that David still wanted revenge on Jud. Why the Sgouros men had allowed Diana to investigate the situation alone—or at all—intrigued Mara, regardless of whether or not either man was aware of what was going on. Mara felt that the combination of individuals with today's events had alarming aspects.

David wondered what Jud was thinking about him. He felt fortunate that Jud's re-entry into his home today would give him an easy second chance at revenge.

Georgina waited for Jud to accuse her of attempted murder in front of everyone. She watched Jud and Mara's silent ease together and considered them each to be lucky. She hoped Mara wouldn't be jealous of her, Georgina, because, although she loved Jud, she still loved her husband and hoped that, since his failed attempt on Jud's life, he would give up his revenge and return to being the loving man she had married. She wanted to return to the life they'd had before he had found out about Jud.

Constantine was angry that David had botched his revenge today and that Mara was here—both situations impacted his own plan for Diana. He had not placed himself in the presence of a heathen just to go home without accomplishing his purpose—tonight.

Stephen knew nothing about the reason for the crowd today and didn't ask. He remained blissfully ignorant.

Jud said, "Constantine, I've been told that you are Diana's future father-in-law." Jud saw Stephen staring at him. Jud faced Constantine again and continued, "How do you feel about that while knowing that Diana is my daughter." It was a stated question.

Georgina choked on her water. Mara held her wine glass in mid-air. David glared at Jud and wondered how he had known about the Sgouroses.

Constantine felt his fury increase. He felt pressure. He didn't know how to answer. When he could speak, he said, "I'm happy for you."

"But how do you feel that she, as the daughter of a profane writer, will be married to your son and have children with him?"

Georgina picked up her napkin and wiped her lips. Mara put her glass down too hard, having misjudged the distance, and David felt responsible toward the Sgouroses for Jud's discourtesy. Stephen felt shamed that Jud, a younger man than himself, acted as an equal with his esteemed father and ignored himself who had a key role in the marriage.

Constantine deliberated and said, "I suppose I might have to reconsider the marriage arrangement. It might not be a good idea, after all."

Jud decided to push Constantine no further but watched his face. He realised that a powerful family alliance would be difficult for Constantine or David to give up. And that giving it up would cause much speculation. Especially if the public discovered that Diana was his own daughter.

Silence ensued for a while. After dinner was over, as was the stilted conversation that had occasionally punctured the taut silence, Jud got up and started clearing the dishes with Georgina. He refused Mara's offer of help to Georgina before Georgina could say anything; David and the Sgouroses made no offer.

David felt secure that there was no danger in Georgina being alone with Jud—she would not tell Jud that he had threatened Diana's life. She still had to accomplish her mission, with a different method, and would think that Diana's life still hung in jeopardy. David had been surprised that Jud had chosen to enter his home again now that he knew that David wanted him dead but David was more surprised that Jud seemed unconcerned that he would try again. As Jud and Georgina carried dishes to the kitchen, David invited Mara and the Sgouroses to retire to the third floor with their drinks.

Jud and Georgina returned to the empty dining room for the remainder of the dishes and platters, putting them on trays. Once in the kitchen again, Jud threw out scraps and helped Georgina load dishes into the commercial-size dishwasher. Georgina had thought that now they were alone he would condemn her actions but he did not.

Georgina could take his silence no more. She asked, "Have you nothing to say?"

"No."

"Why don't you tell me what you're thinking?"

Jud turned and faced her. He stared into her eyes as if he were reading an engrossing book. He asked, "Do you want me to ask why you did it?"

"No." As David had foreseen, Georgina dared not tell Jud about the risk to Diana. She wanted to cry over what Jud must think about her. Another woman might not have done to her lover what she had done to Jud, at any cost, even the death of a child.

Georgina had expected to feel remorse over what she had done after Jud's death but, now, she faced not only her remorse, she faced Jud, alive to know and remember what she had done to him. Yet, the latter was the better circumstance and had no competition from the former. She wished she could tell him that she was happy he was alive. But, no matter how she expressed it, he would disbelieve her, she was sure.

Jud realised that Georgina had made the rape accusations today with the intent to cause his death by anonymous hands. That it was David's plan, he was sure. He felt no anger toward Georgina for what she had done but he had felt sadness when she had walked away afterwards, a reminder of the past, rather than come to him and Diana—and Mara. Yet, he knew that she must be feeling devastated. And that she had done what she had under duress; the way to force Georgina to do what she did not want to do was to strike her Achilles heel, Diana's well-being.

Jud still felt Georgina's love. He knew she did not feel his. When she had stood in front of the gates, he had seen her self-punishing thoughts on her face. She wore them now; he wanted to erase them. He had intended to say more tonight but he had felt emotionally blocked from doing so, either by her or his own self.

§

While Mara and David sat on a couch and spoke on one side of the vast third floor, Constantine had drawn Stephen to the other side, the ocean-view side.

They stood near the glass rather than near the central fireplace which David had lit. Constantine said in a low tone, "We have to talk about a few things. About Diana."

Stephen said, "I hate to admit this, Pater—you are right. We cannot bring her into our family. I see that she is truly Jud Thorensen's child—we can't hide that forever—not now that he knows about her. People will see them together, eventually. He's too well-known to be able to keep the relationship discreet. Why did David bring him here? He's spoiled everything—if Jud had not learned about Diana, we might have had a chance to keep the marriage arrangement."

Constantine said in a quiet voice, "You are short-sighted Stephen. Don't you see—we never had a chance at keeping it. Yet, if we dissolve your celebrated marriage arrangement, we will suffer humiliating questions from every direction. I have asked David to be the one to generate the dissolution but that was based on Mr. Thorensen's death."

"Jud's death?"

"Surely you realise that David enticed Mr. Thorensen here for revenge. You don't think that a man like David can allow another man who has slept with his wife to live? David, himself, is a faithful man. He was such to his first wife and is now to Georgina, despite her own adultery." Constantine kept a watch for Mara and David. He heard them laugh on the other side of the room and continued, "Jud Thorensen was almost killed today. David and Georgina set the crowd against him."

Stephen was stunned, "So that's why you didn't want to go near there or allow me to. Isn't this revenge stuff ancient history?"

"Come to your senses, Stephen. Do you think this technological era has altered the emotions of man? It has not. And I have my own emotions. Just by having made this arrangement between you and Mr. Thorensen's daughter, I will be ridiculed. As the Greek City Planner, I'm known in many circles throughout the world. I cannot handle the disgrace that will come from having pledged my only son to the devil's daughter. I cannot live with myself. People will always laugh at me and point fingers; they will never be able to look beyond my shame and forget the reason for it. I can't live with the gossip. And all branches of the Binakas and Sgouros families will resume the feud—while ours will be subtle, blood will be shed by the poorer members. Only one thing will help."

"What is it?"

"Diana must die. With her gone, the marriage arrangement will be gone. No one will know that a Sgouros has done the deed and so no family feud will erupt. And, if Diana dies soon, there is no one who will learn of the ignobility of her birth. And we will have rid ourselves of our problems."

"Murder. You are suggesting murder."

"Yes."

"I will not agree to it."

"Are you saying you care about Diana?"

Stephen recognised an emotion in his father that bespoke of a warning to answer his question with care. Thus, he played along in the direction his father wanted him to. He said, "No. She's just a girl. She only meant something to me when I thought I would be marrying into her family wealth." He saw the relief on his father's face. But when he continued with, "I love you, Pater—you know that—but aren't you being extreme," he saw anger. He had never seen his father's face become like this before—diffused with red and tightened with fury. It reminded him of himself during his childhood tantrums but without the screaming. The quietness of his father's tantrum disturbed him. Stephen continued, "Why don't we sleep on this and talk tomorrow?" He put an arm around his father's shoulders but Constantine shrugged it off. Stephen moved away.

Constantine said, "There will be no tomorrow for Diana."

§

When Mara left David, she went straight to Jud's bedroom. Jud had finished helping Georgina with the clean-up and left her. Once in his room, he had removed his white shirt and jeans and put on black trousers. He was just putting on the black sweater that he had traveled in. Jud asked Mara, "Where are you staying?"

"In a room in Istron."

"I want to take you there tonight."

"Do you want to stay with me there?" Mara thought he was afraid for his life.

"I will be coming back here."

"She said, "Then, I'll stay here with you."

"No."

She asked, "Why not?"

"I don't want you to."

She said, "All right. I'll go." Jud had never spoken to her this way before.

He should have stopped but he went on, "I'm no good for you, Mara. I know I'm making a decision for you. But my father will likely disown me and, with all the choices I'm going to make and because I can't bear to drag you through events like the one today, I have to be selfish and tell you—we don't belong together." He had said too much.

Mara was afraid. She asked, "Are you breaking up with me?" She was unable to believe it. "Oh, Jud, please don't do this. Don't punish us both."

"Being with me endangers your life or, at the least, your emotional well-being."

"Why are you giving me no option—or is it your own desire to separate? Perhaps you are using today as an excuse." She couldn't bring herself to ask if he was doing this because of Georgina.

"Mara, please don't think that. It isn't that way." It had not occurred to Jud that she would think that.

"Then give me a choice."

"You have a choice to be with someone who wants to marry you and have children and live what is called a normal life. I know you say you don't want those things but you might change your mind. And, if you don't, why would you put up with me? Since my crucifixion book, I am always going to be branded, not by everyone, but by many, especially those who misunderstand the book—and so misunderstand me. And, whether people hate or love the book, I'm tired of being known as the crucifixion author—as if that's all of what I am and ever will be. But that's okay—I can't control other people's ideas about me—or about anything else. But you don't need to be branded with me—especially since you don't know what other circumstances I will create or attract. I can live with them. I don't want to see you live with them."

Mara couldn't help it. As she stood there, she cried silent tears. Jud didn't put an arm around her to comfort her. She felt alone. When she could look at him again, she saw that he had turned his back to her and was looking through the window at the night sky. She looked beyond him and was surprised to see that the moon look rose-colored. She said, "All right. I'll leave. But you don't need to escort me."

Jud turned around to face Mara. He wondered why he was causing pain to her and himself. He questioned if he was punishing himself. If so, he didn't want to punish her, too. Yet, he felt he should decide whether to share their lives together, stained with his concern for her well-being, or to share a penalty of enforced separation. Then, he wondered if the drugs were affecting his mind—he felt self-destructive, unlike his usual self.

And he was shocked that he was treating Mara as if she didn't know her own mind and couldn't decide anything for herself—as if she were weak and couldn't handle all that they had been embroiled in together and what they might become embroiled in, if they stayed with each other—because he knew what he was going to do tonight. And it wasn't a good thing. His mind was in an altered state and he was likely perceiving life though a distorted view but it was the only view he had.

He said, "Mara, I'm not sure if it's been me talking—or effects of drugs. But, through it all, I know I love you. And you know I do. I'm not breaking up with you because of not wanting you and making excuses for it—but in the way of what I've said—seeing you go through the messes I make. That's stressful for me."

"Then let me stay tonight. I can take care of myself—whether I'm with you or not. Jud, let's—" Mara was about to suggest to Jud that he leave the Binakas household and come to Istron with her when he spoke.

"Then, perhaps you will help me out with something."

Mara said, "Yes, I will. But I'm tired right now, I just want to hold you close and go to sleep." Traveling from the Midwest had given her a nine-hour difference—she had lost a night of sleep the night before.

Jud looked at Mara's face. He said, "Mara, I love you. I'm sorry about everything I said." He put his arms around her and buried his face in her neck. He kissed her there—and then on her lips. He said, "I love you. It almost hurts."

She put her arms around his waist and put her hands on his lower back. She felt encased in his strength and warmth. She felt his heartbeat. She put her lips against his.

Jud released her. When he had seen Mara for the first time today, he had never been as glad to see someone. She had come all this way because she cared about his welfare. When Mara and he had dressed for dinner, he had kissed her hand because being with her had given him comfort—and he appreciated her in every way. After dinner, although he had begun to feel more aware of his environment and his own self again, he had become afraid of destroying her along with himself because he had a gut feeling that none of what had been happening today was over.

Jud had come to Crete knowing that he did not know of the reasons he had been invited, other than the one he had been told: David's generous motivation of allowing Diana to come to know her biological father—a reason that Mara had distrusted and that he, Jud, had been deluded by. But when, last night, David had said that Jud would not meet Diana after all and told him to disregard what he had said—and when David had said that Diana's prospective family would be upset that Diana was not a true Binakas, Jud had suspected David of playing more than a psychological game. Yet, he had still disbelieved that revenge was a reason for a man to kill another man, even though he knew it did happen. Today, his disbelief had placed him in a near-fatal ambush.

When he had watched Georgina as she spoke in Greek and brought the crowd from anger to extreme hostility, he had still been shocked at the severity of her charges against him when she repeated them in English. He had experienced insufferable hurt, a feeling of emotional violation, that she would have set up a rendezvous with death for him. Yet, through his haze, he had begun to believe that she had felt backed into a corner with no way out other than what she had done.

He had later realised that Georgina must have cause to worry for Diana's safety. But from whom, he had been unsure. Even though David may have used Diana as leverage for Georgina's help, Jud discounted him because he had loved and raised Diana for twelve years and because he seemed to be out only for his, Jud's, life; he discounted Stephen who had a docile manner and lacked confidence. And he discounted anyone outside of the house. It was Constantine that Jud distrusted.

Constantine was a man who liked control. As he planned cities and controlled environments, he planned his life and controlled his emotional climate. Having Diana in the Sgouros family or barring her marriage into it would cause him great embarrassment either way once it came to light that Diana was his, Jud's, daughter, which Jud was sure would happen soon—anyone seeing them together would know they were blood-related. And since he and Diana had begun a friendship, no one else could end it. Unless by death.

Jud said to Mara, "I need help tonight." He could carry out his venture alone but having help would increase his chance for success.

Mara sat down on the bed. Jud sat down beside her and held her as she leaned her head on his shoulder. He wanted to take her away from here right now, even though he had no time to. Yet, if she said that she didn't want to help him—that she disagreed with his plan of action—he would find the moments to take her from this nightmare.

But Mara said, "Tell me what you want to do."

§

David faced Georgina in his office. After Mara had excused herself, David had said good night to Constantine and Stephen, who had remained on the third floor. Then, he had gone downstairs and found Georgina leaving the kitchen for her studio. He had led her to his office.

Now, he said, "We have a problem. I can't set up a more perfect plan than the one I had today. We would have been blameless—Jud Thorensen would have been dead by hands other than mine and not been around to disclaim what you said." As David spoke, he saw the anguish in Georgina's face that would have told him that she had paid well for her adultery with her betrayal of Jud today if he had not seen relief mingled in with it, which told him that, because Jud was still alive, her payment had been insufficient—even though she must know that Jud must hate her.

David continued, "Jud Thorensen cannot stay alive; yet, I cannot be the one to kill him. You must." He saw the alarm on her face. *Yes,* he thought, *a better payment for her adultery would be if she went to jail for the death of her lover, past—and present, evidently.*

From the wall behind his desk, David pulled down the Turkish dagger, with a six-inch blade, pointed and with both edges sharp. He unlocked a drawer and pulled out the dagger's sheath, into which he placed the dagger, which he then laid on his desk. From within the same drawer, he pulled out a vial and a small rectangular case, which he opened to reveal a small hypodermic needle—about five inches long with the plunger—similar to the ones he had used to first inject the sedative and to later inject an amphetamine into Jud's arm. David tore the foil from the needle and took off its rubber stopper. He unscrewed the vial cap and then with the hollow needle pierced the inner rubber cap and drew the poison made from the deadly red and black seeds of the rosary pea into the syringe barrel. He replaced the stopper to the tip of the needle, which he snapped into the prongs of the case. He closed the case and laid it next to the dagger.

Georgina watched; she stayed silent.

David said, "I'm going to give you a choice, you can kill Jud with a lethal injection while sleeps or with a dagger to the heart. I will ensure that he sleeps well tonight."

David wished he owned a gun, even though he disliked firearms. Still, if Georgina had a gun in her hands, she might shoot him rather than Jud. And, although he, himself, might be able to shoot Jud and frame Georgina for it, he could not bring himself to soil his own hands—he could plan a murder for Jud but not carry it out. And that was why, even if he could be the one to commit the murder with a lethal injection or dagger and then frame Georgina for the murder with the same result of her going to jail as if she had committed the murder herself, he would not frame Georgina— she had to be the one to do the fatal deed.

But Georgina said, "I cannot be a part of any more of your plans."

"You know what I will do to Diana." It had still not occurred to him that Diana's life was in danger by Constantine whose only wish to get out of the marriage arrangement gracefully was by killing Diana. Yet, although David did think that Constantine might kill Jud, he wanted Georgina to be the one to do so.

Georgina said, "Whatever you do to Diana, you will have to do to me first." In her moonlight silk dress and high heel shoes, she left David's office and walked through the moving shadows of the living room, licked by flame reflections from the large fireplace, walked upstairs toward Diana's room, opened the door, and stood in the doorway. By a lamp's low light, she saw that Diana's bed was empty.

§

Diana was asleep in bed. She awoke when her door opened. She thought it was her mother at first but when no light went on, she felt fear. Then, she heard Jud's whisper.

"Diana, it's me. I want to talk with you."

Her eyes began to see better in the dark; she saw him walk from the door to her bedside.

"Turn on your light Diana." Jud wanted to see her face, to watch how she would react to his words. He needed her co-operation. He also hoped that while her lamp was on, the man that Jud had guessed wanted to end her life would make no attempt to do so while he thought Diana to be awake.

Diana turned on a lamp and blinked as light hurt her eyes.

Jud said, "I have no time to explain everything to you now. I want you to come with me."

But as she had fallen asleep with questions, she had awoken with them. She asked, "Why were those people going to kill you today? What did you do?"

"I didn't do anything. They just thought I had."

"Then why didn't my parents help you? Instead, they left you there."

"If you thought I deserved what was happening, why did you save me?"

"At the time, I just knew you were being hurt. I wasn't thinking about why." She looked him in the eyes, "As you do, I hold life sacred—I know that everyone talked about how you would have been justified in killing a man in Washburn—but you didn't."

Jud had hoped she would say she cared about him. He said, "I can only tell you that I am not any of the names I was called today. I'm not going to explain what happened." Jud had no intention of telling anyone, especially Diana, of Georgina's role. Nor would he tell about David's. He did not think that Diana should have illusions about her parents but Georgina had been under duress and David was Diana's father—and he had done nothing that could be proven wrong. Nor was it up to him, Jud, to try to change how Diana saw her parents. He believed that a person could not often be defined by one action or by just a few moments in time. Yet, Jud remained aware that David wanted him dead and that Constantine was not to be trusted with Diana.

Jud said, "Diana, we have no time to talk now. You must come with me." He did not want to tell a child that her life was in danger and that, perhaps, her mother's was. But he would if Diana would not come with him any other way.

Yet, Diana said, "All right." She grabbed clothes out of a drawer and sped into her bathroom to change—not from urgency but from a sense of adventure. Once ready, she came out of the bathroom and saw Mara. In silence, Mara took Diana's hand.

§

Standing in Diana's doorway, Georgina turned around as she heard a sound. Constantine Sgouros had just come out of his room and was standing in the hallway looking at her. But just before she had turned around and just after she had opened the bedroom door, she had caught a glimpse of a shadow move within the room. Yet, now facing Constantine, she asked, "Is there anything I can help with you Constantine?"

Constantine was feeling as David had when his plans had gone awry. He had heard sounds on the staircase landing a few moments earlier and had assumed that Georgina had been checking on Diana, as he knew from his past visits that she always did after her dinner guests retired. Thus, he hadn't expected to see her now—so he wondered just whom he had heard. Constantine said, "I was feeling restless. Perhaps I ate too much tonight. Do you have an antacid?"

"I'll get one for you. Just give me a few minutes with Diana."

"All right—thank you, Georgina. Just knock on my door." He entered his room.

Georgina entered Diana's room and closed the door; she faced Jud.

Jud prayed that he had been right about Georgina when he had been observing her in the kitchen earlier and that she would not betray him now. He beckoned her to the recess of the room. Georgina asked, "Where's Diana?"

"She's fine. I've been waiting for you. I thought I was going to have to come and get you. Do you trust me?"

Georgina thought that she should have been asking Jud if he trusted her. She touched the glimmering diamond-and-gold crucifix, which lay on her bosom. She said, "Yes."

"I took Diana—"

"Why?"

"She's unsafe here." He didn't want to accuse Constantine outright because he could be wrong about him but danger's pungency seeped into his nostrils and its prickling dis-ease permeated the air around him, as it had last night and he had ignored it because he had known that Diana was in the house and wanted to stay to see her. He asked, "Do you have your passports?"

"David locked up mine in his desk after I returned from the States. Diana's was put in there after her arrival last night from Athens." Georgina assumed that Jud was protecting Diana from David.

Jud said, "Where does David keep his desk key?"

"On him, along with the key to his office. The passports might be in his vault now. Jud, where is Diana?"

"She's on her way to Istron with Mara. Do you know Alek Myron? Mara has a room in his house. I don't know how she is going to explain her late arrival and having your daughter with her, especially if Alek was part of today's crowd." He saw the shadow of pain pass over Georgina's face and said, "Don't worry about it Georgina. It's over. We need to focus on this moment. You'll have to come with me dressed as you are. I asked Diana to disarm your security system and to leave it that way—you and I can leave from any exit. I had hoped to take the first plane or ferry boat to the mainland tomorrow morning and then leave Greece—but without your passports we'll have to plan another strategy. Unless you know the combination code of the vault—I have no idea of how to break into one."

Georgina shook her head. "Why should we leave Greece?"

"Until I'm sure of Diana's safety, I think that's our best option." Jud heard a sound outside and continued, "Even if the passports are just in David's desk, we don't have time to get them now." Jud was sure that Constantine had been ready to enter Diana's room just now.

Georgina said, "I'm supposed to bring a medicine to Constantine."

"I'm sure he needs nothing. Let's go now. Check to see if the hallway is clear."

Georgina opened Diana's door and faced Constantine.

Constantine stared. After he had left Georgina and entered his room, he had thought that something had been odd—there had been no light showing from underneath Diana's door in the dark hallway when he had come down from the third floor a short while ago but there had been one just before Georgina had opened Diana's door. It had caused him to speculate about what had awakened Diana at this late hour—Georgina had always maintained that Diana was dead to the world once asleep. Thus, after a pause long enough to allow Georgina to kiss Diana good night and then leave to acquire medicine for him, Constantine had left his room again, walked to Diana's door, to which he had stood close and, because a light still came from underneath the door, had listened for sounds. Hearing none, he had been ready to open the door when Georgina had opened it.

Beyond her, Constantine saw Diana's empty bed and, beyond that, near the open bathroom door, he saw a nightgown strewn on the floor. He grabbed Georgina's arm. Georgina gasped. Jud appeared. Constantine saw the ruins of his plan, a simple one: chloroform Diana, carry her downstairs in the stealth of a sleeping household, put her in a Binakas car, drive her to his chosen site, do away with her, return to his bed, and play the innocent house guest the next morning once she was discovered as missing.

§

In Georgina's studio, David was waiting for Georgina while she checked on Diana. He heard someone come down the stairs and, through the open doorway, saw Stephen Sgouros head toward his own bedroom. David followed him. Stephen heard his footsteps and turned as David said, "Are you looking for me."

Stephen said, "David, my father is upset." How could he tell David that his daughter's life was in danger and not go against his own father. He continued, "You might want to—"

"I don't know what Constantine has told you but don't worry about anything—everything is under control." David put an arm around Stephen and led him to the stairway. He heard a door close upstairs and anticipated his discussion with Georgina.

David and Stephen looked up at the same time. A black figure was descending the stairs. Behind him was a flash of pink and another dark figure.

Jud reached the bottom of the stairs. He was followed by Georgina and Constantine, a dark look upon his face with lines that had deepened in the past moments. It seemed to him as if no one in this house had planned to go to bed tonight.

David asked, "What's going on?" He noticed Jud's change of clothes.

Constantine said, "Why don't you ask Mr. Thorensen. Diana is missing. And so is Miss Sylvan."

David noticed that Georgina looked unworried. He asked her, "Where is Diana?"

Jud stepped forward and said, "I haven't told her. But she knows Diana is safe."

"Safe from what?"

Jud looked at David's face and saw that David had no fear of danger for Diana. Yet, Jud could not tell David, in front of Constantine, that he believed that Constantine intended to kill Diana—Jud felt shards of fear go through him when he thought of harm coming to Diana. With nothing else that he could think to say, Jud said to David, "Safe from harm."

David said, "That's not an answer. Safe from what?"

Jud said nothing. If Jud was wrong about Constantine, David would be able to press charges against him, Jud, with kidnapping Diana; Mara would also be charged. Likely, Georgina would stand by David. And Jud began to wonder just what he had done and what he should do next. He would leave but he knew that David wouldn't let him—by himself or with Georgina. And Jud would not leave without Georgina because he wanted to re-unite her with Diana and because he didn't like the anger in Constantine's eyes when Constantine looked at Georgina—or at David, for that matter. Jud was also sure that Constantine would not let him walk out any more than David would.

Stephen was astounded that Jud had guessed about the danger to Diana and he wondered whom Jud suspected, Constantine or himself. He felt he could not say anything without saying the wrong thing. With relief, he heard his father speak.

Constantine said to Jud, in their circle of five, "It's very late. But I doubt that David is going to retire tonight until he has his daughter back home. I, as her future father-in-law, and Stephen, as her future husband, have a decided interest in Diana's welfare. While Georgina trusts you, the rest of us do not."

Constantine wondered that Jud showed no anger toward Georgina. He knew she had played a major role in Jud's near-death. If she had done that to him, Constantine—and he had survived—he would have wrung her neck. Constantine was a genial man unless something angered him. Then, deep rage thrust through him too fast for him to be aware of soon enough for him to control it. And his anger had been burning hot since he had found Diana missing. When Mara had taken Diana away, she might as well have poured gasoline onto an ongoing fire, the one that had started when Constantine had first found out that Diana was the Antichrist's child.

Since no one else spoke, Constantine continued, "So, let's make this fast and easy—where did Miss Sylvan take Diana?" Mara's role in all of this was of no surprise to Constantine. Mara, unlike his own wife toward himself, was supportive of Jud. Constantine felt jealous of Mara's love for Jud, and his for her, which he had observed during dinner in endless ways, every meeting of their eyes, every touch of their hands. He was losing his patience. He asked, "Again, where is Diana?"

Despite Jud's doubt about Constantine's murderous intent, he continued to keep Diana's whereabout a secret. If he was wrong, he would go to jail for abducting a child. But, if he was right and handed Diana over to Constantine, Diana would die. Thus, he remained silent.

David said, "I'm going to call the police."

"No." Constantine said

David asked, "Why not?"

At this point, Georgina would have left but she didn't want to leave Jud alone with three angry men. She might not be allowed to leave, anyway. Before Constantine could answer David, Georgina said, "We don't need to call an authority. Diana is safe. Why don't we all get some sleep? We can work things out tomorrow." Georgina was afraid that David still meant Diana harm—since Jud still lived and David still wanted him dead. Only this time, he wanted Georgina to kill Jud with her own hands but she had refused. And so it would be better if Diana did not come home tonight.

Georgina distrusted Constantine, also, with Diana. He had been spying outside of Diana's door. When he had discovered Diana missing, he had become incensed. He had checked Diana's room thoroughly and then gone to Jud's room to search for her and then found Mara missing, too. To buy time for Diana's safety, Georgina had hoped that Constantine would feel the need to search the entire house for Diana but he had not. Instead, he had told Jud and Georgina to go downstairs ahead of him. David and Stephen had been standing at the bottom.

Stephen was brooding. No one was paying any attention to his feelings. He had let his father and David control his life before. In this moment, he was struggling to know what he wanted for himself. And then it occurred to him—he should just walk away from everyone. He would not be marrying

Diana Binakas in four years because whatever happened tonight would not allow it. Yet, his problem was that he would not leave his father and thus allow him to commit a murder. And so, resentful yet silent, he stayed.

David said, "We are at an impasse—we have no agreement. But Diana is my daughter. I will call the police."

Constantine said, "We all want to find her and ensure her safety. If we bring the police into this, we will lose our privacy. And they lack the ability to do much, particularly at this time of the night. Let's try to find her first. Is it not true that our common interest is Diana's welfare?"

Now distrustful of Constantine's anxiousness to find Diana, David silently disbelieved that Diana's welfare was his motive. But he went along with Constantine, for now, and said, "Let's go for a drive." And because he trusted no one, he added, "We'll all go in the same car. Constantine, would you please stay here while I close up my office."

David went to the vestibule next to the kitchen. He put on his overcoat. He was tempted to call the police from his office. Instead, when he entered his office, he opened his vault and took out the passports belonging to his wife, daughter, and himself—he put them inside his inner breast pocket along with cash and credit cards. He removed the sheathed dagger and the hypodermic needle from a drawer and put them, one on each side, into his deep side pockets. Although he didn't know what was going to happen next, he wanted to avail himself of whatever opportunity might come to kill Jud Thorensen by whosoever's hand. And after finding Diana, remove his family from within the grasp of Constantine, whose ill-intent toward Diana was now apparent to him. Yet, David believed that finding Diana would not be paramount to placing her life in Constantine's hands—he, David, could protect her. He returned to the living room.

Next, Constantine and Stephen got their coats while David stood with Jud and Georgina. Georgina was about to get her coat when Constantine stopped her and said that she didn't need one. He thought she might cooperate better if she suffered from the cold of the night. David disliked the

way Constantine touched his wife and the way he seemed to think that he
could tell her what to do.

Jud realised that all eyes had turned to him.

Constantine said, "Where is Diana? We need to know before we leave."

Jud knew his latest problem had begun. He said, "She's gone to a hotel
in Irakleío." He wanted David to think that Diana was far away but,
because David would know that Diana had no passport, Jud knew there
was no use in saying that Mara was going to take Diana across the sea to
the mainland and then soon leave the country.

Constantine said, "In what? Miss Sylvan has no car, I believe."

It had not occurred to Jud or Mara to steal a Binakas car but Diana had
suggested that they take one since her mother would be joining them and
so they would not be stealing. It was decided that Jud and Georgina, if she
agreed to come, would bring a car because if Mara took a car and was
heard leaving the garage, then she and Diana would soon be found missing—and then, Jud and Georgina might be found out and disallowed to
leave the house. Thus, Mara and Diana had walked to Istron.

David said, "We're waiting for an answer, Jud."

Jud realised that he could slow down the search for Diana by telling the
truth about their method of travel to Istron but he was stumped at how to
sound convincing that their method would take them all the way to
Irakleío, where Mara and Diana were not really going. He said, "They're
on foot," and waited to be disbelieved.

Constantine had noticed Jud's hesitation. He laughed at the absurd
answer and then said, "That is not the truth."

Jud smiled. He said, "It does sound ridiculous but I was to take one of
David's cars and meet them along the road. We agreed that if someone
should offer them a ride—unlikely but we had to cover that possibility—
they would accept it and I would meet them at the hotel."

Constantine asked, "What hotel? If you are lying to me, someone is
going to get hurt." He looked at Georgina and wondered if she had been
planning to sneak out of the house with Jud.

Jud said, "It's just a small hotel I passed by when I came from Irakleío."
Jud tried to remember a hotel name and said, "It's the Hotel Homer. But
Mara and Diana certainly won't be there, yet. You can go ahead and call
the place if you want to check that it's real but don't ask for our names—
we made no reservations."

Constantine asked, "And what if you didn't find them walking along
the road and then reached the hotel to find that they had not arrived?"

"I would have backtracked and kept looking for them."

"And if you still didn't find them?"

"I guess I would have gone back to the hotel and waited—they would
make it there eventually."

Constantine struck Jud across the face. He said, "You are lying."
Constantine would have hurt Georgina, apparently Jud's ally, to get Jud to
tell the truth if David had not been standing there. Yet, he knew he had
already gone too far regarding his treatment of her in front of David. He
did not want to risk that delicate balance in which hung the finding of
Diana. Then, he noticed that Jud was trying to catch his breath.

The blow had caused Jud to breath harder—the pain in his side had
intensified.

Georgina said, "Jud is telling the truth. I thought it was a foolish plan
when he told me about it. Of course, he didn't tell me the hotel name, just
that Mara and Diana were heading to Irakleío. And contrary to what all of
you think," she looked at David and the Sgouros men, "I believe that
Diana is safe and there is no need to go looking for her tonight. It's true
Jud is paranoid for her safety—he should not have taken her. I don't know
how Mara could have gone along with him. She's too smart for such an
idea."

Jud was amused by Georgina's words and pleased with their ensuing
effect.

David said, "We're going." He was getting hot with his coat on. If Jud
was lying, he would kill him with his own hands. As he walked out the
door, he was followed by Stephen, who was followed by Jud and Georgina,

who were followed by Constantine. Jud and Georgina saw no reason to run away—neither one knew what Stephen, who was close enough to stop an escape attempt, was thinking about all of this. The drive to Irakleío would take them far away from Mara and Diana in Istron. And, soon, Mara and Diana would know something was wrong when Jud and Georgina didn't show up.

CHAPTER THIRTEEN

The five companions, held together by cross-purposes and bonds of distrust, stood inside the underground garage housing three cars. David was about to climb into the driver's seat of the black Mercedes, its keys on the driver's seat, when Constantine said that Stephen would drive. David shrugged his shoulders, took off his coat and placed it on the front passenger side, where he then sat. Stephen picked up the keys and sat at the wheel. Jud opened the back door for Georgina, climbed in, and closed the door. Constantine climbed in next to Georgina from the other side, which placed him behind the driver's seat. With one switch, Stephen locked the automatic door-locks and, at Constantine's request, activated the child locks. Stephen opened the middle door of the garage with a three-way-switch remote, backed up the car, and closed the garage door.

He drove away from the villa and passed Istron, where Mara and Diana waited for Jud and Georgina in Alek's home. He slowly drove north. With no lights along the road, David and Constantine, their eyes accustomed to the dim moonlight, looked out for Mara and Diana but saw no one. Stephen focused on driving—he didn't want to find Diana, for her own sake. And by not finding her, his father would be saved from committing murder, for tonight at least. Jud stared out of his window, while Georgina, from her middle position, leaned against Jud as she stared beyond him through the window. In the intimate dark that promised to tell no secrets, she put a hand on his thigh; he put his hand over her hand.

Once they reached Ágios Nikólaos, David and Constantine assumed that Mara and Diana had hitched a ride, if not all the way to Irakleío, then some of the way. Thus, Constantine told Stephen he could drive faster but not too fast. He still wanted to keep a careful watch for the runaways. He had taken off his coat and thrown it on the seat—he might as well have let Georgina bring a coat because Stephen, who had also removed his coat, was keeping the car heat on for Georgina in her thin silk dress.

Leaving Ágios Nikólaos, they drove north by northwest and, just before Mália, headed west along the north coastline to Irakleío. It was a slow drive but, for Jud, they arrived too soon. Stephen stopped the car along the side of a road on the outskirts of Irakleío. As he switched on an interior light, Constantine saw Georgina pull her hand away from Jud's thigh. Constantine reached forward for David's car cell phone.

Because Jud couldn't recall where he had seen Hotel Homer, Constantine called information for the hotel number and then dialed it. Once he had directions from the hotel clerk, he directed Stephen to the hotel, where Constantine then stepped out of the car with his coat, which he put on. He walked through the hotel entrance and into its lobby; he roused a drowsy clerk, who told him, upon Constantine's descriptions of Mara and Diana, that no one had come to the hotel tonight who looked like that. Once Constantine was satisfied that the clerk had been there for the last few hours; had seen all who had come and gone; had shown him the guest registry and told him that his vacancy sign had been on for the last several hours, Constantine walked out of the hotel, lit only by its vacancy sign.

When he reached the car, he said, "Mr. Thorensen, get out of the car." When Jud got out, Constantine said, "Where in hell is Diana?"

"I don't know. We must have passed by her. Perhaps she and Mara got a ride part way."

"I think not. I think you lied." Constantine wished he knew what would make Jud talk, apart from harming Georgina, who was still under the protection of her husband. Constantine suspected that Jud had been injured today and that he could easily cause him more pain. But not yet. He said, "Get in the car." Jud did as he was told.

Constantine removed his coat and put it into the car trunk. He walked to the driver's door and opened it. He said, "I'm driving, Stephen. Please get in the back." Stephen got out. As Constantine took the driver's seat, next to David, Stephen took the seat behind his father and closed the door.

David said, "Let's head back home. We might still see them."

With all locks secured, Constantine drove the car to the outskirts of Irakleío and headed west again on the main road.

David said, "What are you doing Constantine? We need to head east."

"We are going on an excursion."

Stephen wondered what his father was up to but was glad that the quest for Diana was off, for now. Jud and Georgina were pleased that they would be heading even farther away from Mara and Diana. Georgina, warm and relaxed, fell asleep leaning on Jud's arm. Jud's eyes were closed but he was awake. David looked back at them and felt sick.

And David felt frustrated. It seemed as if he was the only one left who wanted to find Diana tonight. He decided that, at some point during this night, he was going to have to gain control. Right now, he had no allies— he was unaware that Stephen was one. As David watched dark clouds streak the pink moon and slide in front of stars, he fell asleep.

Constantine continued his drive west along the northern coastline. He looked in his rearview mirror and saw that Stephen was nodding off. Jud seemed to really be asleep, this time. Constantine turned up the car heat to keep them all sleeping. He himself was impervious to falling asleep—he relished his upcoming moments.

He passed through Rethymnó. A few miles beyond there, he dropped down to Chora Sfákia on the southern coastline and then headed west past Anapoli to Aradaina. Constantine parked next to the gorge. He climbed out of the car. He opened David's door. It was black outside with a rose glow from the moon. David didn't know where he was. Constantine said, "Come on David, we must make a plan."

David got out of the car and asked, "A plan for what, Constantine?" He started to wake up.

"Come this way, I don't want to disturb the others." They reached the edge of the gorge. He continued, "Let's get rid of Mr. Thorensen. We can throw him over the edge now. No one will ever know—neither of us will be blamed." Constantine put an arm around his shoulders. "Take a closer look. He will have a swift, sure death."

David didn't know he was seeing the Ravine of Aradaina—he had never been here before. He looked down on the dark gorge and began to make out its dark depth. Then, he felt himself begin to fall. But Constantine had not pushed hard enough. David fell onto the edge of the stone path. His body bounced and then rolled over the side before dropping down. The zigzag path went along the gorge's side from top to bottom in a diagonal direction, the only way for it to have been manufactured and be useful. David's body met with no more path to stop his fall down the stoned side. He never had a chance to scream—he lost consciousness upon the first impact. After a few moments, he reached the bottom.

Constantine got back inside the car. David's coat sat on the passenger seat. He pushed it down onto the floor. Stephen mumbled something. Constantine said, "I had to get some fresh air." He was shaking and his hands were ice-cold. But he was elated. He had rid himself of a big problem. And, yet, underneath what he felt as elation was not a conscience but a bleak realisation that he would never be the same again. And that life would hold none of the same joy again. He could feel emotional numbness setting in.

From the south coast, he drove north up to the start of the small peninsula of Akrotíri and then continued farther north into the peninsula until he reached Triados. It was still dark in the early hours of the morning when he reached the Osios Monastery. He wanted to pray there as he often had before. He began to see clearly that getting rid of David was as good as if he had killed Diana. Either way, the arranged marriage would disappear and its traces, with time, would disappear, also.

From the driver's seat, he leaned toward the passenger-side floor and picked up David's coat, which he placed on his lap. He felt a heavy object. He put his hand into a pocket and pulled out a sheathed dagger. With care, he reached into the other pocket and pulled out a narrow rectangular box, which he opened up. He removed the needle, which he supposed that David had filled with a sedative. The discoveries combined with a new growth of concerns stimulated a new idea for him. So he placed the dagger and the needle in the compartment in-between the two seats. He put the case back into a coat pocket. He got out of the car. He put David's coat over his arm and walked to the trunk. Before placing the coat on top of his own, he reached inside the inner breast pocket and extracted a sheaf of flat objects: three passports, a batch of drachma bills, and credit cards. With his hands full, he closed up the trunk, quietly, and went to the driver's door, which he had left ajar, climbed in, and sat behind the wheel. With the sheaf in his right hand he reached for the middle compartment with the back of his hand to lift up the lip of its lid.

"Where's David?"

Constantine jumped. The sheaf of passports, cash, and credit cards spilled out of his hand and onto the passenger-side floor. Constantine closed the car door and looked back at Jud and said, "He wanted to get out some time ago. I dropped him off in Rethymnó. He said that he would find his own way home."

Jud had woken up as fresh air had entered the car. He disbelieved Constantine but knew he would learn nothing from him. As he mused on what Constantine had just dropped, he asked, "Where are we?" It was still dark. The streaks across the pink moon had inflated into masses that had covered the sky's glistening orbs, including the moon. A gale shuddered and shook the car. The next three days of autumn rain were starting.

Georgina opened her eyes. She saw that her husband was gone. She thought she'd heard Jud ask about him. She sat up and asked, "Did David get out of the car?"

Jud said nothing; he let Constantine explain again where David was.

Constantine leaned back in his seat, turned to face Georgina, and said, "David and I had a disagreement. He said he was going to hire a taxi back to your home, get another car, and search for Diana." Constantine glanced at Stephen as he stirred.

Georgina glanced at the car clock and said, "He won't get a taxi at this hour of the morning on Crete."

"I tried to tell him that Georgina. We'll all go home soon, though. In fact, why don't you and Jud get out of the car and take a stretch before we head back?" Constantine released the child-locks so that they could let themselves out. Jud and Georgina got out of the car from the same side.

Within the car, Constantine climbed from the front seat into the middle back seat, next to Stephen, still asleep but stirring. Constantine raised the arm between the two front seats into a vertical position and opened up the compartment, taking care to catch the dagger and the small needle as they spilled out toward him. Constantine inserted the sheathed dagger behind his own back, between his belt and pants, and put the needle on the floor after he had removed its rubber stopper. He undid the cuff of Stephen's right sleeve.

With his eyes still closed, Stephen mumbled, "Where are we?" He knew his father was next to him.

Outside, Jud and Georgina talked about separating from the Sgouroses. But they were in the middle of nowhere, in the small hours of the morning. They had no concern for their safety. They would have to watch Constantine but, with the proximity of Stephen who was innocuous, he could do no harm. The worst that Jud and Georgina thought that Constantine had done to David was to have dropped him off in the middle of nowhere without his consent. And they wondered if Constantine had wanted them out of the car so that he could leave them behind.

Georgina still worried that David might harm Diana, if he found her. She shivered as the cold gale blew around her and whipped her short thick hair around her face. Yet, she felt glad to be outside after the stuffiness of the car. Jud put both arms around her. She held him around the waist and closed her eyes—she felt a sensation of being in a event that, although cataclysmic, could not touch her.

Inside the car, Stephen opened his eyes halfway and looked around him. Down a short road was a tall dark square. He dimly recognised where he was and hoped that he was wrong. He asked, "Are we at the Osios Monastery?" Stephen had sat in a car on many occasions as a child while his father had walked past the grounds of the monastery, one-hundred-fifty years old, descended past the older deserted monastery, and then gone to pray in one of the caves. That it was autumn didn't strike at Stephen's awareness—his father came to pray here only in the summer, if he came here at all.

Constantine said, "Yes." Stephen's coat was behind Stephen's back and leaning against the back of the seat. Constantine pulled the coat shoulders around Stephen's shoulders. He opened his door to an ajar position; the interior light went on.

Stephen then gave the response that Constantine expected. He said, "Wake me up when you're back. But make it soon, please." Stephen closed his eyes again.

In one swift movement, Constantine pushed back Stephen's sleeve with one hand as he reached his right arm to the rear floor for the hypodermic needle, which he swung up and plunged into a vein of Stephen's arm, just as Stephen opened his eyes again.

Constantine could have quickly jabbed the needle into the muscle tissue of Stephen's leg but he had preferred an intravenous shot to Stephen's arm for two reasons. The first was that he had wanted to mimic what he had seen—Constantine had never used a hypodermic needle but, as its occasional recipient in a doctor's office, he had watched the nurse's deft application of the point into his vein and then felt the pressure as she had pressed the plunger, forcing medicine into his bloodstream. The second reason was that, being unaware of a drug's potency and its effectiveness in muscle tissue, he wanted to be sure that Stephen stayed asleep while he took care of his new business.

Constantine had just pulled the needle out of Stephen's arm when Georgina knocked on the window of the driver's door and then opened it. The light that had just gone off came on again. Constantine threw the needle onto the floor and jumped out of the car before Georgina could lower her head and look through the door to talk to him. As he closed the car door, she looked over the car roof to talk to him. Neither one saw Stephen's body convulse and then slip into the phase of physical death.

§

As time passed and Diana grew tired of sitting on the floor with Mara while waiting for Jud and Georgina, she climbed onto the hard cot and fell asleep. She wore a jacket, sweater, and jeans. But it was a cold night so Mara covered her with a heavy blanket.

After more than an hour had passed since she and Diana had left Jud and while Diana slept, Mara risked a visit to the villa. Spotlights lit the grand stucco house and left darkness everywhere else. The house seemed empty. Had Mara not been responsible for Diana, she would have entered the grounds and looked through windows. Yet, if someone were there and she had been found, Diana would have been found soon afterward. Jud had made it clear to her that Diana needed protection from Constantine, until he learned otherwise.

Mara returned to her room in Istron, pulled Diana's blanket from off the floor and put it back over her. Mara sat on the cold hard floor to keep herself awake. Even though wearing a sweater, she pulled a blanket around her shoulders. In a half hour she planned to call the Ágios Nikólaos police—by then, two hours would have reached the deadline she and Jud had agreed upon. Yet, having been awake for over forty hours, she fell asleep.

Diana was restless and kicked off her blanket again. Then, she woke in a cold sweat from a nightmare and lay frozen, too terrified to move—if she moved one tiny muscle, something would kill her. She barely dared breathe. She opened her eyes and heard the wind outside. The cypress trees shouted their indifference to her terror as gales blew gusts around them and gave them their voices. As Diana lay for long moments, she began to see the room in pale rectangles. Nothing seemed to be there that could harm her. She wanted to look at Mara but still feared to turn her head. Almost a half hour passed before she slowly turned her face from the ceiling to face Mara, who was still sitting—her head fallen forward. Diana whispered, "Mara." She whispered louder, "Mara." But her whispers fell into the sound of the wind. She called out, "Mara." And wondered if Mara had stopped breathing.

Mara raised her head.

Diana said, "I can't move, Mara. I'm afraid."

Mara rose and walked over to Diana. She felt her forehead and its cold sweat. Mara recognised that Diana had dreamed up a nightmare as she herself had done years ago—a dream of pure terror. She knew the feeling of being petrified to move. She didn't know Diana's exact experience but hers had been as if some horrible unknown thing would throw her into a deep black abyss from which she would never be able to leave. She stroked Diana's forehead and said, "It's okay Diana. It's just a dream. There's nothing from outside of you that has come to hurt you. Don't worry."

Diana slowly stretched and felt the physical-like restraints on her body movement dissipate. She sat up. Relief dissolved her fear of the unknown. But then, she asked, "Where is my mama—where is Jud?"

"I don't know." Now that Mara realised there must be trouble for Jud and, perhaps, Georgina, Alek's sparse square room seemed to be worth more than all the gold in California. If Jud's concern was unfounded, then Jud would have come to Istron for Diana and brought her back home to the villa but if his concern was real, then he and Georgina would have come to take Diana and the rest of them away from here. Mara did not even want to think that something had gone wrong because Georgina had refused to come and had, instead, informed David and the Sgouros men against Jud.

Mara had suggested to Jud that he should come with her and Diana and then contact Georgina by telephone from whatever city they ended up in so that Georgina would know Diana was safe. But Jud had not wanted Georgina to worry for even a moment about Diana's disappearance and had seemed to think that Georgina could be in danger. Mara looked at her watch and saw that almost two hours had passed the two-hour deadline to call the police. She picked up her belt bag which held her money and documents, in addition to Jud's wallet and passport, and snapped it around her waist.

She left the bedroom and knocked on Alek's door. He had awakened when he had heard Diana call out. He was dressed when he came to his door. He knew who Diana Binakas was but had not interfered with whatever was going on when Mara had shown up with her late in the night—Diana had seemed fine. Alek said in Greek, "What is it?" The only English words he knew were 'room' and 'twenty dollars.'

Mara herself knew few Greek words so she asked Diana, who had come from behind her, to ask Alek for a telephone. Since the Binakas villa had phones, someone in the village might have one—Alek led Mara and Diana to a taverna. He banged on a door and asked his friend if they could use the telephone. The three were let inside.

Diana called the Ágios Nikólaos police station. Mara told her what to say. In Greek, Diana said, "I'm Diana Binakas. My mother is in danger. Please come to this address—" Diana also gave her home phone number. She put her hand over the telephone receiver and said, "He wants to know what kind of danger."

"Tell the police that a man is in your house and that you think he wants to kill your mother—but you're not sure because you are locked outside.

Tell him you are only twelve years and very frightened." Mara loathed giving Diana words like that to say about her mother's welfare but the words had to be strong enough to bring the police. And they could be true.

After Diana spoke Mara's words in Greek. She listened and then hung up the phone. She told Mara that the police would come. Mara paid the taverna owner more than enough drachmas for the call and thanked him. Then, she took Diana to the villa gates to wait for a policeman, who would likely arrive in thirty minutes, despite the short eleven-mile distance, due to traveling along a dark winding road. Mara and Diana paced because they were cold and nervous. Mara began to think about how she would explain to the police why she had asked Diana to call them out here on a false alarm if Jud and Georgina were all right, after all.

A squad car pulled up. A policeman, left his car, and, in English, introduced himself as Officer Theo, and then buzzed the villa intercom. When no response came from within, he told Diana and Mara that there was nothing he could do to help them.

Diana said, "But, Officer Theo, this is my home. And I can't get in. If my parents were safe, they would have called your station to say that I was missing."

The officer saw the sense in that—he radioed his station to explain the situation. He waited and then was told that no one had answered the station's calls to the Binakas household and that he would have to wait until morning to investigate, unless Diana had identification showing that she was Diana Binakas. She did not. Thus, Officer Theo was told to return to Ágios Nikólaos. He said good night, got into his car, and drove off.

Mara and Diana shivered. Mara said, "We have to find a way into your home Diana." They climbed over a wall and approached the villa. They looked through windows and saw no one. All doors and windows were locked. From the front of the house, Mara picked up a heavy stone; she shut her eyes as she heaved the stone through the dining room glass door. She felt a sharp sensation go through her stomach and legs as she released the stone. It smashed a big hole through the glass. Yet, no alarm went off—no one had reactivated it since Diana had disarmed it hours ago.

After the noise of shattering glass, no one came running from within the house to see what had occurred. Thus, Mara and Diana entered the house. With care, they went through the jagged hole and put on all of the lights; they searched for anyone or anything that could tell them what had happened. They discovered that a few overcoats were missing from the foyer closet and that no beds, except for Diana's, had been slept in. Diana called the police again. She said she was in her home and her parents were missing.

Officer Theo had almost reached Ágios Nikólaos when he was radioed by his station. He turned around and returned to the villa, where he buzzed the intercom, and drove through the gates as they opened. He stopped in front and got out of his car.

Diana let him in through the front door. She showed him her school identification. She told him that not only were her parents missing but so were Jud Thorensen and the Greek City Planner, Constantine Sgouros, along with his son, Stephen.

Officer Theo ran through the house and observed what Mara and Diana had. He asked Diana where she thought her parents and their house guests could have gone to. Diana said she didn't know. Mara asked Diana to take them to the garage. The three went through the house's connecting passageway to it. Diana said that the black Mercedes was missing. She told Officer Theo its license plate number.

Then the three went to his car from where he radioed his headquarters because, although it was improbable that anyone would have seen the black car in the black hours of a cold windy night on a scarcely-populated island, it was a large matter that the Greek City planner, the owner of Alpha-Omega Pharmakon, and a famous American were missing. Then— with the usual awareness that Cretan police held inadequate resources to find missing persons, who, often, just had to turn up by themselves, if they could—he left Mara and Diana.

Mara thought about where she would look for everyone if she dared to take a Binakas car. She could think of nowhere. Although a small island, Crete held many man-made structures and many more natural structures.

Inside the villa, Mara rekindled the living room fire and put a fireguard in place. She and Diana turned out all the house lights. Each with a blanket wrapped around them, they sat on the woven rug in front of the warm fire and got to know each other as they hoped for the phone to ring. Mara told Diana that her mother was a talented painter. And as Diana thought about her mother's studio, she was reminded of her father's office and realised something that she had noticed but not registered. She said, "Mara, there is one thing—the Turkish dagger is missing from a wall in my father's office."

§

In Massachusetts, Angela Wynne had a nightmare. *Jud was lying in a stream of cold water, edged by thick woods. He was alive but dead bodies were floating by him. Then, the water turned opaque red, covering him entirely. A man saved him but, then, the man put him on a cross—Jud allowed him to— and drove spikes into his hands and feet; the man raised the cross single-hand-edly. Then, he lay stones high up around the base of the cross; he stacked sticks around it. He started a fire. The flames rose up around Jud and, then, water rose up from ground and above Jud's head. A girl stood and watched. She cried. And it seemed as if her tears were causing the flood. Then the cross and Jud disappeared.* Angela screamed. She sat up. She felt as if she had been trying to wake up from the dream for hours.

Mrs. Wynne came into her daughter's room and turned on a light. Angela said, "It was just a dream. I'm fine." Mrs. Wynne returned to her own bed but Angela did not go back to sleep. She picked up the telephone receiver next to her bed and called Helen Thorensen.

Ogden answered the telephone and passed it to Helen. He told her that Angela Wynne was on the line. Then, he turned on a lamp and lay down again to return to sleep.

Helen said, "Hello, Angela."

"Helen, I am sorry to have called you like this. Why did Jud go to Crete?"

"He went on vacation, dear."

"But is that all?"

"There were other reasons—private ones."

Angela asked, "Do you know how to reach him?"

"No, I don't." Helen had her own concerns but could do nothing about them.

"Would you please ask Jud to call me when you hear from him?" Angela knew she couldn't explain to Jud's mother that the last time she had dreamed a nightmare about Jud, he had been in fatal danger. But, as before, she had been worried, as she was now. Despite her knowledge of dream theories, Angela disbelieved in pre-cognitive dreams. It was her worry about Jud that had given her a bad dream, as before in Washburn. This time, after Jud had left her at Bentilee, she had thought about their lunch together and felt her own worry about the look of concern in his eyes and his manner. Yet, she had not asked him questions. They had held hands and talked about theosophy.

Helen said, "Angela, I will let you know as soon as I hear from Jud." Helen was too tired to ask her why she sounded anxious about him. She wished she could give Angela a phone number for Jud but she truly had none.

They said good night to each other and hung up.

Angela's clock showed that it was a few minutes after eleven p.m. which meant that it was a few minutes after six a.m. on Crete. Angela wondered what Jud was doing. She got out of bed and did the only thing that could take her mind off her worry. She picked up the Fender guitar and played its strings, almost mute without the guitar body being plugged into an amplifier. She closed her eyes and softly sang new words to a new tune, the best way she knew to write a song.

§

From his side of the car, Constantine walked around to Georgina, who had been surprised that he had been in the back seat. She spoke. He wasn't listening. He pulled the car keys from his pocket and, with one turn of a key in the driver's door, locked all doors. Despite feeling cold, he did not go to the trunk to get his coat, which lay underneath David's.

Georgina asked, "What are you doing, Constantine? Didn't you hear me?"

Jud came up to them.

Constantine said, "I'm sorry, Georgina. Tell me again."

"I want to go home, Constantine. Please."

In the darkness, he turned his back on her and walked away. He heard her following him as he reached the edge of the steep incline. And he heard Jud following Georgina. He pulled the dagger from out of its sheath and waited. But Georgina did not come close enough to become his victim. He had lost the moment. He said, "Georgina, I want to pray. There's a small chapel down there. We'll go home after that."

Georgina wrapped her arms around her torso. Her body shook from the cold now that Jud no longer had his arms around her.

From behind her, Jud said to Constantine, "Georgina's shivering. We'll wait in the car for you."

Constantine said, "You might drive off without me. I can't take that chance."

"You'll have the car keys."

"And, as all Americans seem to know how to do, you'll jump-start the car and leave without me."

"There's no reason I would do that, Constantine. But, I'll go with you to your place of prayer. Georgina can go back to the car to get warm."

"Knowing her, she'll leave us both behind. I know what she did to you yesterday. You are a fool to trust her—she will only cause you rivers of pain. In fact, you should align yourself with me. I'll take you back to Mara. Just let me pray for a few moments. You can both join me."

Then, with his back to the steep descent, Constantine stretched out and grabbed Georgina's arm. He wrenched it behind her back so she was spun around with her back, arched in pain, toward him. As he was raising his dagger, which Georgina did not see, she dug a spike heel into his foot. He lost his grip on her and dropped the dagger. She stumbled. Constantine fell aside and headfirst onto his hands. Through the wind sounds, he heard a faint thud as the dagger landed; he felt around for it.

Georgina had fallen and begun rolling over the steep curve; the stone steps slowed her descent. Jud had run past Constantine, who was still on his hands and knees, and stopped short of Georgina, whose silk dress sent a pale reflection to his eyes. He leapt over her rolling form and a couple of feet beyond. With blind fortune, he landed on a stone step. He had barely stretched out his arms to gain his balance before he dropped to his knees to block Georgina's descent and catch her in his arms. Jud took her arm and pulled her to her feet on the narrow path. He looked up to see Constantine, a dark silhouette, standing and holding a dagger, against the dark. The car stood a few yards behind him. Down a long steep depth that eventually met flat land and lying to the distant back of Jud and Georgina was the ocean. Georgina also saw Constantine with the dagger, whose shape she recognised as the same as the one in David's office—in a thought that took no time, she wondered why Constantine had it. She kicked off her shoes, grabbed Jud's hand and pulled him down the steep steps of the path. Constantine was behind Jud. He was familiar with the steps and was quick but Jud and Georgina were faster—they wanted to escape with their lives. Strong wind blew against their faces as they flew down the hill.

Jud and Georgina reached a plateau; they discerned deteriorated stone buildings surrounding a small church. Constantine came within two feet of Jud. Georgina heard Constantine's breathing, despite the sound of Jud's ragged breathing, and pulled Jud farther down the steep side. Her nylons were torn and her feet were bleeding. They stopped at the edge of a sheer side, falling away so that its side was invisible to anyone who stood atop it. To their left was a grass plateau and the black mouth of a cave containing the chapel where Constantine had once confessed his past and future sins. The grass plateau ended at another sheer side but this one went upward— it was the side of a mountain. Georgina led Jud to the mouth of the cave as rain and hail began its pelt downward from the heavens, as if the heavens had waited to accumulate all of their material and release everything at once. They ran inside the cave, eroded and shaped by water, its porous rock now welcoming more water.

Constantine returned the dagger to the sheath, which he had moved from his back to his side since he no longer needed to hide it, and followed after Jud and Georgina. As he did, his thoughts blew in every direction. He was becoming ambivalent about killing Jud and Georgina. His chances to kill them were becoming fewer. If he did kill them, he hoped Stephen would support whatever alibi he created for himself. Fingerprints inside of the Binakas car could be cleaned up, although eradication of all hair, skin, and clothing particles might be impossible. His having been a house guest of the Binakases could cause him to be a suspect in their disappearance—although risky to have David missing, it was more risky to have his hostess and one of her guests become missing, also. If he let the pair live, he imagined that his powerful status as the Greek City Planner would overwhelm any claims that two adulterers might make against himself regarding David's death. Constantine felt a desperate need to reach the holy shrine within the cave. His new debate about whether Jud and Georgina should live or die was becoming his downfall. He must follow through with getting rid of them.

Jud and Georgina entered the cave. Georgina felt on the ground for a string. She grasped one and followed its direction with one hand while she held Jud's hand with her other hand. Instead of letting the string drop to the ground behind them as they moved along its length, she gathered it up so that Constantine might lose track of them, which meant they would have to, later, find their way out of the cave without being able to follow the string. But Constantine knew the cave well and followed their sounds as Georgina pulled Jud along into the water and into an inner recess. The water was above their ankles. Georgina told Jud to continue to watch out for stalagmites thrusting upward and the dripping stalactites, which he and Georgina walked around as they put out their arms to feel for them. She was warm after exertion but the water was cold.

Jud and Georgina came to three tunnels, each similar to the one they stood in but different because the tunnels continued into inner depths with no way out. Still following the string, Georgina led Jud into one of them. She dropped the string when it ended in a recess with a shrine, about two hundred meters in from the cave entrance. Georgina felt along the altar top. There were candles and a damp matchbox. She and Jud heard Constantine wading through the water but could not estimate how close he was. Jud touched Georgina's arm and felt the goosebumps. He knew her body must be bruised and cut. The water, like liquid ice, in the recess was up to Jud's knees and crept up higher as the rains came down outside. Jud pulled off his sweater and pulled it down over Georgina's head. Georgina felt his bare chest and put her arms around him to try to keep him warm. It was then that she noticed his ragged breathing again.

Georgina touched her gold and diamond crucifix; she prayed for Jud's and her safety. She stopped worrying about David finding Diana. She trusted that Mara would have hidden her well. After Constantine's violence tonight, Georgina was beginning to wonder if Jud had been protecting Diana from Constantine, who had shown, until leaving the Hotel Homer, a strong intent to find Diana. She felt that Diana was safe. And for that, she was grateful. She reached her lips to Jud's and kissed him. She tasted his mouth. It was sweet.

Then, Constantine stood beside them. His distant sound had been deceiving—he had moved with stealth. By the flame of his windproof lighter, Jud and Georgina saw him light orange candles, whose flames danced from traces of wind that had decreased from gusts that incessantly wove into the cave and along its passageways. Fresh green smells mingled with the ever-present musty one. The air was alive and electric. Constantine prayed; his past confessions of future sins had come to pass. Though he had thought he would have no more confessions to make of future sins, he did have more, yet made none.

As Georgina saw by candlelight Constantine's face, ravaged by the night—he, alone, had never slept,—she saw the flash of an image of danger for David. Yet, she could not have imagined that he lay dead on a bed of round stones at the bottom of a gorge with animal bones and a broken staff. And that the storm was pounding his broken body.

Georgina glimpsed pain on Jud's face. She caught sight of the large bruise on his side, near his rib cage. She touched him there, realising that he had a cracked or broken rib. The water from hidden streams of rainwater and the saturation of the ground crept higher in the cave. Although Jud's sweater hung below her hips, she shivered again. Jud picked her up and held her in his arms. He was regaining his breath now that they had stopped running. Georgina put her arms around his neck, lightening her weight, and clung to him. Jud started to leave the recess.

But Constantine was alert to his movement. He interrupted his prayer, just begun. He said, "Stay here."

Jud kept walking. Then, as Georgina looked back and glimpsed an orange glint on the blade of the dagger, she said, "Jud," with a voice that held breath and tone twisted into one knotted sound. Jud swiftly let her down. Just as her feet touched the ground, he spun around and dodged Constantine's thrust of the dagger. Constantine lost his balance and fell against a wall, while retaining his hold on the dagger. As Jud and Georgina ran through the water toward the cave opening, water splashed into their faces. When they tripped over stalagmites, they fell into the water. When they got up again, they had lost their sense of direction. With hair and clothes plastered to their faces and bodies, they searched for the cave's mouth.

Constantine followed Jud and Georgina. He was more careful than they were as he followed their sounds and did not fall. He soon found them—they had not reached the mouth of the cave, they had gone down one of the two long tunnels. He had been down both in the past. This one had a slight incline, misleading in its similarity to the passageway, shared by the three tunnels, that led outside. He continued in the blackness. Then, he knew he was close to them. He took the lighter out of his shirt pocket and hoped it was still dry enough to work. The flame shot up. He saw Jud and Georgina in the middle of a deep pool.

They could not touch the ground. When they saw Constantine, they swam to the other side. Constantine put the lighter into his left hand and was about to throw the dagger when his light went out. It had no more butane gas. Jud and Georgina grasped a stalactite near a wall and stayed as still as they could. And hoped that the dagger didn't fly out of the darkness and into one of their hearts.

Constantine was patient. He waited for a long time but his legs were becoming numb from the cold deepening water. When he could no longer hear Jud's breath, he left. He had never been able to hear Georgina's breath. He hoped that she was dead, too. If he had known how to swim, he would have gone to find their bodies. Yet, if they were alive, he still had to leave. He wanted to be back on the mainland today and prepare for Monday, the start of a new life.

As Constantine made his way through the cave, he saw a faint light, paler than the glow of an American firefly necklace fading hours after the capture of its fireflies, pierced, and strung together by a child, as taught by his parents. But the storm still resounded with wild winds, thunder claps that were kept company by blue lightning that filled the sky, and rain and hail hitting the ground and hissing up. The lightning sent an occasional blue shaft that bounced along the cave's inner walls.

§

But the blue shaft of lightning didn't dazzle Constantine's eyes the way the full glory of the jagged veins of lightning dazzled Diana's eyes, raining tears, as she looked out into the lit-up night while Mara lay by the fire. Occasionally, Diana jumped when the winds broke more glass from the smashed door. The storm was finishing the job that Mara had started. Diana was wishing upon unseen stars for the safe return of her parents and Jud. She wished for the safety of Constantine and Stephen, too.

§

As Constantine continued heading to the outdoors, he reviewed how he had expected this new day to be compared to what it had become: Diana was to have lain dead on the flat base of Aradaina gorge as he made a pilgrimage to Aradin Village next to it; he would then have gone to Anapoli to give his promised gift of new guitar strings to the fisherman. And, before leaving Crete with Stephen, prayed at the cave's shrine, for the last time, because he intended to not set foot on Crete again. As he walked up incline, the water became lower, except for the deeper pockets over holes, and, by the time he viewed the storm from the cave's mouth, he stood on damp ground.

He realised he would not be accused of David's death—he had left no clues and there had been no witnesses. And David's fall would likely be considered as an accident rather than a murder. David would be found soon after the storm—the Aradaina ravine was still used as a crossing, down one side and up the other—and, tomorrow, David would be reported as missing by his employees, whom he had been in daily communication with. The bodies of Jud and Georgina would remain unfound for months in a cave rarely visited. And, if Jud and Georgina could be around to say anything, they would have nothing to say—they'd had invisible attempts on their lives and they knew nothing about David. Neither did Stephen. And Stephen would believe anything he said about Jud and Georgina, because he would want to believe him, his father. The dissolution of the marriage arrangement for Stephen and Diana would be unquestioned because Alpha-Omega Pharmakon would no longer be run by David—and Constantine couldn't be expected by his family and friends to be sure that Diana's dowry would be sustainable by a business under the guidance of a new president, with an unproven track record, perhaps.

Constantine pushed against the wind and ascended the uneven stone steps. When, at last, he reached the top, he was breathing heavily. Yet, he ran as he relished reaching the windless, dry interior of the car. Each step held the promise of warmth and luxury. He pulled the car keys out of his deep pants pocket, unlocked the door, and slid inside.

Without noticing a fine odor gradually condensing, Constantine started the engine and turned on the headlights. As he looked in back of him and began backing up the car, he saw Stephen's white face, with a cold drool congealed at the corner of his mouth. Constantine slammed on the brakes. He turned off the engine, put the car in first gear, and pulled on the emergency brake. He got out of the car and climbed into the back seat. He felt Stephen's hand, almost as cold as the water he had stood in while praying. He looked at the hypodermic needle on the car floor. David must have put poison in it.

All that had mattered to Constantine an instant ago mattered not at all now. He put his arms around his son and screamed a gut-wrenching howl that reverberated against the car windows and then out of the doors he had left open. And once he had started it, he couldn't stop it. But when the scream stopped of its own volition, it had not assuaged his pain, which was driving him mad. He thought, *my dear sweet son—what have I done— Mother of God, what have I done. What—have—I—done.* He rocked back and forth holding Stephen until, when his pain had reached intolerable heights, he set Stephen's body back against the seat. He took the dagger from out of its sheath. He kneeled on the back seat and sat on his haunches. He ripped open his shirt. He pushed his head back, his face almost parallel with the car ceiling and, as he released another guttural cry of grief, with two hands, in a diagonal motion, he plunged the dagger into his heart. He raised himself up straight and, as his own life quickly ebbed, he slumped over his beloved son. And as his awareness faded, he realised the grief that he had planned for David, Georgina—and Jud—for the loss of their daughter, Diana.

CHAPTER FOURTEEN

From across the pool of cold water, Georgina had heard Constantine leave. He had been quiet for a while and then, a few minutes after Jud had passed out and his breath had gone faint, Constantine had splashed through the water. Georgina had listened to his sounds until they had become inaudible. Now, she held onto Jud but couldn't for much longer. He was slipping from her grasp. Her arms felt numb. Tears came down her cheeks. She said, "Jud. Jud—wake up. Please." Underbreath, she said "My darling."

From far-off, Jud heard Georgina's voice. He felt a numbing cold. He stirred; he slipped from her arm. As he sank down, below the water's surface, he became aware of where he was. Nothing seemed real. He held his breath; he let himself stay submerged and suspended in the deep dark wet; he felt calm. Then, he felt an arm grab his. He became alert and, using his arms and legs, pushed himself upward; above the surface, he struggled to catch his breath.

Georgina had let go of the stalactite and was by his side; she pulled him in the opposite direction from which they had entered. He knew he was expected to follow her. He did but his side hurt badly as he breathed hard. When their knees hit a ledge, submerged under water, they climbed onto it and stood up. The water came up to Jud's thighs. After Jud caught his breath again, Georgina took his hand and pulled him along. They both staggered as they continued. Georgina saw a glimmer of light and almost collapsed from relief. "Thank God," she said. The night had passed. The day had come.

Jud and Georgina reached the mouth of the cave and faced its curtains of water. Jud lay down. He had to sleep. The damp ground of the cave felt good against the cold skin of his back. Georgina took off the sweater he had put on her and lay its drenched mass aside; she held herself over Jud—lightly so that he could still breathe. She hoped that the closeness of their bodies would warm them both. Then, as her strength ebbed, she lay down beside him and stared at his profile, peaceful and beautiful. She fell asleep.

When she awoke a short while later, he was on his left side with his arm around her. His eyes were open. He kissed her.

The storm still played. They both stood up. Jud wrung water out of his sweater and tied it around his waist. Georgina stood behind his back and stared at the scars on his skin. She had heard what had happened to him but couldn't have imagined its reality without having seen the remnants of pain lying on his back, which she had seen during the times they had made love but never in a stark light that, although not bright was sharp.

Jud and Georgina left the cave. With a north wind at their backs, they leaned forward to climb the steep ascent. With their wet hands, they grasped the steps to help pull themselves up. The sharpness of the stones peeled the skin from their wet hands. Jud and Georgina were both white and shaking from cold. Jud thought he was going to black out during the climb but, because the elements of nature claimed most of his attention and because he wanted to live, he stayed alert and paused when he needed to. Jud had asked Georgina to go ahead of him because, if she fell, he could help her. With the loudness of the storm and darkness of the day, if she were to fall away from the incline while in back of him, time could elapse before he would notice. And, if he should fall, he wouldn't take her with him. When they were almost at the top of the hill, Georgina saw her pink shoes off to the side and a few feet apart. One was lodged in a shrub, the other lay wedged between two rocks. She picked them up and returned to the path. Jud came up behind her.

Georgina reached the top of the hill. By glancing back occasionally, she had kept her pace with Jud's slower one, in case he needed help. So, he reached the top within seconds after she did. He sat down to catch his breath. Georgina sat with him. They were both aware that the car was still there, although it was a few feet from its original spot and two of its doors were open—the driver's and the one to its rear passenger.

Jud and Georgina stood up and approached the car. He went to the rear open door, she went to the driver's. They each leaned down and peered through a door. From their different perspectives, they saw that the son was dead, underneath his father, whose visible life had first ebbed to a pale existence, then become extinguished and reformed into the vapor of departing body heat.

Jud walked to Georgina who had shut the driver's door. He opened it again; he leaned inside, toward the middle of the front seat, and pressed a button on the car phone. It was dead. Jud closed the driver's door. He backed away from the car.

Georgina walked to the other front door and opened it. She wanted to see what lay on the floor. She reached down and picked up the passports. She took a sharp breath when she looked at the first one, David's. She kept it and picked up the other two which she presupposed were hers and Diana's—they were. She kept them in her hand as she took a few bills from the pile of money on the floor. She picked up a credit card and saw David's name. She placed it down again. Georgina feared that David had been harmed or killed. She glanced at Constantine and Stephen; she felt sick to her stomach. She closed the door. She turned.

Jud stood in front of her. He looked at her trembling lips as he took the passports and drachmas she handed to him. He put them inside a trouser pocket.

Although the storm was still strong, Jud nor Georgina considered driving the car or looking for coats or blankets in its trunk. They stood by the car and held each other in the rain. They could not imagine what had happened to Stephen and Constantine. Pellets of hail like the dots of pointillist paintings pattered at their skin and water smeared Georgina's silk dress to her body. Sheets of water ran down Jud's back. His trousers felt like columns of wet plaster. As it had been in Diana's nightmare, so it was for Jud and Georgina, they were frozen in terror and, if they moved, they would die. But as it also had been for Diana, after a while, they began to unlock their frozen limbs. They moved apart. The rain had stopped. The fresh gale was changing into a fresh breeze.

§

Leaving the car behind, Jud and Georgina, carrying her shoes, walked along the road a few yards and reached the section that was bordered with stucco walls on either side and lined with cypress trees. They walked several more yards until the road ended at a large and dismal stone building with a painted copper roof, the Osios Monastery. They saw a monk who beckoned to them from a tall doorway. He, in turn, was beckoned by another monk, who, before leaving, summoned a blond man, who said, "I'm Richard." He was British, in his fifties, and had deep lines in his face.

"Richard, I'm Jud Thorensen. This is Georgina Binakas. Do you have a phone we could use?"

"I'm sorry. We don't have telephones."

Jud and Georgina were anxious to find a phone or a police station but were too cold and weak to go anywhere. Yet, Jud asked, "Are the police nearby?

"No." Richard looked at the cuts and bruises on Georgina's arms and legs as well as those on Jud's torso. The pair looked like drowned rats that had gone through a mill wheel. Richard had been about to step out and was wearing a yellow slicker, in case the rain resumed its flow. He removed the slicker from his thin frame. He continued, "I'll get dry clothes for you."

Jud and Georgina followed Richard from the cold outdoors into the warmer cold of a stone corridor. Jud told Richard that there were two dead men in a car nearby and asked if there was anyone who could drive to a police station. Richard was shocked about the news but, even though it was only afternoon on a Sunday, he said that nothing could be done till morning and that, since the men were already dead, a delay would matter naught to them. He stopped outside of a tall, wide door. Jud and Georgina stopped with him. Jud told Richard that Georgina's husband might be missing. Richard said that Monday morning would be the best time to take care of that, too. He opened the heavy door.

The three walked into a vast rectangular room with thousands of old books behind glass along three of the walls, a fourth end wall had an arched window. A four-foot-high arched fireplace sat inlaid into the second long wall, also with more bookcases on either side. A table filled the length of the center of the room. Tall-backed chairs bordered the table. Richard went to a diamond-paned cabinet and pulled out a bottle of raki, which he poured into three glasses. He put raisins into a bowl, which he set onto the table. Jud nor Georgina sat on the chairs in their wet clothes but they accepted the raki. The strong liquor burned their throats but was not strong enough to heat up their chilled bodies. Richard said, "If you'll just wait here—I'll return in a moment."

Georgina's lips were purple and her flesh was frozen. She couldn't stop shaking. She sneezed. Jud poured her another glass of raki. He handed it to her. As he gazed around the room, he saw an icon, Virgin and Child, an old painting, leaning on the high mantel above the fireplace. From outside, he heard a gunshot. He jumped. Georgina laughed at him. Jud was glad to see her face relax. She said, "Some men are shooting grouse, it's a common thing—although they usually do it on a sunny day."

When Richard returned, he had a wool blanket and a wool monk's robe. He handed the blanket to Georgina and the robe to Jud. He said, "I cannot give a woman, especially a Greek woman, a monk's robe. We do have a community shower here but no hot water. Jud, you are welcome to use that. I'm sorry Georgina but, of course, you cannot." Then, he said, "I stay at a hotel in town once a month so that I can have hot water—it's the one thing I find difficult living without here. Georgina, I will leave the room while you change. A water closet is one door down. Jud, please come with me."

Following Richard, Jud said, "I thought monasteries kept many icons but I noticed this one just has one—in the library, anyway."

"Gunmen come and steal them—then sell them. Osios did have many that were stolen. The monks decided to have just one icon after that—unworthy of a thief's trouble."

They reached the shower room. While Jud showered in cold water, Richard returned to the library. Georgina had wrapped the large blanket around her. Because she was cold, she could only feel its warmth—not its scratchiness. Richard placed logs on top of the kindling, struck a matchstick on the stone, and lit a fire. Georgina was standing near it when Jud returned carrying his wet sweater and trousers. She smiled at him, dressed in a monk's robe. She would have laughed if Jud told her that he had been aspiring to be a monk until meeting her almost thirteen years ago. James placed a large, rounded black fireguard in front of the fire and invited them to lay their wet clothes on top. Jud put the wet passports, drachma bills, and his socks and shoes next to Georgina's shoes on the ground near the fire; then, he lay Georgina's dress, his sweater and trousers on the guard—he left space in the middle so that the fire could be enjoyed. Richard said that he would see if he could prepare food for them. Jud thanked him and said that they would leave after their clothes dried—which he hoped would happen before nightfall, although unlikely.

Jud and Georgina ate what Richard had brought for them: fresh bread, goat cheese, and wild greens. Richard gave them more raki and sat with them; he told them about his adult children in England and how he was going to visit them in the Midlands soon. He asked Jud and Georgina what had happened to them. Jud said that it was a long story, a bad one. Then, Jud asked Richard where he would find the nearest telephone.

Richard said there was a small town close by but it was up in the mountains. He suggested that he and Georgina go to Chaniá, instead. They would be able to take a bus there tomorrow. Richard told them he would see them later and left with their empty dishes.

Early evening soon came. Only firelight lit the library. Full of raki and warm by the fire that illuminated them but sent scant light into the vast stone and glass room, Jud and Georgina lay on her blanket and held each other under the cover of Jud's robe, since removed. They hadn't intended to make love but they did, without consummation for Jud—they had no birth control. Then, they lay in each other's arms—the roughness of the wool cover did not detract from the exquisite comfort that then drowsed them.

During a half-awake state, Georgina reached up and felt that her dress was dry. She got up and put it on. Because Jud's heavier clothes were still damp, Jud put the robe back on; then, because the fire cast warmth only a short distance, he put the blanket around Georgina's shoulders. It was late evening. The room was beginning to cool. Jud threw the last log on the waning fire. With no timepiece in the room, he had no idea what the time was. As Georgina stood up facing the fire, Jud walked up behind her and put his hands on her shoulders. He kissed her hair, dry and uncombed. He asked, "Are you all right, Georgina?"

There was a knock on the door. Jud opened it. Richard told Jud that it was ten o'clock and that he could have a cell to sleep in. In the silence, Richard said that the superior would prefer that Jud, if he and Georgina stayed at the monastery overnight, take a separate room. Jud turned to Georgina, who had come to the door, and asked, "Will you be all right alone?"

She said, "Yes." She kissed his cheek and said good night.

Richard told Georgina that he would be back with another armload of wood and would put it on the fire for her. Holding a candle, Richard led Jud down the dark corridor of narrow doors and opened one of them. Jud thanked him and walked into a small square room with a high ceiling.

Richard closed the door on him. Jud lay on a hard ledge under a blanket. Without a candle, he saw nothing. He wished he could hold Georgina all night. He was afraid she would disappear. He slept for a while.

Jud woke suddenly. He got up and went out into the corridor of cold circulating air. He estimated the distance of the library and then began to feel for the wide door to it. He found it and knocked. There was no answer. He opened it. A large candle burned in the middle of the table. A man was holding Georgina, whose blanket left one side of her dress uncovered. Another man held a shotgun pointed at Jud, whom he took for a foreign monk. One of the men spoke in Greek.

Georgina interpreted for Jud and said, "He is going to take the Virgin and Child icon." She added, "They didn't know I was in here, of course." In Greek, she asked the man holding her to let her pull her blanket around her more—she was cold. He did. And, as he did, he stepped away from her and held his shotgun on her. He spoke again.

Georgina interpreted again, "He wants to take me with them. As a hostage so that you won't follow them. They'll let me go later."

Jud knew two things: that the Virgin and Child icon was considered sacred and that he couldn't let the men take Georgina. He saw through the window that light was dawning. He said to Georgina, "Tell them that if they leave you here and the icon, we will give them something more valuable than the icon. And no one will follow them."

Georgina spoke to the men, listened to one of them, and then said to Jud, "They want to know what we will give them."

"Tell them to let you go, first." The men looked as if they were still celebrating Ochi Day—they were inebriated. They had helped themselves to the raki. Two empty bottles stood on the table.

After Georgina repeated Jud's words in Greek, one of the men nudged her toward Jud, who said, "Tell them I'm going to take down the painting."

After Georgina repeated those words to the men, Jud reached on top of the high mantel shelf for the icon. As he did so, a knock at the door heralded Richard, who walked in with a pitcher of goat milk and a loaf of bread. He saw Jud with the Virgin and Child in his hands. Then, he saw the gunmen. Jud waited for Richard to lay down the bread and milk before he handed the icon to him, who let it sit in his hands and felt sure he would be shot. Jud gleaned that Georgina's money and passports, unnoticed by the gunmen, still lay on the shadowed floor.

Jud asked Georgina to interpret again. He said, "Tell them to let Richard leave with the icon. Then, tell them to stand by the exit door—you and I will go there with them. They can shoot me if I do anything wrong."

The men laughed when Georgina repeated in Greek what Jud had said. They would never understand foreigners. But they nodded their assent—sure, they would shoot him if he did anything wrong.

Richard left with the icon. The men, holding their guns on Jud and Georgina, backed up toward the exit as Jud and Georgina moved forward. Then, as the men stood in the open doorway, Jud turned his back on them and faced Georgina. He put his hands around the nape of her neck, unfastened her gold chain, and slid up, from in-between the blanket and her skin, her gold and diamond crucifix. He whispered, "I hope you don't mind."

She said, "I want no more symbols of suffering. Take it."

He said, "Leave as soon as I start to turn." Jud kept his hands up as he turned around. The men stared up at the dangling crucifix in his left hand. The rising sun, disregarding the autumn pattern of a second consecutive day of dark storm, gleamed on the gold Jesus set on the diamond-filled cross. The men were hypnotised by it. But, as one man reached for it, the other man, seeing the crucifix near Jud's face, suddenly associated the two and recognised the crucifixion author. Jud saw the man's face and cognised what the man saw. Jud grinned at him as he let the crucifix drop into the other man's hand.

CHAPTER FIFTEEN

Richard revived the fire in the library with yet another armful of wood. The Virgin and Child icon stood in its place above the mantel. Richard sat with Jud and Georgina while they ate breakfast and then he left. Jud changed from the robe into his own clothes. Then, because it was too early for the buses to run, he and Georgina slept in front of the fire. When they awoke, they waited for Richard to return.

Jud knew that the crucifix he had given to the two men was worth more money than the Virgin and Child but the icon was irreplaceable. He wanted to bestow money on the monastery if it would be accepted, not as payment but as a gesture of appreciation for what he and Georgina had been given—intangible kindness, manifested as shelter and food—warmth and peace.

When Richard knocked on the door and entered, they thanked him. Jud asked him to thank the monks and their superior for both of them.

Richard said, "The monks don't know who you are, Jud Thorensen. But, if they had known, they still would have allowed you to stay."

Jud couldn't help himself as he smiled and said, "And knowing who they are and what they stand for, I still stayed."

Richard looked shocked. So did Georgina.

Jud said, "I mean—I appreciate what they did for us. My gratefulness to them is truly unbounded. But I would have accepted this help from

anyone who offered it. Human kindness stems from a human's consciousness and not from his vocation. So, I thank them because any one of them
would have offered this to us without his having a label and position of a
monk." Jud smiled again. He shook Richard's hand and said good bye.
Georgina did the same and was thinking that, for all Jud's sweetness,
within his seductive charm lay a forthright edge.

§

As they waited at a bus stop, Jud held Georgina with both arms—because
it was a cold day and he wanted to hold her. She enjoyed having his strong
arms around her and felt cherished. When the Chaniá bus came, they
stepped on. Georgina stuffed a thousand-drachma bill into the coin box.
She shared a verbal exchange with the driver and sat down with Jud.
Everyone stared at the Greek woman wearing a silk dress, as well as her
foreign companion. Each time the driver stopped the bus and a new fare
got on, he covered the coin box and instructed the person to give his coins
to the woman in pink. When Jud asked Georgina what was going on, she
said that the bus driver was ensuring that, since he carried no change, she
would get change from the new fares, even though she had told him it was
unnecessary. And they would likely get off the bus before she got all her
change.

　　Once in Chaniá, Georgina called her home but no one answered and,
because no one from or nearby the Osios Monastery had contacted a local
police station about the Sgouros men, she called the Ágios Nikólaos police
so that they could find out which was the closest station to the Osios
Monastery.

　　Then, Georgina bought a jacket. Because she and Jud were unable to
rent a car without credit cards, she hired a taxicab to take them to the
Binakas villa. Georgina planned to give the taxi driver all the rest of her
money and, if the meter ran up to a higher amount than that, more
money from her home. Almost four hours would pass before they would

reach Georgina's home. In the back seat, she and Jud closed their eyes. Each had his own thoughts.

Being in the monastery had reminded Georgina of how, when she had sometimes become depressed about not having children before Diana's birth, she had thought that she was being punished because she had not kept her childhood vow to God to marry Him by taking vows of chastity and poverty—and then joining a convent. Although the thought was a weak belief, it had added to her depression and a feeling of self-hate. Yet, since reading Jud's book, she had begun to feel that she was already married to God—Who had no dimension or sex—because she felt inseparable from the spiritual. As Jud's written words had seeped into her receptive mind and heart, she had perceived that each person was an individual expression of All-That-Is, the Gap—or Whatever, as Jud had put it.

She knew that Jud would disagree with her that she owed him something in order to pay the debt she felt she had incurred by bringing Jud to what had seemed would be a sure death. Thus, regardless of what would come to pass within the next few days, Georgina knew what she would give to Jud.

And she owed David something. She prayed that he was alive. If he no longer wanted revenge on Jud, he and she could make a fresh start. She felt that they might be able to make a new life together. That Constantine and Stephen Sgouros were dead was tragic to Georgina. And she had liked both of them, especially Stephen.

Jud was hoping that Mara and Diana were all right. The thought was a mantra for him. He sat up and meditated for the first time in years. He had been taught a method when he was sixteen. But, instead of using the mantra he had been given and which he still recalled, he simply slipped into transcendence by not thinking about anything.

§

In the Binakas villa, when morning came, Mara and Diana wanted to stay by a telephone but, because Mara needed her computer powerbook and felt it was unsafe to leave Diana alone, Mara took Diana with her to get her suitcases and powerbook from Alek's house, as well as to pay Alek more money and thank him for his gracious and extensive help. Thus, she and Diana missed Georgina's call from Chaniá.

Mara had to finish writing her last story for the Farnham trial, a summation, which Bos wanted from her as soon as possible. Back at the villa, Mara turned on her computer and Diana took a call from the Ágios Nikólaos Chief of Police, who had the list of persons that Diana had reported as missing last night. He told her that Georgina Binakas had called and was fine. At the moment, he thought it best not to tell her about anyone else, such as her father still being missing and the Sgouros men being dead. Because Jud Thorensen was likely a stranger to Diana, he neglected to tell her that Jud was with Georgina. Before Diana could ask questions, the Chief told her had to take another call and hung up.

Diana repeated to Mara what the Chief had said to her in Greek. She saw the quick tears come to Mara's eyes when she told her that the Chief had not given any word of Jud—or of anyone else but Georgina. Diana put an arm around Mara's shoulders.

Mara appreciated the gesture. She filled her mind with the trial story and typed quickly. Diana made soup and sandwiches for lunch. After they ate, Mara finished the story and sent it to Bos via e-mail; then, she and Diana went for a walk on the cool, sunny afternoon. And Mara found out that she liked having a child around, especially one like Diana.

They were walking from Istron's square when they saw a taxicab, empty except for the driver, driving away from the villa and toward them. Beyond the taxi, they saw Georgina standing at the villa gates. Beside her was a hallucination of Jud. Yet, as Jud and Georgina moved in their direction, as quickly as their hurting bodies allowed, Mara and Diana had to believe their eyes; they ran toward them. Then, Mara was in Jud's arms and Diana clung to Georgina. And then, Diana hugged Jud and Mara put an arm around Georgina. The reunion was sweet with the joy in Jud's and Georgina's return; it was bitter in the sadness of David's absence.

They walked up the villa's drive. Georgina now knew for sure that David had never made it back. Her heart began to pound. Mara and Diana were refraining from asking questions. Once inside, they heard the phone ring. Georgina answered. Her disappointment sliced the air. It was not David. It was the police. The Sgouros men had been found where Georgina had described. David Binakas had not yet been found. Georgina looked at Diana's anxious face. She said, "Your papa is missing."

CHAPTER SIXTEEN

On Christmas Day, Jud sat with his daughter in his parents' home. Diana had gone to church with Ogden, Helen, and Lisbeth. He would have gone with them if his presence would not have caused disruption—he was in newspapers and on magazine covers again, with Diana, Georgina, or both, this time around, but, while they were called Christians, he was called a heathen. His body was almost healed again, including the cracked rib.

Helen looked at her handsome son bending over a book that Diana was showing him. Jud was her favorite child. She loved all her children without limitation but she got along the best with him. She was delighted with Diana. While being a grandparent had not been essential to her sense of well-being, being one was something she had desired. Yet, she marveled that she had become one from Jud, an unexpected source. She had thought otherwise—even though Jared Thorensen seemed to be clinging to a long engagement as if he were afraid of sex and Lisbeth had years of school and university ahead of her before she would consider marriage and children, if at all, according to Lisbeth's viewpoint now.

Ogden Thorensen still felt distant from his youngest son but, while Helen would have fought against his taking legal action to disinherit Jud, Ogden had decided not to do so of his own volition because he thought that Jud had enough difficulties in life. Nor did he disown Jud and thus disown Diana because he, himself, could not deny Diana his love. She was becoming precious to him. He was staying home more often these days and looked forward to her visits, as did Helen. He was proud of Diana's creative nature and savored her sweetness. He saw the sadness in her face—she still grieved over the man who had brought her up during her twelve years—and she missed her mother. Yet, it had been her choice to be here now. That she loved Jud and he loved her was evident. The affinity they had with each other made it seem to Ogden as if the pair had always known each other. Ogden planned to introduce Diana to his friends after the holidays. They wanted to meet the young writer.

Lisbeth looked forward to guiding Diana on how to be a teenager in the United States of America. She felt as if Diana were a younger sister. She knew she would have to be protective of her because, it seemed, that Greek girls were more innocent than American ones and because Diana was soon going to attract boys. She had broad shoulders, a tiny waist, and narrow hips; she was cute, like a female version of Jud but with hair as fair as Lisbeth's own.

Pastor Jared Thorensen couldn't leave his ministry to come and meet his niece but had invited Jud to bring Diana to his home in Maine after the holidays. He did not mention his fiancée. The Harcourts and their daughter had met Diana and welcomed her to the States when she had arrived in November.

Diana Ellen Benthos Thorensen had taken the last names of her mother's family and her father's; she was in the shared custody of both parents, winters with her father and summers with her mother on Crete. She had begun teaching Greek to her father. She was looking forward to attending an American school in January. And, for an American girl, she wasn't overly tall.

Georgina Benthos Binakas was the new President of Alpha-Omega Pharmakon. She would have preferred moving to California to her family's home but David Binakas's last will and testament, done this past summer, had named her as his sole beneficiary. And she had chosen to honor his wish. In January, she would begin study for a master's degree in chemistry at the University of Athens.

Angela had invited Jud to her place several times after his return from Crete. She had been surprised to learn that he was a father but had adjusted to the fact—and found him even more attractive. On a night she was home alone and he was without Diana, they had written their first song together, the beginning of songs by Wynne-Thorensen. Her love and her burning desire for him seduced him and she had taken him to her bed. It had been the same as before—during their one night together several months ago—the rapture and erotic fulfillment and then the timeless transcendent state. Yet, it had been different—a new experience. They knew each other better.

Angela had received three invitations for her Christmas break from Bentilee. With graciousness, she had refused her mother's displeasing one of traveling to Washburn and Helen's attractive of staying at the Thorensen home. Instead, she had accepted the one from Van Silverman and Dr. Sherry Hall which had taken her to Japan, where Romeo was continuing its world tour, giving her a taste of that was like. A recording contract was in the offing for her. She had written a song for Jud.

§

At midnight, as Jud took Diana up to a guest bedroom, until Helen finished another room especially for Diana, he heard the buzz of the intercom, almost indiscernible from here. He sat on the edge of Diana's bed. She asked him to tell her the story she had asked him to tell her a few times during the last few weeks. He began,

"Once upon a time, there was a beautiful white cat named Chalk. He loved life. He loved everything about life. He lived with a little girl, Anna, who loved him very much. Every morning, watching and waiting, Chalk lay curled up on Anna's bed. In the moment that Anna stirred or her eyes blinked open, Chalk spoke in purrs and meows mixed together—they were the prettiest sounds Anna had ever heard—and then he climbed all over Anna, slowly and daintily, until Anna rose from her bed.

All morning, Chalk followed Anna. Whenever she was busy, he was busy. While she played with her dolls, he tossed his toy mouse into the air. He chased spiders away from her toys. When she drew pictures, he jumped upon his cat tower and watched her until he fell asleep. When Anna ate dinner, Chalk ate his. When evening came, Anna threw soft toys for him to catch and wrestle with. When Chalk wanted her to pet him, he arched his back and walked around her, and then looked back to see her notice him. He purred with great noise when Anna rubbed him behind an ear and under his chin. He did the same when she stroked his back.

He followed her when she went to brush her teeth. Then, he followed her to her bed and waited until she climbed into it—then, up he jumped and lay upon her chest. He kneaded his paws on her and rubbed his head against her chin. Then, Anna and Chalk went to sleep. And so their years went.

Then, one day, a door was left open. Chalk sauntered outside. But as he chased a mouse across the road, a car ran over him. Through a window, Anna saw what had happened. She ran from the house to Chalk. She saw his body twitch. Then, he was dead. She cried.

Chalk could not understand why she was crying. He looked at the body that had once been his. He didn't know human language nor did he have a voice but he tried to tell Anna, "Don't cry for me. I'm not dead. What you see on the ground is no longer me." But Anna was unable to pick up his message because she was too sad to hear any happy thoughts. And Chalk was happy. He had enjoyed this life as Anna's white cat. He knew he could experience physical life any time he wanted to.

After Anna and her father buried Chalk's body in the garden, he was gentle with her when he said, "Anna, let's get another cat. Not today if you don't want to—but soon. He won't take the place of Chalk—he won't be the same—but he will be a happy creature, as Chalk was. Chalk won't mind. I promise."

One day, Anna asked her father to take her to an animal shelter to pick out a cat. At the same moment that she thought she had picked out a small gray cat, she realised he had picked her out, too. She called him Mouse. And even though, he was different from Chalk and she would never see Chalk again, Anna loved Mouse and he loved her. He loved life, too. And when he was extra happy, he lay in Anna's lap and purred."

As always when Jud finished the story, Diana felt an ease about life.

Jud leaned forward to kiss Diana's cheek. He still felt overwhelmed that Georgina had given him, on the condition that Diana would want it this way, this gift of sharing Diana. He felt a surge of emotion rise up. Diana put her arms around him and held him tightly. She said, "I love you, Daddy."

"I love you, too, Diana."

§

Jud went to his room, different from how it had looked when he had been a child and from what it had changed into when he had been a teenager. The only furniture other than the bed—upon whose middle pillow, one of many, lay a small wrapped box—were a writing desk with a chair, and two bedside tables with lamps. His guitar, usually kept at home in Ocean City, leaned in a corner. He saw that his bedcover had been turned down and that the candles Mara had long ago interspersed around his room were lit. He opened the drapes to the large paned window and saw the view similar to the one from the conservatory below.

Snow fell on the garden. He opened the window to smell and breathe the crisp air. He stooped down to light the gas fireplace and then stood up in front of its mantel with the large mirror, in whose reflection he saw Georgina's painting of Diana with the rainbows and a larger one that Georgina had recently done of the Aegean Sea, its waves in multitudes of blues and stretching endlessly back through the canvas, never reaching the gold sun in the azure sky. On the mantelpiece sat a framed photograph of Georgina and Diana. Next to it lay Diana's gifts to him, her hand-made illustrated book of Chalk & Mouse and a windproof lighter, which he picked up. Then, he left the room.

As Jud came down the stairs, he heard his mother laughing in the living room. A few of his relatives entered the foyer and wished him a good night as they went upstairs to their rooms. Jud wished them a Merry Christmas and reflected again on another book he wanted to start.

He walked into the conservatory. With Christmas lights wrapped around every tree, it looked festive. There was a sack of Christmas cards he had started to open. Some letters from the public had found their way in there—some letters that were wonderful and others that were not. The newest label that his detractors had given him since Desire; Sex & Spirituality had been published was subversionary but there were his supporters who were calling him an enlightened visionary—he would call himself neither.

He was getting more marriage proposals than he had after the Washburn event and more women offering to have his children—a few offers were entailed with the hope that a child with him would bring the real Antichrist. At least, fewer women were offering their teenage daughters to him. Yet, the oddball letters were as valid as the uncountable intellectual and spiritual ones. He appreciated the attention to his writing, even though it sometimes seemed that the more he explained, the more he was misunderstood—for one thing, just because he disbelieved Jesus' crucifixion didn't mean that he disbelieved his birth. Yet, what meant the most to him about many of the letters was that people were telling him they felt good about themselves or simply felt good. And he felt good about that.

Jud opened the conservatory doors and stepped into the falling snow. With Diana's gift, engraved with Eros, his arrow ready to fly from his pulled-back bow, he lit a fine cigar. He thought about Angela's song for him. And her beautiful voice. He looked forward to seeing her when she came home.

He ground out the barely-smoked cigar, walked back inside, closed the doors, and stood looking outside across the back garden while he waited for Mara, who had spent Christmas Day with her mother's sister's family, composed of her pseudo parents and pseudo brother, as she always had during her entire childhood and often had during her adulthood. Jud knew that Mara didn't mind not spending Christmas with Van and Sherry, even though this was the first year that she could have openly done so. That Angela, instead of Mara, was in Japan with Mara's parents was ironic.

Romeo's Mythos World Tour had kicked off in Greece. Jud and Mara had taken Diana to their concert and then backstage to see Van and Sherry, who had said everything she had wanted to say to Jud about his latest misadventure with one look that, if looks could kill, would have slain more than one man. Yet, as Jud had stood there, she had put her arms around him—because she liked him and because, despite his unfaithfulness to Mara, he was loyal to her in a sublime way and he loved her to the degree that she could misuse the power that she allowed her to have over him and, yet, he would still love her. *He has no pride*, Sherry had thought.

On the day of Romeo's tour, the news media had covered the Sgouros double-funeral. On the same day, David Binakas's body had been reported as found by a shepherd, who had made a pilgrimage to a police station, four days since David had been missing. Days after that, the news media had covered the large funeral Georgina had organised for David Binakas. Jud had not attended. A few days after that, he and Mara brought Diana to the States.

Regarding Georgina or Angela, Mara had an air about her that disallowed his confessions—which he had no plan to make. Jud heard more relatives laughing as they went upstairs—he had left the conservatory doors open. They were calling out their Christmas wishes and good nights.

When Mara touched Jud's shoulder, he turned around. Her hair, longer than it had been a year ago, lay in gold strands on her bare shoulders and almost reached the top of her low-cut green dress, its velvet almost as smooth as her skin. She wore her father's gift, as she had during one night last spring, a necklace and earrings of bloodstone, green with blood-like spots of jasper. Her green eyes looked like jade stones in the low light. She stared into his storm-colored eyes that, tonight, were as dark as his black shirt. She touched his darkening, silk hair. He pulled her close to him. When she smiled, so did he. The night was theirs.

Note from the author:

Thank you for reading my book. By the way, there are phrases, sometimes titles, of songs used within the text of this book. My use was unintentional and, as I noticed what I was doing, I resisted an urge to continue to do so. Yet, more phrases did appear and, occasionally, variations of them appear—but not at the expense of the characters and their story.

If you care to, please send an e-mail to me of the phrases that you notice and the name of the songs they are from. I may be unaware of some. Unless you state otherwise, I will put you on my list to receive e-mails of new books.

Example of phrase: *"She showed me her room." from Norwegian Wood*

—a Lennon-McCartney song. This phrase appears in Chapter Ten.*

Example of phrase variation: *"—left Jud standing all alone." from Crying*

—sung by Roy Orbison. This phrase variation of *left me standing all alone* appears in Chapter Eleven.*

I hope to hear from you!

Best regards,
R.M. Gál

rmgal@jps-productions.com

* At the moment I am writing this, I don't know on which page this line will appear, once the book is published.

0-595-25576-0